Perchance to Dream

A Twist Upon a Regency Tale
Book 4

By Jude Knight

Text by Jude Knight
Cover by Kim Killion

Dragonblade Publishing, Inc. is an imprint of Kathryn Le Veque Novels, Inc.
P.O. Box 23
Moreno Valley, CA 92556
ceo@dragonbladepublishing.com

Produced in the United States of America

First Edition September 2023
Trade Paperback Edition

ARE YOU SIGNED UP FOR DRAGONBLADE'S BLOG?

You'll get the latest news and information on exclusive giveaways, exclusive excerpts, coming releases, sales, free books, cover reveals and more.

Check out our complete list of authors, too!

No spam, no junk. That's a promise!

Sign Up Here

www.dragonbladepublishing.com

Dearest Reader;

Thank you for your support of a small press. At Dragonblade Publishing, we strive to bring you the highest quality Historical Romance from some of the best authors in the business. Without your support, there is no 'us', so we sincerely hope you adore these stories and find some new favorite authors along the way.

Happy Reading!

CEO, Dragonblade Publishing

Additional Dragonblade books by Author Jude Knight

A Twist Upon a Regency Tale, The Series
Lady Beast's Bridegroom (Book 1)
One Perfect Dance (Book 2)
Snowy and the Seven Doves (Book 3)
Perchance to Dream (Book 4)

The Lyon's Den Series
The Talons of a Lyon

About the Book

Life is richer than he expected.

John Forsythe abandons London for the furthest reaches of England after a series of betrayals leave him with the shame of a very public divorce, a poor opinion of Society ladies and a heart armored against love. Protected from intruders by his servants, the Thornes, he spends his days with his daughter and in a workshop where he makes clockwork automata.

Life is better than she deserves.

Pauline Turner has reformed in the years since she joined in her mother's attempts to destroy her stepbrother. Eschewing social position and forgetting dreams of marriage and her own home, she is content with her status as a favorite sister and aunt and the space to breed roses.

A kiss awakens them...

When a storm forces Pauline to defy John's ban on visitors, she and John each strike a chord in the other. Though they awaken to the possibility of love, they each have their own lives.

... but the trials that follow tear them apart.

When his ex-wife's husband steals John's beloved daughter, Pauline steps in to steal her back. The journey that follows takes them across the sea to Paris and into the depths of their hearts.

Preface

Essex, 1818

JOHN FORSYTHE PLACED a tender kiss on the cheek of his baby daughter, then passed her to her nursemaid, gently, so as not to wake her. "You have worn her out, my lord," the nursemaid whispered, smiling.

John returned the smile. He had collected Tina Jane from the nursery after her breakfast and carried her with him on his rounds of the stable, the dairy, the barn and the poultry yards. He couldn't say who enjoyed it more—him or the baby girl, who loved the animals, the bustle, and being with her father.

His hour and a half outside with his little girl had cemented the decision he'd been coming to for weeks. In a few days, she would reach her first birthday. It was time for John to resolve his difficulties with Tina Jane's mother. Yes, their marriage had begun in lies and continued in discord, but surely, they could build on their joint love for their daughter and create a real marriage? John was going to find his wife and ask her to try.

The name had been the cause of one of their fights. Augusta had wanted to name her baby Philippa Augustina, uniting her own name with that of Philip Spindler, the treacherous rat who had impregnated her then abandoned her to marry the bride who was his grandfather's choice.

John had been flabbergasted at her sheer effrontery. She wanted to name the child born in their marriage after her former lover? Augusta reacted to his unequivocal 'no' with a six-week-long sulk. She shut herself in her room and refused to talk to him. She had not even visited the baby.

As he searched the house for his wife, John's mind continued to revisit the sorrowful memories. The saddest part was that it had been six weeks of bliss. None of her tantrums or weeping jags or other dramatics. John could get on with the work of the estate, and spend all his spare time with the baby. He had fallen in love with the wee mite from the moment she had been placed in his arms on the day she was born, and tumbled more deeply every hour he spent with her.

In the end, he had given Augustina Jane her first name as an overture of peace to his wife.

After all, however it came about, however he and Augusta felt about it, they were married. His compromise had, to a degree, worked. Augusta emerged from her room, resumed her place at the dinner table, accompanied him to social events in the neighborhood and did her best to behave well in public.

She even began to show an interest in the baby, or at least in having Tina Jane's nursemaid trail behind Augusta with the little girl dressed in a gown made from scraps of fabric left over from whatever Augusta was wearing. "Do we not make a picture, Lord John?" she would simper.

"Where is Lady John?" he asked each servant he met, but she must be restless today, for she was not in any of the rooms to which he was sent. *Lord and Lady John.* She insisted on the ridiculous courtesy title rather than his preferred use of the military rank he had earned fighting Napoleon's armies, and retained as a part-time soldier in the local militia.

Again, allowing her the title seemed a small price to pay for a relative degree of marital peace.

"She is very young," he reminded himself. Only nineteen

when he met her, and much younger than her years. Her parents had alternatively ignored her and given in to her many whims. She had always been able to get anything she wanted, often merely by asking, and if that failed, by having a tantrum.

Even John, though she had not wanted John himself. Only a fool with an estate and noble connections who could be trapped into marrying her without asking too many questions. An older man she could manipulate as she had manipulated her parents, but not as old as the friend of her father that her parents wanted her to marry.

She had been disappointed to discover that the worn-out soldier she'd conspired to trap had a will stronger than her own, and would not bend to her pleading or her histrionics.

Though he gave way to her in minor things, all the sulking in the world had not convinced him to allow her to redecorate the house that had been fully refurbished eighteen months ago, or to take her to London for the Season where they would inevitably meet Spindler and his wife, or to fire Thorne, his manservant, who had been with him since Salamanca in the Peninsular Wars, after Thorne had come across Augusta beating the nursemaid with a riding crop, and had taken the crop from her.

John, appealed to by both Augusta and Thorne, discovered that the nursemaid's crime had been to argue that Tina Jane should not go visiting with Augusta on a cold and blustery day, since the poor little girl had the sniffles.

John had been coldly furious. "Miss Embrow was right to protest, Augusta. Taking our daughter out in this weather when she is already ill would have been foolish."

"But Lord John," Augusta protested, "it was not her place to question my instructions."

"It is her place to put the welfare of the baby first. But even if she was wrong, you should not have beaten her. I will not have any in my household subjected to such violence. You will never raise a hand or any other implement to a servant again."

She had been cowed by his anger, perhaps, for she slunk away and treated him to a week-long sulk, after which she emerged to demand that Thorne be dismissed for laying hands on her when he took the crop off her.

John's refusal earned him the silent treatment for a further two weeks.

Still, she had not persisted, so perhaps she was learning. She was, after all, nearly twenty-one and had become a mother. She might be maturing. He'd seen a firm hand and kindness transform many a wild young man into a steady officer.

Indeed, for the last few days, she had been smiling, sometimes even at John. She had even spent an hour in the nursery yesterday, ignoring Miss Embrow as she had since the incident, but playing pat-a-cake and peek-a-boo with the baby.

But now, where on earth could the woman be? She was not in the house, and she was hardly one to spend hours in the garden. He checked with the stables, and discovered that she'd ridden out, and refused to take a groom with her.

John was worried. Augusta was not the most accomplished of riders. *Perhaps she has fallen.* He ordered his own horse saddled and rode off in the direction the grooms indicated.

The path split, with one branch entering his woods, and the other joining the lane that led out to the village road. John rode a short way along the lane, but he could not see Augusta or a horse, so he returned to the woods. Perhaps she sought shade.

The path led to a clearing where the woodcutter had a cottage he used from time to time, but this was not the season for harvesting or planting or clearing undergrowth. So why were two horses tied up at the side of the cottage, and why was smoke rising from the chimney?

John stopped just inside the trees to examine the scene. He couldn't be sure, as it was in the shade and partly obscured by the larger of the two horses, but he thought the smaller one was Augusta's mare. He was still processing the implications of that when the cottage door opened and two people came out. One was Augusta. The other he could identify by the man's white-blonde hair. It was Spindler. The swine bent to give John's wife a tender kiss.

John nudged his horse into a walk. Spindler looked up at the clop of hooves, started, and ran for his own horse. John resisted the urge to give chase as Spindler threw himself into the saddle and kicked the beast into a gallop. After all, what would he do with the man if he caught him?

Rearranging the dirty dog's pretty face would be satisfying, but it wouldn't solve the problems in his marriage.

Augusta looked up at him without a hint of remorse or concern, trying but failing to compose her face into a serious expression. But a beaming smile of absolute delight kept breaking through. "Lord John, don't be cross. We didn't do anything, honestly. And he brought such good news."

He didn't trust himself to speak to her. He dismounted, tied his horse beside hers, and walked past her into the cottage. Didn't do anything? The blankets had been thrown from the bed and the room reeked of sex.

Augusta followed him, to stand in the door. "You must try to understand, Lord John. We have not been together for nearly two years."

Nor had Augusta and John. Not once since they wed. Not at all, if his suspicions about the night she came to his bed were true.

John had been patient, thinking she would accept their marriage in time. He had also been celibate, since he had long since promised himself he would never break his marriage vows, as both his parents had.

And she thought he should understand? "No, Augusta." When Captain Forsythe spoke in that tight clipped voice, soldiers knew to stand to attention and keep quiet, for retribution was about to fall. "I do not understand how you can expect me to countenance you and your lover meeting in secret, right here on my lands, less than a mile from the nursery where our daughter sleeps."

Augusta was not one of his soldiers. "My daughter," she

insisted. "Mine and Phillip's."

A touch of panic spiked his fury. "Not according to the law," he reminded himself as well as her. "She was born within our marriage. I have claimed her. Spindler has no rights here."

At that, the smile blossomed again, though her eyes remained wary. "Not Spindler. Lord John, that is what he came to say! Kingston is dead! Phillip is free!"

The Duke of Kingston was Spindler's grandfather, and in some ways the orchestrator of John's misery. Spindler had been the duke's pensioner, as had his mother and father. Disliking his grandson's attachment to Augusta, who had only beauty to recommend her, being of modest family and wealth, the duke forced Spindler to choose between poverty and Augusta, and riches and a bride of Kingston's choosing. Either he did not care that the scoundrel had impregnated Augusta, or her condition did not become apparent until after her lover married the selected lady.

Kingston's death was not a surprise. Even John, who took no notice of Society gossip, knew he had been failing since the apoplexy that followed the tragic deaths, months ago, of his heir and his heir's son. Their deaths made his second son, Spindler's father, the heir apparent. Now that second son was the Duke of Kingston. Spindler's father, who had never refused his son anything except his attention.

"He is not free," he told Augusta. "Your lover is married and so are you. You both have a spouse and children."

She stared at him as if he was speaking in a foreign language. John did not want to look at her. He moved around the room, picking up a chair that had been knocked over, folding the blankets, pulling the underblanket off the mattress and throwing it into a heap by the door to take to the laundrymaid.

"We can be together," Augusta insisted. "Tenby—he is Earl of Tenby now—does not have to please his grandfather ever again."

John faced Augusta. She was clenching her fists and jutting

her chin, ready to fight. "Augusta, talk sense. You are both married. Tenby lives in London. You live here, with me." His voice dropped to a growl. "And you can be sure I will not turn a blind eye to you meeting your lover here or in London."

He took a deep breath. She was not listening to him. Instead, her eyes were fixed on some mythical and impossible future that only she and Tenby could see.

"Augusta, we could make something of our marriage. Would life not be better if we were comfortable with one another? Would you not like more children?"

That caught her attention. "No!" she declared. "I do not ever want to go through that again, getting lumpy and ugly. And then the pain! No, my lord, not even for Tenby. But he says he has his heir and that cow is pregnant again, so there might even be a spare. He will not ask me to bear another child."

John shook his head. It was like arguing with a river. You could talk all you liked, but it wasn't going to stop flowing in the direction it had chosen. "You and Tenby cannot wed," he pointed out. "You are both married to other people."

At that, she crossed the room, laid a hand on his arm, and looked up at him pleadingly. "Yes, but we could live together. Tenby says that, if I move in with him, you can easily sue him for stealing me away (though I was always his, so that part I do not understand), and then petition the church for a legal separation. You get to keep Augustina, and you will not have to pay for clothes and the like for me ever again. And I get Tenby."

"You will be cast out of Society," John warned. So would John. Not so much because he would be blamed, but because he would be laughed at. People might pity a cuckold, but they did not admire him. Still, he could live without Society.

"We can live in Paris, Tenby says," Augusta said, airily, "where they understand these things. It is the best plan, my lord. Everyone gets what they want."

"What of Lady Tenby? What does she want?"

John's appeal to Augusta's sympathy for another woman fell

on deaf ears. She had none. "She gets to call herself Countess and live at Spindler Palace with her sons. I don't care about her. It is me that Tenby loves."

"My answer is no. Your plan is foolish, Augusta. You and Tenby owe it to your children to make the best of your marriages. Come. We shall return to the house. I shall write to Tenby and tell him that, if he approaches you again, he will regret it."

That was not the end of it, of course. Augusta was convinced she was the female half of a romance for the ages: a Helen of Troy, an Isolde, a Guinevere, an Eloise, a Juliet. Nothing would be allowed to stand in the way of her happy ending. She blocked John's every attempt at a reconciliation, raised the option of a legal separation at every opportunity heedless of who else might be listening, and in the end forced his hand by running away to France with Tenby.

By then, it was almost a relief to see the end of what would have been a total disaster from the beginning, except it had given John his little Jane. Not Tina Jane. Not anymore. He couldn't go back and refuse to give his precious girl her mother's name. But he didn't have to use any part of it when he spoke to his little darling.

When Lady Tenby died shortly after the church courts had granted their legal separation, John barely argued at all about taking a case to the House of Lords for a full divorce.

John signed the papers when they were put in front of him, sold his estate in Essex, and bought another, in a remote part of the northwest of England, where his woes would not be the leading topic of conversation in every parlor and at every hearth fire. There, far from the place of his misery, he could shelter his darling Jane from gossip and the evils of the ton.

Chapter One

Spring, 1825

PAULINE TURNER WAS never happier than when among her roses, so her current low mood was evidence of her general dissatisfaction. She refused to call it "unhappiness". After all, what did she have to be unhappy about?

Eight years ago, she'd had cause enough for her misery. But eight years ago, she had been a harridan-in-training with no friends, largely ignored by her more ruthless mother and younger sister except when they had a use for her.

If she was in the mood to count blessings, the succession houses she was currently within would be high on the list.

She was making her way along the seedlings in one of her most important seed beds, examining the opening blooms to see if any of the offspring of her controlled fertilization efforts had the characteristics she hoped for.

She would ever be grateful that her stepbrother Peter had taken her in and made her part of his family. She showed her gratitude by lending a hand wherever she was needed, with the house, with the children, and especially with the garden, which had become her great joy—and with roses, her passion.

As well as with Peter, she lived with three sisters, only one of whom was related by blood. Her sister Arial was her stepbrother's wife. Her sister Rose was her stepbrother's base-born half-sister. Her sister Vivienne was known to the world as half-sister to both Pauline and Peter, though the truth was that Pauline's mother had played Peter's father false.

It didn't matter to Peter or to Arial. It had ceased to matter to Pauline. She loved them all, and she loved being Auntie Pauline to the children that filled the nursery and the schoolroom, four of them Arial and Peter's offspring, and the others three cousins of Arial's.

Her life was full, productive, and rewarding, and her current mood was an aberration, not to be tolerated.

In January, when she'd opened the rosehips produced by her breeding program and planted them in the succession houses, she had been full of joy and hope.

Then, Rose and Vivienne had made their debuts, being presented first at Court and then to the ton in a magnificent ball. She smiled at the memory. They had been so lovely, and had from the first attracted much attention.

Now, Rose was betrothed to the son of a Scottish peer, and was soon to be wed. Vivienne had admirers by the dozen and was expected to make an even more brilliant match, though she declared she would not marry without the love Rose had found. Pauline was so pleased and proud.

And yet… It seemed like only yesterday they were little girls, and she was the debutante, full of hopes and dreams. Her mother and sister Laura had blamed poverty for the Turner sisters' failure in the marriage mart but the truth was they had sabotaged their own chances by being horrible people.

Pauline had made amends—was *still* making them. Today's debutantes knew her only as the older sister of Rose and Vivienne, the one with the odd hobby of designing gardens and breeding roses. But still, Society abounded with people who remembered her as she had been. She would never truly be comfortable around them.

No. Pauline did not envy Rose and Vivienne their success. Their hopes and dreams though; those made her wistful. "I will be thirty on my next birthday," she told her roses. "My time to marry has long passed." She tried to make her voice cheerful, but it was a maudlin thought. Without a husband of her own, without children, she would always be an extra on the edges of family life.

I am very fortunate. She knew it, though today she did not feel it. She never needed to worry about a roof over her head. She had a generous allowance, much of which she spent on her gardens. Peter's and Arial's gardens, that was. Though Pauline had made them, she did not own them.

It does not matter who owns them. In a sense, that was true. She was guaranteed a free hand and given all the labor, materials, tools and building she required. But none of it was truly hers.

You are also appreciated, she scolded herself. Arial, a busy mother and countess, as well as an investor and owner of a number of businesses, said she did not know what she would do without Pauline.

She was needed. It was enough. It would have to be enough, and this lachrymose mood would pass.

She bent to examine another of the new blooms, the hybrid children of *rosa centifolia*, with its lovely heads of many petals, and *rosa mundi*, whose pretty varicolored white and magenta she hoped to replicate in other shades. None of her babies had the yellow tones she had been hoping for.

Some of the plants are worth keeping for another season, she reassured herself. She would grow them on to multiply by making cuttings. But none of the dozens of hips she'd harvested for seed and the hundreds of plants she'd planted had produced the blooms she had seen in her mind's eye. *Perhaps that is the reason I feel so low today.*

Here were the centifolias, beautiful in shades of pink and cream. She had hoped for a deep pink. A friend of her brother had given Arial a bunch from his garden that was the exact shade she had in mind. It had, impressively, survived in water on the long journey to their home in Leicester from the Lakes District in Cumberland, where the man lived. But none of the stems she planted from the bunch grew, and when she asked him for cuttings, he did not reply.

She had, in fact, sent four polite letters and received not a single acknowledgment, which was rude. Her misery flared into irritation. She should write to him again, and tell him exactly what she thought of him.

Chapter Two

Rosewood Towers, May 1825

"ANOTHER LETTER FROM that Miss Turner, Captain," Thorne reported.

"Throw it in the fire," John commanded. Thorne didn't comment, but put the letter into his pocket, no doubt to store it with the others.

John didn't need to read it to know it would be another question about the roses that rambled everywhere at Rosewood Towers. At least, he assumed that all five letters were on the same topic. Not that he'd read them, but Arial, Lady Stancroft, whose letters he did read, said that Miss Turner was going to write to him about his roses.

As if it was roses the besom wanted. He would not trust the female a single inch. John remembered Pauline Turner from his time in London years ago, before he married Augusta. The Turner sisters had been friends with Belinda, John's first betrothed, who'd jilted him when his brother's wife gave birth to twin boys, shifting John out of the line of succession.

I know that female by the company she kept. Arial, who was kind and good, might think the harpy would travel all the way to Cumberland for the sake of roses. John was sure the Turner female had other motives, those to do with her being single, and him, lacking a wife.

John knew only three honest women. Arial, wife of his dearest friend, Peter Ransome, Earl of Stancroft. Cordelia, wife of his half-brother, the Marquess of Deerhaven. Thorne's wife, Maggie Thorne, who had once been Maggie Embrow, and who had raised his darling Jane since she was born.

He certainly could not count his own mother, who had died with her lover while attempting to escape her marriage, leaving him behind as an unwanted souvenir of a previous liaison.

Nor his ex-wife, Augusta, who had trapped him with a lie, presented him with a cuckoo chick, abandoned both him and her daughter without a backward look when her lover became rich enough to keep her in comfort, and then demanded a divorce so she could remarry.

Belinda, the woman to whom he had been briefly betrothed, was even worse.

Mama was foolish. Augusta was spoilt and selfish, and lived in a dream world with herself as the female half of a pair of star-crossed lovers. Belinda was grasping and cruel. She had hidden her nature until he had made a public promise to marry her. Fortunately, he convinced her he was miserly, tyrannical, and determined to drag her around the world behind the army. She clung like a limpet, for his brother and Cordelia had only daughters. Until the twins.

"If that's all, Thorne," John hinted.

"No, sir. I came to remind you that you promised to take Miss Jane fishing this afternoon."

He had, too. He cast a wistful glance at the pieces of mechanism scattered across his work table.

"Tell Mrs. Thorne I will collect Jane in ten minutes," he said. "I had better change into something old."

Not that he had anything new. He had last bought clothes not long before he married Jane's mother. However, Mrs. Thorne would growl if he went fishing in anything that was still presentable enough for visitors. Not that he had visitors to be presentable for. Anyone who arrived, except for Deerhaven and Peter, was turned away at the door on his orders, and they had long since ceased coming. Deerhaven and Peter still visited, but rarely and never without a letter announcing their intent.

Jane was waiting impatiently when he arrived at the other tower. "Papa, I thought you had forgotten me," she scolded.

"Hush, Miss Jane," said Mrs. Thorne, throwing him a worried glance. "Your Papa would never forget you."

That hurt on two counts. First, that Mrs. Thorne could think he would be cross with his darling girl for challenging him. Second, the only reason he had remembered, as the Thornes well knew, was his standing order to remind him of any promise to his daughter. When the melancholy was bad, he forgot everything.

"I am sorry I am late, darling girl. Shall we go and catch some fishies?"

She gifted him with a sweet smile, took his offered hand, and for a moment, his world righted.

The world held four good females, he amended, and the best of them all was Jane, who was only seven. She was something of a tyrant, but she had a good heart.

They passed the rambling manor house and walked through the wild overgrown garden and down the hill to the trout stream. Jane described the fish she was going to catch, speculated on when her wiggly tooth might fall out, spelled for him the words she had learned that morning, and described the new dress Thorny was making for her, which was the same color as the roses. Thorny was what she called her beloved nurse.

The roses reminded him of Miss Turner. Five letters! The woman was determined. He hoped the latest would be the end of it.

And it would have been, too, had Pauline's sister Rose not begged for Pauline and Vivienne to come north for Rose's first Christmas in her new home.

Chapter Three

February, 1826

"IF THE ROAD from Carlisle to Newcastle is worse than this," Pauline said to her sister Vivienne, "I am glad we are not on it."

Vivienne shuddered. "I know. This is dreadful."

The coach inched forward through the rain, jolting through ruts and puddles, sliding on mud. Only the strength of the horses and the skill of the driver maintained their progress to their next stop.

"With this storm, there'll be landslides in the hills," the stable master at Carlisle had told the two women. "Normally, I'd say go east. The Great North Road is well maintained, on the whole. If you get to Newcastle, you'll travel south faster than through Cumberland and Lancashire. The trouble is, you're unlikely to get there. You'll be driving into the worst of the storm. Going south, you'll be on the edge of it."

Were those lights out of the window? Pauline leaned forward. *Yes*. They were coming into a settlement—a small village, if the number of lighted windows she could see was any indication. "If we have reached Lancaster, we have made better time than I expected," Vivienne commented.

Pauline shook her head. "I do not think it is Lancaster." The town was a day's travel from Carlisle in good conditions, and they had been on the road for nearly a day.

She put speculation to one side as the coach drew to a halt. Muffled by the rain, she could hear voices, arguing. She recognized the coachman and one of the two guards that Rose's new husband had insisted on sending with them. The other voices were strangers.

The random words and phrases that reached her ears had her sighing. "...bridge is out...", "...inn...full...", "...go back...".

She was prepared, therefore, when the coachman knocked on the door to report.

"I am sorry, Miss Turner, Lady Vivienne. We cannot go any farther tonight. The middle span of the bridge has been taken out by the flood, and they won't be able to rig a fix until the storm is over."

Worse than that, they would not be able to stay in the village, which had nothing more than a hedge tavern totally unsuitable for gentry, and especially for ladies. Further, the villagers claimed that they'd sent so many people to the farms and cottages up and down the river that, even if the coachman could drive them safely down the narrow and slick roads along the river banks, they would find nowhere to stay.

"Could we go back to the previous village, Mr. Riddick?" Pauline asked.

The coachman shook his head. "I doubt it, Miss. There were two small slips on the road when we went through. Managed to make it over them, but we were coming downhill. Uphill? I wouldn't want to try it." He grimaced. "And we've had more rain since then."

"We will have to throw ourselves on the mercies of a local family," Pauline decided. "Mr. Riddick, is there a local squire? Or a rectory? If they cannot accommodate us, they may know who can."

The nearest squire was beyond the bridge, apparently, and

the village had no resident vicar. But the churchwarden's wife took them under her wing, and Pauline and Vivienne, inadequately protected by a large umbrella, followed her from door to door. Pauline hoped that Vivienne's courtesy title, her age, and her clear refinement might prompt some kind soul to squeeze them in a spare room.

The next hour was frustrating. Every household within reach of the village had already taken all the visitors they could accommodate.

The best anyone could do was a blanket in a barn or in a parlor. "Not suitable for a lady," was the oft-repeated opinion. Pauline would not mind for herself, but if anyone in the London ballrooms discovered Vivienne had slept the night on a farmer's floor, even when there was no other choice, her reputation would be shredded in no time.

To make things worse, another coach that arrived after them reported being barely missed by a slip that made a return impossible. Nobody was going anywhere till the storm passed and repairs could be made.

In the end, the churchwarden's wife agreed to ask her husband whether they might be allowed to make up beds for Pauline, Vivienne, and their maid Betsy in the choir loft, while Mr. Riddick and the Shaw brothers, the guards, slept in the church.

"It will be cold, I fear," their reluctant hostess said, "but at least now the road is closed in all directions, there will be no more people seeking a place to stay. Perhaps them at the Towers might be able to supply some blankets?"

Pauline stopped, and had to take a double-quick step to get back under the umbrella. "The Towers?" she asked. "Is that Rosewood Towers? Where Captain Lord John Forsythe lives?"

Vivienne's eyes lit up. "Peter's friend John? Surely, he will give us a bed for the night?"

The churchwarden's wife shook her head. "He does not allow visitors," she insisted. "Not even the vicar, when he comes to the village. Threatened to shoot him, he did. Still, if you know him…" She did not seem convinced. "I don't know if anyone will show you the way, though, Miss Turner."

"I am sure he will be happy to help us," Vivienne said, happily. "He was very kind to me when I was a little girl. We must go and ask him, Pauline."

Pauline was certain the man would not want her as a visitor, but she did not see how he could refuse his friend's baby sister. "We will," she decided. "Please explain how we find the Towers, and I will have our men escort us there."

⸙

AFTER A DISCUSSION with Vivienne and the servants, Riddick stayed with the vehicle and the horses, which had been accommodated in a farmer's barn.

"I can sleep in the carriage," he assured the farmer, whose family, servants, and farm hands filled every bed to bursting."

"You can eat with the family," the farmer's wife assured him, her eyes gleaming at the thought of the coins Pauline had offered.

With Riddick comfortably placed, the rest of them set off up the hill on the path that led to the Towers, carrying a bag or a satchel each. Pauline hoped that at least some of the clothes packed within would be dry enough to change into once they had traversed the mile that separated the estate from the village.

Certainly, the ones she had on had long since soaked through. Even her bonnet, which should have stayed dry under the umbrella, was saturated, and the sodden brim channeled the rain that drenched it into a waterfall each side of her face, while the bonnet's ribbon ties siphoned more water down her jawline and throat, and even down her chest to soak through to her corset and the breasts beneath.

The light was fading as they approached the house. Pauline gained an impression of a large sprawling mansion anchored at each end by much older, stone towers. Only the towers showed light.

Neil Shaw knocked on the door of the nearest tower and they waited in the rain. He knocked again. After a further wait, he said, "Shall I walk 'round to see if I can knock on a winder, or try yonder big house?"

"Walk around," Pauline decided.

Neil had taken only a few paces when the door suddenly opened. For a split second, Pauline thought it had opened by itself, that no one was in the doorway. Beyond, a shadowy sitting room was only partially lit by a five-branch candelabrum on a table on the other side of the room, where stone steps curved up into darkness.

A child's voice said, "I do not know you." When Pauline dropped her gaze, a little girl with white-blonde hair and large blue eyes stood there, frowning at her.

"Are you visitors?" the child asked. "I did not know we were going to have visitors."

Vivienne stepped up beside Pauline. "You must be Miss Jane Forsythe," she said. "We hope to be visitors. I am Lady Vivienne Ransome, and this is my sister, Miss Pauline Turner. I think you know our brother, Lord Stancroft."

The child nodded. "I know Uncle Peter," she said. "I had better fetch Thorny."

She started to shut the door, but Pauline put a foot out to stop it. "Can we wait inside, out of the rain?"

Jane hesitated. "Visitors are not meant to come into the towers," she said.

"We do not have visitors." The gravelly voice came from a dim corner, where a shape was moving out of the shadows. In the candlelight, it resolved into a man. Pauline barely took in anything about his appearance, her eyes being riveted on the rifle that he cradled. Perhaps the story of the owner of the tower threatening to shoot the vicar had not been the exaggeration she'd thought at the time!

"Thorne, Uncle Peter's sisters have come to visit," said Jane. "I will tell Thorny." In a few quick steps she disappeared up the stairs.

"You can go back where you came from," the man addressed as Thorne insisted, approaching the door. Neil and his brother Keith stepped closer, one on either side of the two sisters. Pauline felt a little safer with them there.

"We cannot," she told Thorne. "The road is blocked. The bridge is out to the south, and a slip prevents travel to the north. The village is full of travelers, with not a single bed to be had."

Thorne shook his head and brandished the rifle. "You cannot come in, and you cannot stay here."

Surely, he would not actually use that thing on them? "You must see that we cannot return down the path in the dark," she told him. Where was his master? She hoped Peter's friend would not turn Peter's sister from his door, much as he might wish Pauline herself to perdition.

Thorne was still shaking his head. "Not my problem. We don't have visitors."

Technically not true, since Peter had been here several times since Captain Lord John Forsythe moved so far north, and at least once, he had brought Arial. The man's brother, the Marquess of Deerhaven, had also visited.

Perhaps Thorne's objection was to women visitors.

He added some weight to that theory by saying, "You can't stay here. Unmarried young women with no chaperone? I know what you're about."

Pauline was perilously close to losing her temper. She could feel the scalding hot words bubbling up inside her. She breathed deep and forced them down.

Vivienne took her hand. "What are we going to do?" she whispered.

Through the wet gloves they each wore, Pauline could feel Vivienne shivering with the cold. "My sister is wet and cold and can go no farther tonight," she said. "You will find us a place to sleep out of the rain."

Thorne sneered. "Or what?"

Beside Pauline, Neil squared his shoulders and opened his mouth, but before he could speak, someone else did. "Or I shall have a word or two of my own to say, Nathaniel Thorne?"

Jane Forsythe scampered back into view, leading the speaker, a woman of about the same age as the man Thorne. "The idea of leaving Lord Stancroft's sisters on the doorstep in the rain! Or any other Christian out on a night like this. Put that silly gun away and go and light a fire in the blue bedchamber. Come in, you poor dears." She nudged her husband out of the way, and beckoned them forward.

Pauline kept a wary eye on Thorne as she followed Vivienne into the tower. Neil and Keith, close on her heels, also watched him closely, waiting for him to make a wrong move. He stood there, indecisive, as Betsy dropped the bag she had been carrying.

Mrs. Thorne hovered over Vivienne, helping her remove her coat and bonnet while lamenting their sodden condition. Thorne put the rifle back on a couple of wall hooks and walked off through an interior door, muttering, "It is not as if it was loaded."

At a nod from Neil, Keith followed the man, and Miss Jane skipped off after them both.

Mrs. Thorne turned her attention to Pauline. "Off with those wet things, Miss Turner. I shall just set the kettle on to boil. And is this your maid?"

"Yes," Pauline acknowledged. She introduced Betsy and Neil. "Neil's brother Keith has gone to help your husband with opening up the room."

Mrs. Thorne looked a bit uncomfortable. "It will just be the one for the two of you," she said. "And your men will have to share, too. It's not that we don't know how to entertain guests, but we are a bit out of practice, and Thorne and I are the only live-in servants, so you see…"

Pauline spoke hastily to reassure her. "Vivienne and I are very happy to share. If you have a pallet, and the room is big enough,

Betsy can stay with us as well. We are easily able to help with the chores. We are so very grateful you have allowed us to stay."

"I could not turn you out into that storm," Mrs. Thorne said. "Even the master would not expect that," she added, but the crease between her eyebrows hinted she was unsure of the last statement.

Another thought wiped the crease away. "He will have nothing to complain of if you just stay clear of him, which will be easy enough, for he seldom comes out of his own tower, and then only to see Miss Jane. If you keep to your rooms, all shall be well."

Chapter Four

JOHN FOUND OUT about the visitors from Thorne, who came to suggest that he might like Jane and his dinner brought to him so he did not risk running into the intruders. "Mrs. Thorne has told them she will bring them dinner in their rooms," he said.

There was no point in being angry with the Thornes. If the road was, indeed, blocked in all directions, then offering a bed to a stranded traveler, especially a sister of John's closest friend, was the right thing to do.

John had his doubts about the road, but even if it was impassable, what were two ladies from London doing on the road between Carlisle and Lancaster in the first place? Given Miss Turner's determined correspondence, only a fool would believe chance played any part in her unexpected and unwanted appearance.

He was no fool, but he was also not going to allow the scheming wanton to disturb his normal habits. "I shall take my meal with Jane as usual."

He would not put himself out to meet people who had invited themselves under his roof, but if he happened to come across the ladies, he would be polite. Distant, but polite. Lady Vivienne, at least, was probably innocent.

He was ready for battle when he strolled over to the other

tower for dinner, and a little disappointed when he found the visitors had taken Mrs. Thorne's admonitions to heart, and had not stirred from the rooms allotted to them.

Not that he missed all mention of them. Jane was full of *Miss Turner this* and *Lady Vivienne that*. She had, apparently, taken herself over to the main house. "We must make sure our visitors are comfortable, Papa," she explained. "Like the princess had to do for the Frog Prince in my book."

"They will only be here until the rain stops," he warned his little girl.

"Yes," she agreed. "For Lady Vivienne is going to London to dance at balls and wear beautiful gowns, and Miss Turner is going to be her chap… Her chapper-wrong."

John discovered he was not above pumping Jane for information. "Why are they all the way up in Cumberland if they are traveling to London?"

Jane, who could have taught a few tricks to some of the interrogators he remembered from his time in the army, knew the answer to that. "Because they have been visiting with a lord and lady in Scotland. I forget the name. But the lady is Lady Vivienne's sister, Rose. She got married and Lady Vivienne and Miss Turner went to Gallows to visit for Christmas."

"Galloway," John suggested, and Jane nodded. Come to think of it, Arial *had* mentioned her sister-in-law's marriage to a gentleman from the west coast of Galloway. Very well, then. Perhaps they had reason to pass through this part of the country. He had no doubt Miss Turner had taken full advantage.

THE RAIN WAS even heavier the next day. John's unwelcome guests would not be moving on. He did not have to see them; he trusted the Thornes for that. Nonetheless, their presence in his house and on his land distracted his attention, so he failed to lose himself in his work. The total concentration he needed was broken by concern about what the she-devil who had schemed her way onto his property might be up to. He kept admonishing himself to forget about her, so he could ensure that every part of the mechanical he was making was placed just exactly where it belonged.

This particular automaton would have over five thousand precisely-made parts, so the potential for disaster was very real. He covered the work and moved to another bench where a simpler piece, a children's toy in the form of a monkey drummer, was waiting for spots of paint to disguise the places where the metal pieces had been joined together with pins so they could move.

Painting was more mindless than constructing a clockwork engine, which had the disadvantage that he had more time to wonder what game Miss Turner was playing. Presumably, she—and probably her sister—were done up in their best gowns, all primped and pretty, and ready to charm him. He was almost tempted to go and see the show.

Mrs. Thorne insisted both ladies and their three servants would remain in their quarters. John snorted his disbelief. Mrs. Thorne did not know ladies of the ton the way that he did.

He finished touching up the monkey drummer and set it aside to dry. According to the workshop clock, Mrs. Thorne would be putting together a meal about now. The visitors were making extra work for her. He could at least help lighten her load by going over to the other tower and fetching his own food.

He knew it was an excuse, even as he thought it. So was his rationale that going through the house would help him avoid the rain. He unlocked the door that separated the tower from the picture gallery in the main wing of the manor, locking it carefully behind him.

He should be honest with himself. He wanted to see the visitors, to prove to himself they were not staying where they had been put, that they were lounging around in fine clothing expecting his overworked servants to wait on them.

Perhaps not Lady Vivienne. He had met her years ago in London, when she and Rose, her sister, ran away from the manipulative, self-centered harridan of a mother she shared with Pauline to beg refuge with Peter. She had been a sweet child. But eight years on, she was no doubt on the marriage market like all the other young women of her class, and lacked a thought in her head beyond marriage and clothing.

The ton and its ways destroyed innocence. He had learned that lesson at his mother's knee, and had had it confirmed first by Belinda, and a second time by his duplicitous wife. He hoped Jane didn't want a Season in London, for either she would be too different to all the other ladies and they would turn on her, or she would make herself over to be like them, and that would destroy him.

He heard nothing in the house. No voices, no movement. Down the main central passage he went, from one end of the main wing to the other, and then up the branch passage that led to the other tower.

When he reached the other end of the main wing, he knew he had been right. The visitors had not stayed put. He could hear them downstairs in Mrs. Thorne's kitchen, laughing and talking. What on earth were ladies like that doing in the kitchen? Making a nuisance of themselves, he'd be bound.

He wasn't going to be kept out of his own kitchen by a pair of Society ladies. And if they were bothering Mrs. Thorne, they could simply get back to their rooms, and so he would tell them.

He walked down the servants' stairs to the kitchen, which was in the lowest level of the main wing of the house. It and its associated store rooms were the only part of the main wing in regular use, though Mrs. Thorne had women from the village up several times a year to give the whole place a good clean.

When he reached the bottom of the stairs, he was struck dumb by the sight of a pretty young lady in a simple day gown slicing a loaf of bread, while an older one whom he recognized as

Miss Turner was helping Jane to sprinkle powdered sugar over the top of a cake.

That was the most startling part of the scene, though all of those currently in the kitchen were busy. Another strange female, presumably the maid, was buttering the slices as Lady Vivienne cut them, and a large, lean man had stopped setting the empty end of the table with crockery and cutlery to eye him suspiciously.

Jane looked up from the cake and flung up her hands, scattering sugar all over Miss Turner. "Papa!"

Mrs. Thorne twisted her hands in her apron and eyed him warily. "Captain, sir."

John heard her, but couldn't tear his eyes off Miss Turner, who was nothing like the besom of his imagination. She wasn't even much like her former self except in general appearance, somewhat modified by the passage of time. The haughty female who had been bosom friends with his former betrothed had worn her discontent on her face and looked down her nose at the world.

This older version of the woman he had met years ago was altogether softer. More rounded, for a start. Eight years ago, she had been slender to the point of gaunt. The extra weight was distributed in all the right places, too, which he shouldn't be noticing.

Nor was she dressed in the height of fashion. In fact, he was fairly certain he had seen the dress under the capacious apron that had caught most of the sugar. If he was right, and it was one of Mrs. Thorne's, she certainly didn't seem to be bothered by it.

She was laughing as she dusted sugar off her nose and cheeks. When she darted out a tongue to taste her own lips, he tore his eyes away, embarrassed by his reaction.

"Papa, did you come to have some of my cake? Miss Turner and I made it our own selves!"

There was only one possible answer. "I would love some cake you made, Jane of mine." For his darling girl's sake, and not because he was at all interested, he added, "Will you introduce me to our guests?"

Jane went to jump down from the chair she was standing on and appeared to realize two things in swift succession. First, that she was still holding the sieve of powdered sugar. Two, as she turned to hand it to Miss Turner, that the lady had been soundly dusted.

"Oh dear," Jane said. "I threw sugar on you."

"These things happen," Miss Turner said, with a twinkle in her eye. "You were excited to see your Papa." She took the sieve and held out the other hand to help Jane jump to the floor.

Jane grabbed John by the hand and pulled him towards the table. "Lady Vivienne and Miss Turner, may I present my Papa, Captain Forsythe?"

She looked to Mrs. Thorne for approval and that dear woman beamed and whispered, "Nicely done, child."

"Papa," Jane continued, "these are Lady Vivienne and Miss Turner. Also, Betsy who is Lady Vivienne's maid and Mr. Neil Shaw, who is a guard who works for…" She wrinkled her brow. "I forget his name," she whispered to Miss Turner.

"Ruadh Douglas, Master of Glencowan," Miss Turner whispered back. "It is a long name to remember, but perhaps your Papa remembers our sister, Rose. The laird is Rose's husband."

Jane nodded. "Mr. Neil Shaw and Mr. Keith Shaw work for Rose's husband, and Rose is Uncle Peter's sister, like Lady Vivienne and Miss Turner." Again, she turned her furrowed brow on Miss Turner. "Should I say Mrs. Douglas instead of Rose?"

John's irritation, always soothed in the presence of his daughter, was rising again. Clearly, Miss Turner had ingratiated herself, not only with the servants, but also with his innocent little girl.

She was explaining that, if Jane met Peter's sister Rose, it would be proper to address her as Lady Douglas. *The family by-blow had done well for herself, then.* John was ashamed of the sour thought as soon as it crossed his mind.

"I understand you have been visiting your sister and her

husband," he said to Lady Vivienne. She was a pretty child, tall and willowy, with fair hair and blue eyes.

"Yes," she said. "It was Rose's first Christmas away from home, and she invited us all up to spend it with her, but Arial was not up to the travel, so Pauline and I went. Then, in January, the weather was too miserable for travel."

Her next remark was made to Miss Turner, "Although travelling in the snow might have been easier than this terrible rain. Here we are stuck, no more than two days travel from Glencowan."

"The rain cannot last forever," Miss Turner told her sister. "Captain Forsythe, we must thank you for allowing us shelter," she added.

The sound of men's voices just beyond the kitchen saved John from having to be polite in return. Thorne had come in the lower door, the one that let onto the kitchen courtyard and a warren of outbuildings, and he had someone with him.

When they entered the kitchen, the resemblance to Neil Shaw identified the other man as the brother, Keith. "Bridge is still down, and village is full nigh to bursting," Thorne reported. "Churchwarden even has half a dozen latecomers sleeping on the floor in the church."

"What about the road blockage north?" John asked. It sounded as if the ladies' story was true, then.

"No one's been up to see it," Thorne said. "Our own hill was treacherous enough in the rain. The travelers who saw half the hillside come down reckon they slid more than they drove the rest of the way to the bottom of the hill. They were lucky to make it. It'd be suicide to go back up Shap Fell before the rain stops."

Miss Turner was asking Keith Shaw about the wellbeing of the driver and the horses. Quite proper that she should, of course, but he hated that he couldn't find a thing to disapprove of since he had entered the room.

Her past history is enough. She is a scheming, social-climbing gos-

sipmonger. I may have to tolerate her presence while it rains, but I won't be fooled by her, or any woman. Never again.

"We were about to eat, Captain," Mrs. Thorne told him. "Shall I make up a tray for you to take back to your workshop?"

"I will have it here," John heard himself saying. "To save work." *And to keep an eye on the intruders.*

Chapter Five

THE WAY CAPTAIN Forsythe behaved at that first meeting—cold but civil—must have reassured the Thornes, for Pauline heard nothing more about her and her party staying in their rooms. It appeared that the tiny household generally spent most of its time in the kitchen, and the temporary residents soon got into the habit of joining them.

They had ignored the prescribed confinement when Pauline realized that the Thornes were the only resident servants. Five extra people who sat about doing nothing was too much of a burden to put onto a staff of two.

Pauline gathered from the surprised reaction of Mrs. Thorne and Jane that the captain seldom joined them for meals. For some mysterious reason, he hated being addressed by his courtesy title, so she must remember not to call him Lord John.

Apparently, Captain Forsythe spent most of his time in the second tower which contained, as well as his living quarters, some mysterious place that the Thornes and Jane referred to as his "workshop". No one explained what he did in that room.

However, after his surprise appearance on their first day at Rosewood Towers, he apparently instructed Thorne to call him whenever they were gathering to eat. The departure from usual custom was a matter for much muttered discussion between

Thorne and Mrs. Thorne, and Pauline's unusually good hearing made her party to it whether she would or not.

Thorne's view was that the captain was keeping an eye on the intruders, and making sure they did not in any way upset or harm his little girl. Mrs. Thorne took the more charitable view that he had been smitten at first sight by Lady Vivienne's sweetness and beauty.

The second was possible, though he showed none of the signs of infatuation displayed by the army of suitors who had swarmed after Vivienne since she was first judged old enough to attend a private dinner or a village assembly.

However, he was markedly warmer to Vivienne than to Pauline. Indeed, he addressed Pauline as seldom as possible, was rigidly cold and polite to her, and always eyed her with suspicion. It was to Vivienne that he addressed permission to move freely anywhere in the main wing of the house, and to make whatever use she pleased of his library, but Pauline availed herself of the same opportunities and he said nothing.

The captain's attitude to Pauline annoyed Vivienne far more than it did Pauline. "He is horrid to you, Pauline darling," she complained as they walked along the picture gallery on the third morning of their stay. "So cold and formal. When he is talking to Jane, I really like him. He is pleasant enough to me. But when he speaks to you, I want to slap him. I really should say something."

Pauline begged her not to do so. "We are uninvited guests under the gentleman's roof. Please do not insult him. He has reasons for his opinion about me."

Vivienne shook her head. "It's just because our mother and sister were horrid and they made you be horrid with them. You were never mean to me or Rose, and anyway, you made up for it. When Mother plotted to get rid of Peter and Arial, you were the one who saved them. We all love you very much, Pauline."

Her words were a comfort and her hug more so. However, Pauline was more inclined to agree with Captain Forsythe than with her sister, who was prejudiced in her favor. When he'd met her eight years ago, she had been—in her sister's words—horrid.

Yes, she had done what she could secretly to look after Vivienne and Rose, but she had never stood up to her mother, or even to her sister Laura. Not even for the two little girls.

With her mother and Laura, she had spent money on gowns and bonnets and fripperies with no thought to how the bills would be paid, even after her stepfather died and Peter discovered that the estates were badly in debt.

In Society, she had helped to spread malicious gossip, with no care as to its truth. She had delighted in mean and cutting remarks that sapped the confidence of others. She believed her mother, who claimed other young ladies were doing the same behind her back, and winning their own excellent matches at the expense of Pauline and Laura.

The change had begun when Peter married Arial. She well remembered her step-brother telling the three of them that his father had spent their dowries and most of the dower fund that was meant to support his widow. Peter proposed to reinstate them, and continue Mother's allowance, even double it.

Mother and Laura had been offended and furious, especially when he made the benefits contingent on them ceasing to spread nasty stories about him and his wife. Pauline was surprised he had been so generous, and inclined to give the credit to Arial.

Over the following weeks, she found it was easier not to be nasty about Peter or Arial if she avoided all gossip, and all unpleasant remarks. It would be worth it, though. She was twenty-two, and Peter had promised to pay out her dowry in full when she was twenty-five. She set herself to earn her freedom.

She was surprised to discover that some of the other wallflowers were quite pleasant to her when she stopped being unpleasant to them. Laura was scathing, but she mostly kept her criticism for the privacy of the townhouse Peter had provided. Rent free. Peter really was more generous than they had any right to expect. Especially when his stepmother and stepsisters had been so unkind to him.

The realization that Peter would have been justified in leaving them all to starve had only been the start. Another major step had been her revulsion when she overheard Mother plotting to have Peter killed and Arial confined to an asylum, so that her own daughter, Vivienne, would inherit everything. Pauline chose sides by going to her stepbrother and telling him what she had heard.

Mother and Laura had fled overseas, and Pauline had heard from them precisely once since, when Laura was married to an Italian count and wrote to crow about her newly married status and her townhouse in Paris, in a letter full of mock pity for her spinster sister.

So really, how was Captain Forsythe to know how much Pauline had changed since they last met?

"Captain Forsythe's opinion of me would have been true before Peter married Arial," she told Vivienne. "He has been living out of Society ever since. I do not blame him for remembering me as I was before, and you mustn't either, darling Vivienne. I am not offended. I am just glad he is not openly rude."

"He has been living out of Society because he chose to sue his wife for a divorce," Vivienne insisted. "That tells us a lot about his character, I think."

Pauline disagreed. She had been at the house party where he announced his betrothal after being caught with a young lady under circumstances that left the captain's friends distressed on his behalf. And as the divorce had been so much a topic of conversation within the ton, she could not help but know that, as soon as the decree was made final, Mrs. Forsythe had married the man for whom she had fled her husband and daughter.

"On the basis of gossip and hearsay, I refuse to judge either his character, or that of his ex-wife," she told Vivienne. "As to his attitude, you must remember we were uninvited and unexpected guests."

Vivienne was not convinced. "I know we were not invited, but it is not as if we planned to be trapped in this place."

Pauline was sure John suspected she had travelled this road in the hopes that they would be forced to seek his hospitality.

"He probably thinks it too much of a coincidence," she said. "I have written to him several times asking for cuttings from his roses. He has not ever replied. It is odd that, of all the places I might have been trapped, and of all the people who might turn up at his door, it is one whose correspondence he has been ignoring."

Vivienne snorted. "Silly man. As if you could have planned a storm, a bridge collapse, and a landslide in the mountains. Besides, even I know that you can't take cuttings at this season."

Pauline chuckled. "To be fair, darling, you have helped me out in the garden often. Given how much I talk about roses, it would be hard for you not to have learned at least a little."

"True, sister dear," Vivienne agreed. "Do you think the rain is a little less heavy? I would so love to walk outside and see something new!"

"Soon enough," Pauline soothed. "Shall we go to the library and choose another book to read to little Jane?"

Chapter Six

WHAT HE'D OVERHEARD gave John much to think about. Perhaps Miss Turner was not as bad as he'd thought. Certainly, Jane liked her. She liked Lady Vivienne, too, but Miss Turner dominated her conversation. Miss Turner showed her how to paint a rose. Did Papa know that Miss Turner grew roses? Miss Turner read to her every afternoon and made all the voices. Not as well as Papa, because Papa was the best, but it was nice to be read to twice a day.

Miss Turner sewed Clarabella, Jane's much-washed rag doll, a new face and made the poor toy a new wig out of plaited wool.

Miss Turner tried to teach Jane to plait, but Jane made a tangle. Miss Turner said it was her own fault, for trying to teach Jane too early, but Jane was so clever that Miss Turner forgot she was only seven. Jane was going to try to learn to plait when she was eight, and Miss Turner said she should try each year until she managed it, and then she would know she was old enough.

John had tried to convince himself the female was just trying to ingratiate herself with John by being nice to Jane, but she ignored him except for common courtesy and was sweet to Jane whether John was watching or not.

He had been consoling himself with the thought that being nice to children did not preclude being a harpy in every other respect. But Lady Vivienne clearly loved her, Mrs. Thorne was favorably impressed, and even Thorne had allowed that she was not as bad as she'd been painted.

She was even polite and friendly to her own servants, and they did not seem to be surprised. That could not possibly be an act for his benefit.

And now this conversation. She could not have known he had been just on the other side of the door to his tower, which was hidden behind a curtain at the end of the picture gallery.

Perhaps her letters really had been about his roses. But what did she want cuttings for? A person could get all sorts of roses anywhere in England! He would not check the letters to find out what she had said. He had told Thorne to burn them, but he was almost certain the man had put them somewhere. It wasn't worth facing Thorne's knowing looks to ask for them, but he was beginning to think he might have been a bit hasty in his judgement.

By dinner time, the rain was decidedly easing. The winds had dropped, too; the storm was at last passing.

"Perhaps we will be able to leave tomorrow," Lady Vivienne said, hopefully.

"It will take a day or two to fix the bridge, I imagine," John warned. "It is likely to depend how quickly the river goes down to its normal level." He found himself adding, "You are welcome to stay until it is safe to travel."

From the look on Mrs. Thorne's face, he had been more of an ogre than he had realized.

JOHN WOKE THE following morning to sunshine. His window looked over the valley below, so he had a good view of the sodden landscape. Lakes and ponds glittered in the sunlight where barley normally grew or animals grazed.

He could not see the village or the bridge, which were close under the hill, but the river ran into view in full spate, the turbulent waters stretching from bank to bank and, in places, spilling over on one side or the other.

Still, it would go down nearly as quickly as it had risen, if rain had stopped falling in the hills.

Thorne must already be up, for a bucket of hot water waited in his dressing room for his morning ablutions. He would have to give the Thornes both some time off after the guests left, to make up for the extra work, though the guests were helping far more than he expected, and with better grace.

In the meantime, now it had stopped raining, perhaps Mrs. Thorne could persuade a few of the villagers to come during the day to help with the cooking and cleaning.

Dressed, John first of all checked on his work. The automaton he was building for the clock tower in Carlisle was beginning to take shape—four mechanicals, each taking up a quarter of a circle, each powering a scene.

It illustrated the town's history, and had been commissioned by the Town Council. The first scene would show a Roman fort, with soldiers marching to and fro. Carlisle was nearly at the Western end of Hadrian's Wall. The second was intended to depict towering castle walls, with arrows raining down on besiegers who raised their shields in protection. Carlisle's place in the borderlands ensured there had been many such incidents. The third showed a market, complete with moving peddlers and a hand cart. The fourth celebrated the current prosperity; the woolen loom that was its centerpiece was giving John more trouble than all the rest.

When finished, with the sets painted and populated, the whole device would activate on the hour, and shift a quarter turn every ninety seconds until all four scenes had showed through the front aperture of the clock tower. It was the most complicated, and the most lucrative, automaton John had ever made.

The monkey drummer was finished. It awaited just the jacket

that Mrs. Thorne had not yet had time to make. The jacket would cover the mechanism inside the monkey, which would be accessible from the back.

On an impulse, he put the device into a box to take across to the kitchen with him. If he had the chance while Jane was out of the room—the monkey was intended as a surprise for her—he would ask Mrs. Thorne about the coat.

LURED BY THE sunshine, Pauline went for a walk before breakfast. Fortunately, her walking boots had dried out since their arrival, and one of the Shaw brothers had oiled the leather again. The grass paths through the gardens were soggy underfoot, with wide puddles in places, but none of them too deep to walk through without the water leaking in around her laces.

The gardens showed signs of a ruthless sort of care. What was probably a herbaceous border in the summer was buried deep under layers of straw. Shrubs and heathers had been clipped into regimented mounds. Here and there were signs of a more naturalistic imagination. Primroses sent up their hopeful flowers in shady corners. Drifts of snowdrops starred the grass under a small grove of trees.

She came around a corner and the bare frames to find scaffolds of rose bushes everywhere. They had been mercilessly pruned to hardened wood, and the first soft new leaves would not appear until spring warmed the earth.

She stopped, nonetheless, wondering which was the rose from which Arial had been given so lavish a bundle.

"Good morning," said a voice, startling her. She shrieked and then clamped her mouth shut, blushing at her own startled response.

"I beg your pardon," said Captain Forsythe—for it was him, of course. He offered her a smile, sad-edged like all his smiles, though this was the first he had ever directed her way. "It is pleasant to have the sun, is it not? I see you were tempted to make its reacquaintance, as was I."

"I hope you do not mind, Captain Forsythe."

"Not at all. Please feel free to explore wherever you like in the garden. You like gardens, Arial tells me."

"I design gardens, and I breed roses," Pauline corrected, and could not resist adding, "as I explained in my letters." If she could have bitten the words back, she would have. Here he was being pleasant for the first time in their entire acquaintance, and she could not resist a sniping comment.

However, Captain Forsythe did not retreat into his cold disdain. Instead, he colored. "I apologize, Miss Turner. I did not read your letters."

For a moment, Pauline was flummoxed. She had known he had chosen to ignore them, but she had never dreamt he'd not even read them. "I see," was all she could think of to say.

"I am most sincerely sorry," he said.

She had never blamed him for thinking ill of her, though she had regretted it, so her answer was prompt. "I accept your apology," she told him.

"They were about your roses?" he asked.

Because the cold disdain was gone from his voice and face, she gave him her honest answer rather than a polite one. "About yours, actually. I think the roses you gave Arial during a visit some years ago may be just what I need to achieve the deep pink I am trying for." He looked interested rather than disapproving, so she continued with her explanation. "I've come close to the color I have in mind, but the resulting cross-bred seedlings were weak and disease-prone. I was hoping for cuttings from whichever bush carries that glorious cerise, for Arial said your bushes were vigorous and healthy."

"So, you want my bushes to be parents to a new breed?" he asked. If she had been forced to put a name on his expression, it would be intrigued. That was hopeful.

She nodded. "In essence. Or grandparents. From the cuttings, I could grow plants that were identical to yours, then pollinate their flowers from several other roses that I think may give the results I want, while also using their pollen on those other plants." She had allowed her enthusiasm to carry her away and forgotten that an unmarried lady did not talk about pollination with an unmarried man. She turned away so he could not see her blush.

However, his response was neither salacious nor disgusted. "I see. Then you plant the rose hips, is that right?"

"Plant the seeds *in* the rose hips," she corrected, "and hope the seedlings will grow, and that one of them will give me all the qualities I want."

"A deep pink color, disease-resistance. What else?"

"Deep-pink streaked in a golden yellow," she corrected. "Plus, a vigorous growth habit, a sizeable double bloom, fragrance." She chuckled. "I do not want much, Captain Forsythe. Just perfection."

"You have done this before," he observed. "Tell me about the other roses to which you have been midwife."

She studied him for a moment. He seemed interested, and he had asked, so she told him about the Rosalind Douglas, a soft white with a pink blush, named for her sister, and the Countess of Stancroft, whose white and magenta streaks made it stand out in the crowd.

"I would love to achieve a true purple," she said, a little wistfully.

"The Lady Vivienne?" he asked, and she laughed.

"Exactly," she confirmed.

"You are very fond of your sisters, are you not?"

This version of Captain Forsythe was easy to talk to, and since he knew her past, she had no reason to measure her words. "You probably know I am not actually related to any of them except Vivienne," she confessed. "She and I share a mother. But I love them and they love me. All of them, even Arial and Peter, though they had more reason than most to hate me. I would do anything for them, Captain Forsythe."

He sounded slightly surprised when he said, "I believe you."

Pauline should just leave it at that, but she had been disturbed by his hostility, and shaken by the knowledge he had not even read her letters. "I'm glad. But if you did not know about my desire for rose cuttings, I cannot imagine why you thought I was writing, or why I intruded unannounced. I suspect you thought I arranged to be stranded here, but I do not comprehend what you thought was my purpose." Surely, he didn't think that he was such a marital prize that she would take such extreme measures to attract him as a husband? Even if she knew how to do such a thing.

He flushed again. "Foolishness," he said, stiffly.

Good heavens. He *did* think she was out to trap him. *Or he had.* Since his attitude appeared to have softened, she would try to ignore it.

"May I escort you to breakfast, Miss Turner?" he asked, with a touch of his former stiffness.

He moved the box he held under one arm to the other side so he could offer her his elbow. She used that as a pretext to change the subject. "What do you have there, Captain, if I may ask?"

He seemed relieved by the shift in the conversation, for he grinned. "A toy for Jane. I will show you, if you like. Perhaps we could sit in the summer house for a moment?"

He showed her through a gap in the yew hedge to a sheltered garden.

Within the yews, a circular garden slept under its mulch. At the center a little eight-sided summerhouse was accessed by shallow steps on the nearest side. Captain Forsythe invited her to sit on the bench that wrapped around the other seven sides and sat beside her.

"We would be warmer in the house, but I don't want to risk Jane seeing it yet."

"I am warm enough," Pauline assured him, as she looked

around at the mulched beds. She wondered what they held.

Captain Forsythe was opening the box, and she turned her attention back to that. He pulled out a model of a monkey bent over a drum, and held it up for her to admire. It was made out of metal, and painted—the monkey in shades of brown and white, and the drum in bright yellow, red, and green.

"It is quite realistic, isn't it," she said, not quite sure what else to say.

"Wait," he said with another of those boyish grins. "There's more."

The captain set the box to one side, and held the monkey on his knee, showing that the back was open and contained some sort of metal mechanism. He produced a key and poked it into a hole in the little device, and turned it several times.

Then, he let go of the key.

Chapter Seven

MISS TURNER'S FACADE of polite interest was very different to the enthusiasm she'd shown a few minutes ago over her roses, but then the little toy's arms began to move up and down, the sticks fell on the drum, and the monkey's head bobbed back and forth, keeping time with the drum beat.

Miss Turner laughed, a delighted chortle, and clapped her hands together. "It plays the drum," she declared. "Oh, Jane will love it."

"It's nothing, really," he demurred. "Just a bit of nonsense."

"I think it is wonderful. So clever! Mrs. Thorne said you had a workshop. Is this what you make in there?"

"I make mechanicals," he confessed. "Automata, as they are called."

Miss Turner was so interested that John found himself telling her all about the hobby that had become something of a business.

"I started making them at a time when I needed something to do," he told her. He'd made the first in the months after his marriage, a distraction from the cold disdain of his new wife and his growing certainty he'd made a terrible mistake.

"I found I enjoyed it, and kept it up." Through the misery that followed, tinkering with automata had been his refuge.

No one had been more surprised than him when one he had

given away attracted a sponsor at the highest level. "Then, after a couple of years, the Prince Regent saw an automaton I had given to my sister-in-law, Cordelia, and hinted strongly that he'd like one, too. And when other people saw that one and started clamoring for their own, Deerhaven advised me to make them on commission. So, I found myself in trade, quite without meaning to."

"My own story is similar in a way," Miss Turner mused. "I began gardening as a way to help Arial, and found I loved nurturing things and making them grow. Then, I offered advice to some of Arial's friends, and that led to others asking for my help with their gardens. Peter suggested I charge a fee, and so I also found myself in trade." She chuckled, and said, with some scorn, "As if those who make beautiful things with their own hands are somehow less worthy than those who make their income off the labor of others."

"Yes, indeed," John agreed. "I do not understand what is so worthy about living off one's relatives and so despicable about making one's own way."

"Perhaps Society's opinion is formed by the drone bees rather than the worker bees?" Miss Turner suggested, dryly.

John gave a snort of laughter. He rather liked the lady's sense of humor.

She was quite pretty when she smiled. He'd noticed that before, though she had not smiled at him until this morning. He rather liked it.

She lowered her eyes and looked away towards the opening in the hedge. "I ought to go in. Vivienne will be wondering where I am. Are you giving the monkey to Jane this morning?"

John shook his head. "It needs a jacket. I am going to ask Mrs. Thorne to make one, when she has time."

"I could do it," Miss Turner offered. "It is our fault that Mrs. Thorne is currently short of time, and I would enjoy making some small recompense for your hospitality."

John's conscience gave him a firm boot in the rear end. "I

have not been at all hospitable, Miss Turner, as you well know."

She shook her head. "After the first shock, you have been very pleasant to Vivienne and the servants, and you didn't turn even me out into the rain. Let me make the little jacket, Captain Forsythe. It can be a symbol of our truce." Humor danced in her eyes, and that decided him. That and his residual guilt for his harsh judgement of her.

He finished packing the monkey into the box and handed it to her. "Here you are, then. And thank you."

She stood, the box cradled in one arm. "What sort of a jacket do you require? What color and shape? Do you want it trimmed?"

He waved a hand. "Whatever you do will be excellent. It is just to cover the mechanism. As long as it has a hole in the back for the key, Jane and I will be delighted."

She walked away down the steps towards the gap in the hedge, still talking. "I shall hide it in my room when I run up to take off my coat and scarf, and I shall see what scraps I can find to make the jacket this afternoon."

He hurried after her. "You may take any cuttings you like," he offered.

She gifted him with another warm smile. "Thank you. I appreciate the thought, but I am afraid that, even if I knew which of the bushes carries the rose I want, they will not produce material suitable for taking cuttings for months."

He fell into step beside her, and found himself saying, "Then perhaps you will come back in the summer, if it suits."

She stopped and stared at him for a moment, her mouth open, then gathered her composure again and resumed walking. "Thank you, Captain. I will hope to take you up on that offer."

Chapter Eight

Captain Forsythe returned to his tower after breakfast. When Vivienne offered to take Jane's morning lessons, Mrs. Thorne was delighted. "I want to turn the pantry out, and make a list of things we'll need once we can get up to Carlisle," she said. She was even more pleased when Betsy offered her help in the kitchen.

Pauline, after briefly explaining her self-imposed task to Vivienne and Betsy and swearing them to secrecy, locked herself in their bedchamber. Between her workbasket and Vivienne's, she soon found enough pieces to make a bright red jacket trimmed with gilt braiding and a stand-up black collar, also trimmed with braiding. She fastened it with tiny mother-of-pearl buttons that she had removed from some gloves she had thrown out. The gloves had been so mud-stained on the day they arrived, they were ruined. She also created a buttonhole in the jacket back from which the key could protrude.

She glued some of the red fabric to stiff paper to make a little stand-up cap, also trimmed with braid and with a braid chin strap. She was quite delighted with it, and so were Vivienne and Betsy when they returned to the bedchamber so Vivienne could change out of the old gown she'd worn while she and Jane painted.

"Captain Forsythe made this himself?" Vivienne was astounded.

Betsy knew all about it. "Spends all his time at it, Mrs. Thorne says. Much as her life is worth to clean in there, except once a month when he puts everything away and goes to Carlisle for business. Makes all sorts of clever little things, he does. Absolute wonders, says Mrs. Thorne."

"I had no idea," Vivienne marveled. "I wonder if he would show us?"

Vivienne was much inclined to wonder about Captain Forsythe's new attitude to Pauline, and Betsy wanted to pass on some of the details of the captain's sad history, as related by Mrs. Thorne, but Pauline stopped them both. "You know I cannot abide gossip," she said. "If Captain Forsythe wishes us to know what has happened to him and how he feels about it, he will tell us. Shall we go down to our noon meal?"

THE CAPTAIN ARRIVED late, after the rest of the household had already been served a bowl each of hearty stew, with fresh bread that Mrs. Thorne had somehow found time to make while sorting the pantry.

"Please accept my apologies, Mrs. Thorne, ladies," he said. "I got caught up and didn't notice the time. No, Mrs. Thorne, don't get up. I can serve myself."

For a marquess's son, he certainly did not stand on ceremony.

He brought his bowl over to the table and took a seat next to Jane. "How was your morning, darling girl?"

Jane chattered away about her painting lesson, which had largely consisted (to hear Jane tell the tale) of mixing different colors to see the result. Vivienne added a word or two of explanation. Apparently, they had written a story and then made a painting to illustrate it. The blending lesson followed a minor crisis when an over-enthusiastic painter attempted to blotch her green dragon with purple spots, and was most unhappy with the resulting brownish gray.

Pauline gave Captain Forsythe credit for keeping his amusement to dancing eyes as he gravely agreed that knowing how to mix colors was an important skill for a painter.

"When I am big, Papa," Jane told him, "I can help paint your mechanicals."

"That will be excellent," he said.

Thorne and the Shaw brothers had been down to the village. "Bridge will be a couple of days," they reported. "Slip on the hill could be a week."

"Jane will miss our visitors," Captain Forsythe said. "Won't you, Jane? Perhaps they will visit again next time they go to see Lady Douglas."

What a contrast to his attitude when they arrived!

Pauline followed him out of the tower after the meal, and gave him the box. "I hope this is what you want," she said. "Let me know if anything needs to be changed."

Before he could look, Jane came running from the tower door, followed by Vivienne. "Miss Turner, we are going to get some eggs from the chickens. Will you come with us, Miss Turner?"

Captain Forsythe tucked the box under his arm and gave Pauline another of his wistful smiles. "I'm sure what you've done will be perfect." And they went their separate ways until later that afternoon, when Captain Forsythe gave Jane her new toy.

Jane was thrilled, and had to wind it up straightaway and set it drumming on the kitchen table.

"The jacket is marvelous," Captain Forsythe told Pauline. "I love the hat. That was a really nice touch. I put a spot of glue to hold it in place when the playing gets too enthusiastic."

Just as well, for Jane had tipped the monkey over again to rewind it for the fourth time. After that, she had a kiss and a hug for her Papa. "I am going to call him Matty," she said. "Matty Monkey."

"You must thank Miss Turner, too," said the captain. "She made Matty's coat and hat."

The young lady then required Pauline, too, to bend over for a kiss and a hug. Jane pronounced the monkey's clothes to be perfect.

"I quite agree," Captain Forsythe murmured to Pauline. "I wondered… if you and Lady Vivienne are not busy, would you like a tour of my workshop?"

⋙⋘

JOHN HAD SHOWN his brother Deerhaven and Peter Stancroft through his workshop, but no lady had ever stepped inside. Except Mrs. Thorne, to clean. She did not see his work, because he packed everything away into boxes, which he put into cupboards, each month before she was allowed in.

Lady Vivienne was intrigued by the little figures and other items that were to populate the scenes for the Carlisle clockwork, but the mechanisms themselves did not interest her. Miss Turner, on the other hand, was truly examining the pieces, asking intelligent questions, and listening to his answers.

Lady Vivienne's eyes glazed over when Miss Turner began to ask about how the mechanicals would work and the purpose of the various tools. "Some of my samples are in the bookshelves near the stairwell, Lady Vivienne," he said. "The doors are not locked, if you would care to examine the pieces more closely. I only ask that, if you wish to wind them up, you put them on the nearby table, first."

She thanked him, and the alacrity with which she stepped away confirmed his sense she had been politely bored.

"The key for each should be in the mechanical at the back," he added. "Five full turns should be enough to set the automaton working."

Lady Vivienne opened the first pair of glass doors, and was

soon absorbed in examining what lay within.

"Will overturning damage the mechanism?" Miss Turner asked.

He showed her how the key tightened the long coil of a flat spring.

"The uncoiling of the spring turns the gears, levers and cogs to move the automaton," he explained, releasing the key so that the spring relaxed. "Once the tension has gone from the spring, the mechanical stops. Wind up clocks and pocket watches work the same way."

He touched the loose coil. "If the coil is over tightened," he added, "the spring may break, usually at the joint to the rest of the mechanism. I am not concerned about the ones Lady Vivienne is looking at. Those are mostly for display. Besides, she will be careful, and if anything goes wrong, I can always fix it."

Miss Turner touched the spring. "Will the device you are building also be worked by a key and a spring?"

John frowned as he thought about how to explain. "They are going to be mounted under a tower clock, which is powered by a dropping weight that swings a pendulum." He went on to explain how he would attach a separate mechanical to open the doors in front of the scene as the minute hand reached the hour, and to turn it one quarter at a time as each set of figures finished their action.

"It will also trigger each scene mechanical on the turn, and stop that mechanical when it ends," he said.

Each scene mechanical was powered by a mainspring. Since these unwound slowly and were stopped after a minute and a half, they would need to be wound only once a week, at the same time as the clock weight was pulled back to the top.

By this time, Lady Vivienne had ceased making any attempt to pretend she was listening, and was looking longingly at the door. Miss Turner, however, appeared rapt.

"I apologize," John said to them both. "I tend to get carried away. I do not mean to bore you."

"You haven't," Miss Turner assured him. She smiled at her sister. "Vivienne is used to enthusiasts. Heaven knows I have bent her ears often enough about the intricacies of rose breeding."

"If you are truly interested," John said to Miss Turner, "would you like to watch me finish assembling and testing the first mechanical? It is my task for tomorrow morning, after I've broken my fast." He bowed to Lady Vivienne. "That is, if you are prepared to come and play propriety, my lady. You could, perhaps, bring a book?"

Miss Turner's eyes lit up. "I would love to. Vi, darling, if you would be unutterably bored, I shall bring Betsy."

Lady Vivienne laughed and said she was happy to sit by the window with a book, and they arranged that the ladies would present themselves at ten the following morning.

After they left, John wondered what on earth had got into him.

Have you not learnt your lesson, man? Just because they smile and flatter!

He had to be honest. It was more than that. It was more than guilt for his coldness to Miss Turner, whose unpleasant behavior was eight years in the past. Although, to be sure, her earnest self-blame had heaped him with remorse. He wanted to spend more time with her, even as he recognized the danger inherent in indulging his wishes.

She could have been acting. If so, she was a much better actor than anyone he'd ever known. His love for his mother had not prevented him from recognizing her inherent selfishness. Even blinded by infatuation for his first betrothed, he had developed concerns about her attitude to those she saw as different or of lesser status.

As for his former wife, he had understood her to be conniving from the very first, although not well enough to avoid the trap she laid for him. Just how conniving, he did not realize until later.

Everything would be fine. Miss Turner would have Lady Vivienne or her maid with her, and in a day or two, they would be on their way south. He had no reason to feel under siege. She had made it clear that all she wanted out of him was a few cuttings of his roses—that is, if she was telling the truth.

He pulled his box of parts closer to the part of his work bench where he was building the next mechanical. It was a wooden tray divided into multiple boxes: every size of cog, gear, wheel, hook, lever, rod, screw, and wire in its own place.

"The problem is, John," he told himself, "you like her. You don't trust her, but you do like her. If it is just a façade, it's a good one."

It was worse than that. He wouldn't say the truth out loud, even if he was the only person in the entire tower building. He wouldn't have believed it just a few days ago, for she was really rather plain and no longer young. *You desire Pauline Turner. You fool.*

Chapter Nine

WHEN THEY CAME down for breakfast, Mrs. Thorne told Pauline and Vivienne that Captain Forsythe had turned up early for an apple and piece of cheese, and would not be joining them for breakfast.

Pauline wondered if he regretted his invitation, but Mrs. Thorne did not have a message withdrawing it, so she was determined to go. The clockwork mechanicals intrigued her. While the large one he was so proud of was too complicated for her to fully understand, she had been able to follow Captain Forsythe's explanations. She hoped he would show her something simpler—she was sure that she would be able to figure out how and why it worked.

Vivienne was far less enthused. When the Thornes announced they would go to the village this morning to see if they could replenish any of the household stores, Vivienne looked hard at them and then turned pleading eyes on Pauline.

"May I go, too? I am desperate to retrieve another gown from our luggage. I know you are anxious to watch Captain Forsythe at his work, Pauline, so I will stay if you need me, but you did say Betsy might do, instead."

Pauline hoped Betsy wasn't keen to clamber down the still slippery hill to the village and back again, for the maid was to be disappointed. Pauline was determined to have her treat. Her imagination fed her an image of Captain Forsythe bent over his workbench; his legs outlined in his form-fitting moleskins. *Learning more about automatons*, she corrected her errant mind. *That treat.*

"Of course," she told Vivienne. "Take one of the Shaws with you, dearest, and stay close to Mrs. Thorne."

In the end, both of the guards left with Vivienne, the Thornes, and Jane. They planned to consult with Mr. Riddick to find out whether they could resume their journey tomorrow, and if so, to hire the necessary horses and arrange for the carriage to be ready.

It was nearly ten, and Pauline's heart should not be thumping like a debutante's about to step into her first ball. Heavens, she was not even sure that she liked Captain Forsythe. He was certainly a nicer man than first impressions would indicate. He was loving with his daughter, and treated his servants well, and she certainly admired his craftsmanship. *And his legs.*

But he had judged Pauline and found her guilty without reading even a single one of her letters. He was arrogant and suspicious.

Even so, she liked him. No, she would not lie to herself. She was not sure whether or not she liked him, but she was attracted to him. He made her tingle, and she could not remember when that last happened. Certainly not in a long time.

Pauline was technically an innocent, but she had a theoretical knowledge of the mechanics of lust. Her mother had not been discrete in her liaisons, nor had her mother's lovers entirely ignored Pauline and Laura. She had never been in the least tempted to risk even the mildest of assignations.

Perhaps it was as well she knew he had suspected her of engineering their visit. If she showed in any way she found him desirable, he would undoubtedly return to his first opinion of her.

Pride, as much as her wish for his respect, would keep her from showing him anything of her feelings.

The clock in the hall chimed ten times. Pauline called Betsy to her, and they walked across the carriageway from the house to Captain Forsythe's tower, and knocked.

They waited. She was about to knock again, thinking he hadn't heard, when he opened the door.

"Miss Turner! And Miss Betsy, too. Please, do come in."

"Everyone else has gone down to the village, Captain Forsythe, but Betsy has been kind enough to join me so I can accept your invitation and learn more about making automatons."

Captain Forsythe smiled and asked Betsy, "And do you wish to learn about how to make automatons?"

Betsy denied any such desire, and chose a chair by one of the windows, where she could sit in the shade, but have her hands in good light for the mending she had in her work basket.

Captain Forsythe beckoned Pauline over to the workbench. "I am about to make the final linkages to the Roman scene and then test it," he said. "Would you care to watch?"

The mechanical was raised up on a stand, so he could access the parts beneath the painted and molded cover, which formed the land on which the scene took place. Small pieces of metal poked up in various places through slots in the cover.

Pauline found herself not merely watching, but holding various figurines in the air above these connection points so Captain Forsythe could maneuver them gently into place, and secure them. Once the little centurion and four of the six legionnaires had been fitted, Captain Forsythe offered her the tools and held the final two legionnaires for her.

They exchanged grins as she let go of the last little soldier and he stood firmly in place.

"Now to test it," Captain Forsythe said. He ducked down and reached around the side, where an l-shaped lever stuck out from the mechanical. "This is a temporary key," he commented. "Once I am certain all four mechanicals work, I can secure them in their frame and connect them up to the master." He was turning the lever around and around as he spoke.

"Here goes," he said.

He let go, the centurion raised his arm, and the six legionnaires marched across their stage, three from left to right and three from right to left.

Pauline grabbed his arm in her excitement, bouncing with delight. "It is wonderful!"

Betsy, who had crept closer to watch the demonstration, let out a sigh of awe and brought Pauline back to sobriety. She dropped Captain Forsythe's arm as if scalded. "I beg your pardon." She was sincere, but she could not wipe the grin off her face. "But it is exciting, is it not?"

"Every time," he reassured her. "Mind you, I still have quite a bit to do. But at least I know it works. All the rest is just about perfecting the timing and adding the final flourishes. When the whole thing is done, there will be a set of bells and hammers to play a tune, but I haven't even begun that part yet."

Pauline shook her head at the wonder of it all. "It is most marvelous. Thank you so much for showing me."

"Would you like to build one of your own?" Captain Forsythe asked. He led her to another work table that held a little model stage with clowns, an equestrian, a juggler, a ringmaster, and a high wire walker who perched above the rest.

Next to it, sat another stage with the figurines laid out on the table beside.

"Here is a set of tools," Captain Forsythe told her. "Use the finished one as an example, and ask me if you have any questions."

He returned to his own work, and Pauline immersed herself in the little world he had given her to create.

She had to interrupt him once, but for the most part she was able to copy what had been done. The hardest part was attaching the pole and feet of the high wire walker correctly. The pole was attached at each end to a near invisible thread at the figurine's shoulder height. The thread, she could see, went around a pulley at each end, and down into the mechanism. The tightrope did the same thing, with two thicker threads so that each foot could move past the other.

Eventually, she was done. She straightened, set her tools

down, and looked around her. The sunlight had moved from one side of the window to the other, and Betsy was fast asleep in the sun. Captain Forsythe was preparing a plate of food from a tray of bread, meat and other items.

He grinned at her. "All done? You were so absorbed I did not want to disturb you, or Betsy, either. I crept out and fetched some food and a jug of Thorne's cider from the kitchen, in case you were as hungry as I am."

Pauline *was* hungry, she realized. But more compelling than that was the desire to test her automaton to see if it worked.

Either Captain Forsythe knew how she felt, or he could see her eagerness, for he said, "But first, let's see how well you have done."

He gave her the key for the mechanical and showed her where to insert it. She wound the key five times, looked up at him standing close beside her, then turned her attention back to the automaton and let go of the key.

A music box began to play somewhere within the mechanism. The horse moved around in a circle, with the dancer on its back spinning as it went. The juggler's circle of balls also began to spin. The clown ran back and forth, the ring master cracked a whip, and high above them all, the high wire walker walked from one end of the wire to the other.

It was wonderful.

MISS TURNER HUNG over the little show, her mouth open with delight, her eyes shining, watching every movement until the last note, the last step, or glide, or spin.

"It worked," she breathed on a satisfied sigh.

"You put it together perfectly," John told her, and she turned away from the table to face him. If she was surprised to find him so close, she did not show it. She had to tip her head back to smile up at him, and he was uncomfortably aware of her feminine curves, only inches from his chest.

Her brown eyes were wide, and shining with delight. She was really much prettier than he had realized.

"I had such fun," she confided. "I wish I could do more. Perhaps when I am home in Leicester, I can learn how to create such mechanicals!"

"I thought you were going to London?" He had not stepped away, and nor had she moved from between him and the work bench.

She wrinkled her nose as if smelling something bad. "To chaperone Vivienne," she agreed. "Weeks of meaningless conversations with people I don't particularly like and events I'd rather not attend. But Vivienne enjoys it all, so it will be worthwhile. It means, though, I will have little time to myself before returning to Leicester."

Her breathing had become quicker and shallower, and her color was mounting. When she nibbled at her lower lip, John's control slipped for a moment. Before he had formed the intention, his lips had touched hers.

She froze for a moment, and he almost stepped backwards and apologized, but then her hands came up to rest on his chest and she moved closer.

He fought his urge to crush her to him and devour those delectable lips, because by now he had realized she had no idea how to kiss. He set out to tutor her, first with gentle movements of his lips, and then with a softly murmured request to open. He kept the exploration of her mouth slow and unthreatening. It was surprisingly intoxicating.

His hands found their way to her hips, and hers slipped around to his back, so they were pressed together. He didn't mold her to him, didn't move a hand to her glorious breasts as his baser-self urged him to do. This was… he didn't quite know what it was. An expression of friendship. Something, anyway, kinder than lust.

Oh, the lust was there, raging behind his tight control. Had she given him the least invitation, he might have released it. She responded sweetly to everything he did, made a few tentative forays of her own, but not as if she had ever done anything of the kind before. He would not treat her like a wanton when she clearly was not one.

At last, a noise outside penetrated his concentration—the distant sound of voices. The others were returning from the village. He drew his lips away and smiled down at Miss Turner. She looked back, her eyes dazed, her lips red and slightly swollen.

"I did not mean to do that," he confessed.

She blinked and gave her head a quick shake as if she'd fallen asleep and was trying to wake herself up. "I am glad you did," she replied, to his surprise. "I have always wondered what it was like to be kissed." Her lips spread in a glorious smile and her eyes glittered with unshed tears. "I feel I should say thank you, for it felt like a gift, but I suppose that would be inappropriate."

John could not help himself. He drew her back and placed a kiss on her forehead. "We have, perhaps, stepped away ever so slightly from appropriate. Thank you, Miss Turner."

Perhaps she heard the others coming, for she stepped sideways and then away, saying over her shoulder, "You are kind to say so, but I daresay it was nothing out of the common for a man."

She was wrong. John had not kissed anyone since a couple of stolen—and, in retrospect, considerably more torrid—encounters during his ill-fated betrothal. He could not remember ever engaging in a kiss like that—sweet, innocent, and satisfying in itself.

He could not remember ever being so affected—as if he himself had woken from a long sleep, and now he was alive again. He could understand Miss Turner's head shake.

He opened his mouth to say so, and then shut it again. *She is leaving again, perhaps as early as tomorrow. No point in making more of this than it was.* "I enjoyed it very much," he said, instead.

She was checking her maid, still asleep near the window. She tossed him a smile. "I am glad."

Chapter Ten

THOSE WHO HAD been to the village brought the news that the bridge repairs were almost complete.

"We will be able to resume our journey tomorrow morning," Vivienne told Pauline. "Isn't that good news?"

It was, of course, and for more reasons than one. After that kiss, Pauline was afraid she would make a fool of herself if she stayed any longer. *I will not,* she determined. *I have enough pride and enough common sense not to pursue a man, however much I might desire him.* Captain Forsythe had kissed her, and pronounced it very nice, but he showed no signs of wanting more.

Thank goodness Betsy was so good at feigning sleep, and even better at keeping secrets. No one except she, Pauline, and Captain Forsythe knew about the kiss, and only Pauline and Captain Forsythe knew how enthusiastically she had responded.

She let Vivienne tell her all about the storm damage in the neighborhood, some problems that had arisen between residents and trapped visitors, and the shortage of nearly everything.

In spite of this, Mrs. Thorne had managed to buy, beg or trade the makings of a fine roast dinner, centered on a leg of ham she had wheedled out of the farmer who had been hosting Mr. Riddick and the carriage, and a roast chicken that had been one of last year's surplus roosters, clucking in the Tower's kitchen yard just this morning.

"It is your last dinner with us, my ladies," she said, "and I wanted to make it a special one."

For the first time, they ate in the dining room, in the main wing of the house. Captain Forsythe insisted that all the servants join them. "Just because we are not eating together in the kitchen, does not mean we will change our practice of eating together," he decreed, when Mrs. Thorne argued it was not proper.

Everybody helped to carry the dishes to the table, and everyone sat around to eat the meal, which was simple fare by London standards, but included three meat dishes, five vegetable dishes, and four sweet dishes, as well as bread, cheese, and fruit from the manor's winter stores.

Even Jane stayed up to join the dinner party, and Captain Forsythe allowed her a sip of watered wine in a tiny glass for the toast he proposed, to happy accidents and new friends. Jane screwed up her face at the taste, but drank it all.

Pauline had two glasses of wine, which did not prevent her from helping to carry the dishes down to the kitchen, where Mrs. Thorne put them in to soak. "I will deal with them in the morning," Mrs. Thorne said. "I have three girls from the village coming up to help me."

"What a strange trip this has been," Vivienne commented, as they were preparing for bed. "I haven't eaten with the servants since I was a little girl, until this trip. Even at Ruadh's, though it felt strange, it wasn't quite as it is here."

"The Shaws and others in the Douglas household eat at the same time and in the same hall as the laird, his family, and his guests, but at lower tables" Pauline said, to show she was listening and understood.

Vivienne nodded. "Exactly. They are a kind of a big family, so it isn't like London or even Leicester, where the family lives upstairs and the servants live downstairs. Here is different again."

"I think the Thornes feel like family to Captain Forsythe, and certainly to Jane," Pauline commented.

Vivienne looked up as Betsy entered the room with a jug of hot water. "Here, let me take that, Betsy. I like it, Pauline, and I have liked helping with the work. I would not have expected to enjoy it so much. It is very satisfying eating something you have helped to prepare." She giggled as a thought struck her. "Can you imagine what Mother would say?"

"Only too well," Pauline said, dryly.

"Best you not talk like that with your friends, my lady," Betsy advised. "They wouldn't understand."

"Have you not enjoyed yourself, Betsy?" Vivienne wanted to know.

"It has been pleasant enough, Lady Vivienne. But I'll be more pleased to be back in London where people know their place and behave as they should." The stern look she sent Pauline's way hinted she was not referring to gentlefolk eating with servants.

"As if any of us have forgotten our place," Vivienne huffed.

"That's as may be, my lady, but just as well we are leaving now before worse happens, that's what I think."

She was braiding Vivienne's hair, so Vivienne did not see her narrow her eyes at Pauline. *She is talking about the kiss.*

"One meal eaten in the dining room with servants is not going to bring down the established order," Pauline said. *And nor is one kiss that was witnessed only by one disapproving maid.*

"True enough," Betsy replied. "As long as it stops there."

IN THE MORNING, Jane, the Thornes, and Captain Forsythe all escorted the travelers down to the village. Riddick had the carriage ready and waiting outside of the church, and the rest of their baggage was soon stowed aboard.

There were farewells all round. Pauline found herself being hugged by Jane. Mrs. Thorne pressed a basket of food on her. Mr.

Thorne touched his cap and wished her well.

Captain Forsythe was by the carriage, assisting first Betsy, then Vivienne up. He held out his hand to help Pauline.

"Thank you, again, for your hospitality," she said, placing her hand on his. Even through her gloves and his, she felt a tingle run through her core at being so close to him. His smile, as he looked down into her eyes, had something intimate about it. Betsy was right. It was best they left today.

His response, however, was mere politeness. "We enjoyed your stay. You are always welcome, Miss Turner. At the very least, you must come back to get the cuttings you mentioned."

He handed her up into the carriage, and then bent in to hand her the bag he had been carrying. "This is for you. Something to remember your visit by."

Pauline opened the top. Inside was a box.

She raised her eyes to his, and he said, "It is the little scene you made, Miss Turner. I like to think of you playing it, and remembering our time together."

Pauline could feel herself blushing, and from the heat in Captain Forsythe's eyes, he was remembering the same part of their time together as she was. "I shall treasure it," she told him, her voice thankfully firm. And she would. Both the little toy and the memory of the kiss.

Chapter Eleven

PAULINE WROTE A thank you letter. It was, after all, only polite to express her gratitude. She enclosed it in a note to Jane, which was a little story about how pleased her roses had been to see her arrive home.

The reply came within a fortnight—a letter from Jane, full of misspellings and illustrated by a drawing that Pauline took to be the monkey mechanical and Jane's doll Clementine, for Jane had written that they had resolved to be friends. In it, a note from John wanted to know whether the music box had traveled safely, and whether Vivienne was enjoying the Season.

After that, Pauline and the little family at the Towers exchanged letters every couple of weeks.

John wrote about the wet spring and Thorne's rheumatics. About Jane's lessons, which she was now sharing with a farmer's daughter of the same age. About problems with the Carlisle clocktower automaton, and how he was solving them. He signed his letters, "Your friend, John". Every letter was enclosed in another from Jane, usually a drawing with a few words.

Pauline replied to Jane with further little stories and messages from the birds and animals in her garden. She sent a small present for Jane's eighth birthday.

To John she sent the recipe for an herbal posset against

rheumatics from a friend who was a gifted herbalist. She gave him news from Arial and Peter, wrote little anecdotes to illustrate the lengths to which Vivienne's suitors went to impress Vivienne, and described musical performances, plays and lectures she had attended. She signed herself, "Your friend, Pauline".

In late May, she made a lightning trip to Leicester to examine her seedling roses. She traveled with Arial and Peter, who were going home because measles was rampaging through the nursery and schoolroom. Vivienne was left in London with the Marchioness of Deerhaven. Cordelia Deerhaven was a close friend of Arial's and her second and third daughter were also out in Society. These days, when Pauline met her, she was always conscious that Cordelia was also John's sister-in-law.

The Stancroft children had mild cases and were on the mend by the time, a week later, their father decided to go back to London for the closing of Parliament. Arial decided to stay, so only Pauline and Peter made the return trip.

"Is there something I should know about these letters between you and John Forsythe?" Peter asked her.

Pauline should have expected the question. After all, he had been franking her letters, and the latest, sent just yesterday, had been a large package, since it included a painting she'd labored over that captured the colors and shapes of the best of her new blooms.

"Captain Forsythe and I became friends when Vivienne and I were staying with him. There is nothing more to it than that, Peter." Apart from that one kiss, which she could never forget. "You need not be concerned I will disgrace the family."

Peter was sitting opposite her. He leaned forward and touched her hand—just a fleeting brush of comfort. "I know you would not," he assured her, "and if you did, Arial and I would still love you. I am concerned you may be getting in over your head. If you say it is just friendship, I am relieved."

"I know I would be a fool to imagine anything more," Pauline assured him, trying not to be hurt that the man she loved as a brother was warning her off his friend. "I have never been pretty. I am well past my debutante years. I might be able to lay claim to being gentry through my father, but Captain Forsythe is the son of a marquess, even if he does refuse to use the courtesy title. If I had any thought of such thing, I would dismiss it immediately. We are friends. I can talk to him about my roses. He can talk to me about his automata. He has given me no cause for expectations, and I have none."

She shut her mouth then, realizing that the very volubility of her response betrayed the foolish dreams she claimed not to be entertaining. Peter had noticed, of course. His worried frown told her that.

He took both of her hands in his. "I meant none of those things, Pauline. You are an attractive woman in the prime of your life, and a gentlewoman, at that. It's just that I don't believe John will ever marry again. He likes very few women and trusts none. I'm glad that he has you for a friend, but he is not capable of more. He has been too hurt."

His words were a huge challenge to Pauline's determination never to discuss the business of others without their knowledge and consent. She managed to keep her questions behind her teeth, and said only, "Thank you for explaining."

Peter let go of her hands and sat back against the back of his seat. "You will let me know, won't you, if you ever need my help in any way? Or if you need someone to talk to?"

She reassured him, and changed the subject to Vivienne's suitors, several of whom had petitioned Peter for the privilege of her hand. Vivienne had refused them all.

"Perhaps a latecomer to the Season has caught her attention while we were gone," Peter said, without much hope.

"She is only eighteen," Pauline pointed out. "She has plenty of time to find a husband who suits her."

Peter groaned. "And next year, we will be presenting the first of Arial's cousins. By the time we are done with the three of them, my own daughters will be ready." He shut his eyes and shook his head slowly. "I shall go gray before my time." He flashed Pauline a smile. "Thank all the powers for you, Pauline. You have been a godsend with Rose and Vivienne. I hope you know how grateful Arial and I are."

Pauline brushed his words off with a deprecating remark, but the warmth of them stayed with her. If she did have to dwindle into a spinster, dependent on her stepbrother for a roof over her head, at least he and Arial treated her with kindness, respect, and true appreciation.

Cumberland, June 1826

JOHN HAD ONE of the windows open in his workshop.

He told himself it was to let in the soft breeze and the heady scent of the roses that were in full bloom around the foot of his tower. It also had the advantage that he could hear the cheerful conversation, and sometimes the sweet laughter of his dear Jane, her new friends, and her teacher, who was the wife of one of his tenant farmers.

Mrs. Elliot had benefited from a dame school education in her Scots birthplace, had passed on her knowledge of reading and numbers to all of her own large brood of children, and was happy to do the same for Jane as well as her youngest daughter and others in the neighborhood whose parents agreed to let them come to Rosewood Towers for a full morning, three days a week.

John had set up a room in the main wing of the manor as a schoolroom, but on a fine day, they would, like as not, carry their slates outside to write about and count what lay around them in the gardens.

Mrs. Thorne had been delighted to hand over her teaching duties. Until he began spending more time in the main house while Pauline Turner and her entourage were here, he'd had no idea how much work he had loaded on her shoulders.

To further relieve the burden on her, John had added another maid to the set of young females who trudged up the driveway from the village every day to help with the housework and cooking, and he had commissioned a carpenter and a painter to restore a couple of rooms at the top of the other tower so that two or three of them could stay at night if inclement weather closed the paths and roads.

Mrs. Elliot really was a gifted teacher. Jane's writing and reading were going ahead by leaps and bounds, and she also showed a flair for numbers. *I suppose I shall have to employ a governess sooner or later.*

His mind's eye pictured Pauline, bending over her work on that last afternoon. *She would make a wonderful governess.* John rejected the thought, shoving it away with something akin to horror. Even if the lady was looking for employment, which she wasn't, he could never have her living under his roof.

Witness his frequent thoughts of that visit, of the growing desire that made him both anxious for her presence and eager to avoid it, of how he struggled with lust that last afternoon as he viewed her lovely rear, neatly outlined in her woolen gown as she bent over the little automaton.

She is a friend, and has become a good one over the past few months. That was all it could be.

His inner self asked, snidely, *So, is that why you are hovering by the window instead of getting on with your work*?

He had to admit, if only to himself, that he was waiting for Thorne to come back from the nearest Royal Mail stop, some five miles away by road. The manservant had been sent to post some letters and to collect any mail that might have been waiting.

You had a letter only a week ago, he scolded himself. She had written that she was traveling to Leicester. He hoped Peter's children were recovering. He hoped she found treasures in her new rose blooms.

Thorne had taken his letter in reply. It carried an invitation. He was nearly ready to install the Carlisle clock tower scenes, and would be taking it up to Carlisle within the fortnight. Yesterday, the town council had sent him the date for the opening ceremony. The Thornes and Jane would travel up for it, of course.

He should not hope for Pauline to come. *It is a long way from London to Carlisle.* On the other hand, with Parliament dissolved on the second of June, the ton were abandoning the stinky hole that London became in the summer, and she did, after all, have a sister to visit in Galloway, only a day's journey from Carlisle.

Against that, it was high summer, and she would be desperate to get back to her garden after the long months in London.

The clop of hooves had him crossing the room to look out at the carriage way. Thorne was home.

John drew away from the window before Thorne could see him, and busied himself tidying his work desk, and then his tray of parts. Doubtless, Thorne and his wife had figured out how besotted John had become. It was hard to keep such a secret from a man who had been his soldier-servant for years in the army and with him ever since. John could, however, at least *pretend* to be indifferent.

It was a very long half hour before Thorne knocked on the door and entered.

"A good trip?" John asked, attempting to appear casual.

"Fair to middling," Thorne allowed. "I got your letters off, Captain." John had also invited Peter and Arial, and his brother Deerhaven and Cordelia, and any of their family who cared to make the trip.

"Any mail in return?" He hoped his enquiry sounded casual, but he was wound as tightly as one of his own automatons, just before he released the key.

"Just this." Thorne handed over a letter on thick, official-looking paper, with a seal John did not recognize. He held it for a moment, letting the disappointment sink in.

"What have we here?" he wondered, as he turned it over. The postage had been paid, but the signature was illegible. He broke the seal, unfolded the letter, and glanced at the valediction, frowning at the list of names under the signature. Solicitors.

As he read from the top, he felt his blood turn to ice. He fumbled for a chair and read the letter again.

"Bad news, Captain?" Thorne asked.

As bad as he cared to imagine. "My cheating, lying ex-wife and her new husband are suing for guardianship and custody of Jane."

Chapter Twelve

PAULINE CAME BACK from Leicester to a London abuzz with the arrival of the Earl and Countess of Tenby. The hostesses of Society were faced with a quandary. Should Lady Tenby, a notorious divorcee, be received?

One did not wish to offend the Marquess and Marchioness of Deerhaven, whose brother had been the injured party in the infamous divorce. Equally, one would prefer to avoid upsetting Tenby's father and mother, the Duke and Duchess of Kingston, who had recalled their prodigal from his exile in Paris. After all, they said, he married his mistress once his wife died, and she would one day be his duchess.

The Kingstons were determined it was time for Society to accept the scandalous couple. Her Grace of Kingston had been heard to point out to the recalcitrant that Lady Tenby would herself, one day, be the Duchess of Kingston, and therefore take precedence over Lady Deerhaven.

The question had been largely resolved by the time Pauline arrived at the Stancroft London townhouse. Only the Deerhavens and their closest friends continued to hold out against the Kingston campaign.

"It is rather embarrassing," Vivienne told her. "When their carriage passed ours in Hyde Park, we all had to look the other way, and the same when we met on the stairs at the Opera."

To Pauline, Vivienne looked more excited than embarrassed. Pauline was torn. On the one hand, she had adamantly set her face against gossip eight years ago. She should not encourage her sister.

On the other, she was desperate to hear more about the woman who had married John Forsythe, given birth to Jane, and then abandoned them both for a married man.

Vivienne needed no encouragement. "Lady Deerhaven says she behaved very badly. It came out at the trial that she had been carrying on with Lord Tenby—the Honorable Mr. Spindler, he was then—even before she married Captain Forsyth."

Pauline had been at the house party where John Forsythe and Augusta Pilkington-Smythe, as she was then, had been caught in bed together. According to Peter, John had stayed up playing billiards with Spindler while the others went to bed. Spindler, as Peter recalled much later when John's wife absconded with the man, had been seen several times in close conversation with Augusta.

When John woke to the sound of Mrs. Pilkington-Smythe screeching, Augusta was naked beside him, claiming that he had invited her, and that he had taken her innocence.

They had married by special license within the week. Jane was born six months later, and Tenby ran away with Augusta thirteen months after that. Those in the know pointed out that this was after the previous duke of Kingston had died, and therefore no longer held the pursestrings.

Those were the facts, as Pauline knew them, and as Vivienne now repeated. "The Kingstons are saying how wicked it was for John to keep Jane, when she is really the daughter of the Earl of Tenby. Do you think she is?" she asked.

That was exactly what Pauline thought, but there was a deeper truth. "Jane has been acknowledged, raised, and loved by Captain Forsythe. In every real sense, he is her father."

"How wicked, to trap the captain into marriage," Vivienne

decided.

Pauline agreed, but had some sympathy for a pregnant unmarried lady, although she had not found Augusta at all likeable when she met her all those years ago. Thanks to her mother and her sister, and even herself in those days, Pauline found it easy to recognize ladies whose honeyed words and sweet manners hid a contempt for the feelings and needs of anyone else.

She had no sympathy at all for Tenby. How wicked of him to get his lover with child, conspire to pass her off to another man, then interfere with the marriage when his own circumstances changed. *How like Society to heap all of the blame on the much younger female half of the pair.*

"She was very young, only nineteen when she married Captain Forsythe, and not yet twenty-one when she ran away to Paris," she told Vivienne. "It is always possible that her trials have wrought a change." After all, Pauline was proof that harpies could change.

Pauline had the opportunity to judge for herself a few afternoons later. She had accompanied Vivienne on a walk near the Serpentine in Hyde Park. Vivienne had fallen into conversation with a friend. From the little Pauline heard before stepping a few yards away to give them privacy, the girl was suffering from unrequited love.

She took station near a bed of roses, where she could admire the blooms while keeping watch over her sister. With her attention divided between the flowers and her charge, she was conscious of, but ignored, the person who came to stand near her until the woman spoke.

"Miss Turner? It is Miss Turner, is it not?"

Pauline recognized her instantly. Lady Tenby had changed little in eight years except, perhaps, to grow harder and yet, more beautiful. The man beside her must be Lord Tenby. She vaguely recalled him as one of the gentlemen from the house party—one of those who did not bother with politeness to poor relations. The true identification came from the white-blond hair he shared with Jane Forsythe.

Pauline bobbed the shallowest of curtsies, and inclined her head. "Lady Tenby. Lord Tenby."

"Tenby, darling," the lady said to her husband, "you remember Pauline Turner?"

Lord Tenby held out a languid hand. "Flora Turner's other daughter," he drawled, then snickered. "Flora Edwards since she married her butler. Charmed." He did not sound charmed, nor did he look directly at Pauline. She imagined he was watching those nearby to see whether anyone had noticed him interacting with a peasant.

Pauline dipped another shallow curtsey rather than touch the man's hand, and after a moment he dropped it again.

"Miss Turner, Tenby and I had to come and talk to you. We have heard about how you were trapped by a storm in the remotest wilderness in England, and forced to take shelter with Lord John Forsythe."

"Dreadful for you," Tenby offered. "Place is barely civilized. Man is a brute and lives like a peasant."

Pauline kept her temper under control, but it was a close-run thing. "Lady Tenby, you are correct that my sister, our servants and I enjoyed Captain Forsythe's hospitality for several days when a bridge was washed out by a storm. Lord Tenby, I do not know where you got your information, but it is incorrect in every particular."

Lady Tenby waved an impatient hand. "We know your step-brother is Lord John's friend, so you are bound to be polite about him. But that is not the point, is it, Tenby darling?"

Tenby looked momentarily confused, then anxious.

"Augustina," Lady Tenby hissed at him.

His face cleared. "Ah. Yes. The child." He glared at Pauline. "Lady Tenby wants to know about the little girl."

Lady Tenby clasped her hands to her bosom, turned her lips down, and opened her eyes wide. "My darling baby. My little Augustina Jane. Miss Turner, you cannot know the pain in a mother's heart, to be separated from her only child. To fear for that child's safety at the hands of a man who cannot care for her as a father ought."

She had raised her voice even as she lifted her eyes to the heavens, and a small crowd was edging closer so they didn't miss any of Lady Tenby's theatrics. "I blame myself for not taking her with me when I fled. She was only an infant, and my future was uncertain, but every day since, I have longed for her, worried for her, felt the wound of our separation!"

"I daresay," Pauline replied, investing her reply with all the doubt she felt. She smiled, and raised her own voice to reach the crowd. "You will be delighted to know, then, that Captain Forsythe loves his daughter dearly, as do his servants, his tenants, and the local villagers. She receives every attention and, as a niece of the Deerhavens, will have every advantage."

"Except a mother's love!" declared Lady Tenby, nudged Tenby with her elbow, and added, "And the love of her true father." When he said nothing, she nudged him again and repeated it. "The love of her true father."

Tenby cleared his throat and looked uncertainly around at the crowd that had gathered. "Yes. Er. Well. Quite. Extenuating circumstances, don't you know. Would have loved to fetch the brat—"

Another none too subtle elbow from his wife. "—the, *er*, *dear little girl* away with my beloved Augusta, but circumstances, don't you know? Time to make things right." He beamed at Lady Tenby like a boy who had repeated his lesson and expected praise.

Pauline had had enough of the couple. "Excuse me," she said. "I must join my sister." She took a step away and then turned back. "If you cared at all about your daughter, Lady Tenby, you would not have cast aspersions on her legitimacy in front of this crowd. You might wish to think about how such claims reflect on you. If what you said happened to be true, would you expect people to support a woman who trapped one man into marriage while with child by another? Or a man who abandoned both lover and child to another man? Whether you are lying now, or the falsehoods were in the past, you and Lord Tenby, in making such claims, have proven yourselves deceivers and cheats."

The pair of them stood gaping at her as she took a breath to calm herself. "Fortunately for Captain Forsythe's daughter, your cruel assertions so many years later are of no significance. Do not speak to me again, Lord and Lady Tenby. I will not recognize you."

She marched off, and the crowd parted to let her through. She was shaking with anger and with reaction at her own temerity, but she hoped she at least appeared calm and dignified.

Behind her, she could hear Tenby declare his horror at her words. "I say, Augusta, did that woman just threaten to cut me? *Me*? Who does she think she is? Uppity nobody! I am the son of a duke, don't you know? Disgusting behavior!"

JOHN'S FIRST IMPULSE was to send off a stinging rejection. A night's reflection convinced him that he needed to consult his solicitor. He rode up to Carlisle that day, and saw the man the following morning.

The solicitor read the letter and looked at John over his glasses. "This letter presumes that you wish to give little Miss Forsythe up to her mother?"

It was a question, rather than a statement and John answered it. "The presumption is wrong. Jane is *my* daughter. I am the only parent she remembers, and she belongs with me."

"You are in the right of it, Captain Forsythe," the solicitor assured him. "The child was born during your marriage, and the law assumes you are the father, unless you deny paternity at the time of the birth."

John sighed with relief. "I accepted Jane as my daughter," he confirmed. He had wondered whether he should. He knew she could not be his, and had thought of repudiating her, but he'd taken the innocent little baby from the arms of the midwife, looked into her eyes, and fell in love.

The solicitor nodded. "You asserted paternity. And the child's mother gave up all rights in the divorce, so the legal case, I would think, is cut and dried."

Augusta had never shown any interest in Jane. She had demanded a wet nurse, had only looked at the baby when the nursemaid brought her to John of an evening, and had objected vociferously to the time that John spent in the nursery.

The solicitor made a thoughtful hum. John could tell that a "however" was coming, and spoke first. "Do you think I should ignore the letter, or write and tell them they have no rights?"

"I would not recommend that you do either, Captain Forsythe," said the lawyer. "I suggest that the next step is a letter from your solicitor, asserting your parentage, guardianship, and custody of the child, and declaring that they have no standing in the matter."

That sounded good to John. "Very well," he said.

The solicitor had not finished. "I am, of course, happy to draft such a letter, if you so instruct. However, in my professional opinion—though I regret the truth of it—such a letter will have more weight coming from a firm of London solicitors, rather than from my own pen. Regrettably, while I flatter myself to think my reputation in Carlisle and Cumberland is second to none, I am not known in London."

"I used Fortescue, Bryant, and Fortescue for the divorce," John said.

"An excellent choice," the solicitor agreed. "If I might suggest…?"

John inclined his head. "Of course."

"I shall write an opinion for you to send to them. I trust such an esteemed firm will not see that as a presumption."

"I am sure they will not," John assured him. "I would be

grateful."

He left the solicitor's office feeling much comforted. Augusta and her husband would have their teeth pulled—no, they would discover they had no teeth—and Jane would be safe.

His next stop was the mayor's office, to decide final arrangements for the opening ceremony, and then back to his hotel, where he slept better than he had since Augusta's lawyer's letter arrived. His last thought as he drifted to sleep was to wonder if Pauline would come to the opening.

Chapter Thirteen

PAULINE SPOKE TO Peter about her encounter with Lord and Lady Tenby, and they agreed she should write to John and warn him about what his ex-wife and her new husband were saying.

"Jane is his in-law," Peter reassured her. "She can make a fuss, but she can't change the law."

Pauline thought a fuss might cause damage enough. Perhaps what she said might mitigate the damage a little, but many in Society would choose to align themselves with the heir to a duke and his wife, rather than the reclusive second son of a marquess.

"I am by no means convinced she even wants Jane," Pauline told Peter. "I am very sure that Lord Tenby does not, but he is entirely under Lady Tenby's thumb. It is my view that Lady Tenby wants to punish Captain Forsythe and blacken his name in Society."

"John didn't do anything wrong," Peter said. "He married the woman, even though he had no part in bringing her to his room. He acknowledged her child as his own. He tried to make a go of the marriage until she ran away. He even agreed to divorce her so she could marry Tenby."

Peter didn't understand envy and hate, and Pauline loved him for it. "That is why," she explained. "First, he let her go without a fight, when he should have been desperate to keep her. I know what vain women are like, Peter, and she has not forgiven him for not wanting her. Second, she knows she behaved badly. If he had not been so admirably compassionate and forgiving, he would have given her a reason not to stay with him, and she might not hate him so much."

Peter shook his head, as if the reasoning escaped him. "It is unfair he has to go through this all again. He suffered badly while the divorce was going through Parliament."

It was cruel, but Pauline could see no way to stop it.

She sent the letter to John that same day, reporting Lady Tenby's words as nearly as she could remember and resisting the urge to bother him with her own worries.

The fallout had already begun when she and Vivienne attended a ball that evening. From the stares and the rising buzz of conversation, Pauline guessed people had heard about the encounter, and were taking sides. No wonder. Gossip travelled through the ton faster than water ran downhill.

It was an evening to which the Deerhaven party had been invited and so the Kingstons and their known allies had not. Nonetheless, several of the suitors who normally flocked to Vivienne's side were notably focusing on other ladies this evening, and some of the older women who would normally come and talk to Pauline turned their backs and pretended not to see her.

Cordelia Deerhaven, however, crossed the ballroom to greet them as soon as she, her husband, and her daughter, Lady Delia, arrived. Cordelia kissed Vivienne's cheek and tucked Pauline's arm into hers. "Vivienne, you shall go and talk to Delia, who is over there with her father, and Pauline and I shall take a stroll around the room."

By this time, Deerhaven and his daughter had joined them, so Pauline said to the marquess, "Do watch over Vivienne. I fear she will bear the consequences of my outspoken tongue."

He gifted her with one of his rare smiles. "From what I hear, you spoke the truth. My family and I are grateful."

"You shall tell me exactly what you did say," Cordelia commanded. "There are several versions doing the rounds, and some of them, I am sure, have been created out of whole cloth."

Pauline repeated the conversation word-for-word, as far as she could remember, and chuckled at some of the misrepresentations being circulated. Would people really believe that she had marched up to an earl and his countess in front of an interested crowd and announced herself as Captain Forsythe's lover, there to scratch Lady Tenby's eyes out for being the love of the poor man's life?

If so, some people were fools enough to believe anything.

Of course, the caricaturists and gossip columns picked up that and other rumors, some even more ridiculous. The Tenbys, too, came in for their share of shame. One artist even pictured Lady Tenby as a monster eating a baby, while dragging Lord Tenby behind her on a chain.

Pauline, who had avoided such things for years, became an avid reader. *The Teatime Tattler* was more balanced in its reporting than most, though many of its speculations were far from true.

A few days after the fuss started, she received John's letter inviting her to Carlisle for the opening of the clock. The date was three and a half weeks away.

"If I left now," she said to Vivienne and Peter, "I would have time to visit George and Lucy Chomondeley in Clitheroe. We have been corresponding about their experiments with crossing the China tea roses with the Gallicas. Vivienne, would you mind if I asked Cordelia whether you could stay with her and Delia until Peter is ready to leave London? Peter, would that be acceptable to you?"

Vivienne said she was ready to go at any time. "This Season has turned into a complete bore," she declared. Pauline suspected that the defection of the suitor she most liked was behind that statement.

"I should be home for the election anyway," Peter told them,

"Our candidate is being returned unopposed, but he is going to make a few speeches, and I should be there to clap. When could you be ready to leave?"

The ladies agreed that the following day would be time enough to pack up the house and write notes to their friends. Pauline felt her heart lift. In a few weeks, she would see John again!

BEFORE HE LEFT Carlisle to return to Rosewood Towers, John wrote to the lawyer who had managed his divorce and to his brother, enclosing a copy of the letter from Lord and Lady Tenby's lawyers. He asked Fortescue to write a response, and requested Deerhaven to act as his proxy in approving the letter before it was sent.

His letter must have passed the one Deerhaven wrote when the scandal broke, for Deerhaven's was one of a stack from London. John piled them up, with his brother's on top, Pauline's next, then Peter's, then those from other friends, and finally those from people he barely knew.

Deerhaven was begging for John's authority to act on his behalf as the situation in London escalated.

"Fortunately, most people are leaving town now that Parliament is dissolved," he wrote, "but the Tenby bitch has been spreading the most disgusting lies about you, and some people are believing them. She claims her only concern is to rescue her child.

"Not that people of sense believe her. Not after she claimed in public that Jane was her child's and Tenby's, and Peter's stepsister Miss Turner ripped strips off her and Tenby, pointing out that whether they had lied in the past or were lying now, they had proven they were not to be trusted. Deceivers and cheats, she called them, and the half of London who wasn't watching has heard about it since."

Good for Pauline. He hoped she did not suffer for it. Tenby was a duke's heir, and Society could be unforgiving.

Her letter also covered the incident to which Deerhaven had referred. "Lady Tenby accosted me in Hyde Park, I believe as pretext to lay claim to Jane in front of a crowd. She seems convinced that you will give up your beloved daughter without a murmur. I hope I did not speak out of turn when I gave a rousing speech in response, referring to her own abandonment of the child and your deep love for her."

Both Deerhaven and Pauline described some of the rumors going around Society and included some newspaper clippings. Peter went further, including those caricatures and articles that libeled Pauline, which the other two had not mentioned.

He worked his way through the letters. Some warned him about what was being said. Some merely offered a vague support. As he got towards the bottom, he reached the ones from Tenby supporters and Kingston acolytes who demanded he give up his claim on his daughter to her rightful parents. One or two of those sounded decidedly unhinged. If he did have to go to London to confront his ex-wife and her adulterous lover, he had better make sure he had somewhere safe and secure to leave Jane.

It took him three days to read them all, and by then, Thorne had collected the mail again and there was another stack. Again, he sorted them, again reading Deerhaven's letter first. The lawyer's letter had been sent.

"In Forsythe's opinion," Deerhaven wrote, "the Tenbys know they do not have a leg to stand on, and so are trying to influence you by having you tried and condemned in the court of public opinion. I took it upon myself to visit Kingston to tell him that the lies have to stop. He was polite but refused to discuss the matter, saying it is between you and Tenby. I told him I would be satisfied if he made it clear to his pensioners that he is not taking sides in the matter. Since he clearly is taking his son's side, he made some noises and then claimed another appointment. I have spoken to Dellborough and Haverford, asking them to have a word with Kingston, and I have an appointment tomorrow with the King." The two men he named were dukes whose peerages were senior to Kingston's, and King George, of course, was senior to them all.

Pauline's letter this time was a breath of fresh air. She did not mention the Tenbys at all, and she did say that she was coming to Carlisle, to the opening of the clock automaton.

"My companion will be Miss Pettigrew, whom you may remember as Vivienne's and Rose's governess. She is still in charge of Peter's schoolroom, but has agreed to come with me on this trip. She claims it will be a holiday, and given the number of children she is currently responsible for, she may be right."

Her letter left him with a smile and the fortitude to plow through the rest of the letters. She was travelling to friends in Lancashire first, and would be with him by the third or fourth of July. In less than two weeks!

Chapter Fourteen

If she hadn't been invited to Rosewood Towers, Pauline could have taken her cuttings from most of the gardens in the village, for the rose she sought was blooming everywhere. As the carriage climbed the hill towards the manor, more grew wild in every clearing. Not just the brilliant blend of orange and red she was seeking, but whites, yellows, deep maroons, and every shade in-between.

She hoped that the carriage following had enough of the special mix into which she would put her cuttings. She had taken cuttings from more than a dozen roses in Clitheroe, but she could already see twenty more that, if they proved to have the other attributes she was looking for, were worth growing for her own breeding program.

Then roses went entirely out of her head as they came over the crest of the hill and saw the people waiting.

They stood on the main steps of the manor, John hovering protectively over Jane, with the Thornes on either side, all of them beaming a welcome.

John was the first to the carriage, outpacing both Thorne and Pauline's coach guard, even though he kept Jane at his side, holding one of her hands. With the other, he opened the door.

"Miss Turner, Miss Turner," Jane shouted. "I am coming with

you and Papa to Carlisle to see his Romans march on the clocktower!"

"You may tell Miss Turner all about it, darling girl, after we have welcomed her back to Rosewood Towers," said John, laughing, as he held his free hand out to Pauline.

Pauline placed her hand on John's and felt the warmth of it tingling up her arm. Her ribs were suddenly too tight to encompass all the feelings that surged within her at his touch. She paused on the carriage step, her eyes caught in his.

"Papa," Jane insisted, "Say welcome to Miss Turner."

Broken out of her trance, Pauline laughed. He laughed, too, repeating obediently, "Welcome, Miss Turner," as he handed her down and turned to offer a hand to Miss Pettigrew and then to Betsy, the maid.

Jane orchestrated the introductions and the welcomes, and then commandeered Pauline's hand to lead her inside, "for you will like a nice cup of tea, Miss Turner."

She looked over her shoulder to her father who was following close behind, and added, "*Now* may I tell Miss Turner?"

Pauline already knew the general outline of the plan. They were leaving the morning after tomorrow, and would be staying at The Bush, a coaching inn where John had taken two suites of rooms, one for his party and one for Pauline's.

Jane wanted to share all sorts of detail, from what toys she was permitted to take, to what sights they would see on their journey and while they were there.

John had had more of the house opened up. They took their tea in a little sitting room that was not in use last time Pauline had been here. Jane still slept in the Tower, she told Pauline, but she now took her lessons in a schoolroom that Papa had made in one of the downstairs reception areas.

Mrs. Thorne let Miss Pettigrew into her room and led Pauline to the next one along the corridor.

"Separate rooms," she said, "and I've already shown Betsy where she is to sleep. The extra maids the captain has employed make all the difference." She closed the door to the bed chamber, with her and Pauline on the inside. "He has been a different man since your visit Miss Turner," she confided. "As if he had been sleeping for the past six years, and is now awake." She made a disgusted harrumphing sound. "Such a shame that besom has come back to cause trouble. Not that I should be commenting on my betters."

"Not that I should be listening," Pauline acknowledged. "You can be sure, Mrs. Thorne, that what you say to me remains between us." She turned in a circle to take in the room, including a large vase of roses. "It is lovely." She cupped one of the roses and bent to take in its perfume. "These are gorgeous."

It was not until after dinner that she and John had the opportunity to talk alone. She accepted his invitation to a walk in the gardens. "You won't be able to see the colors very well," John acknowledged, "but I think the scent is better at night."

"Miss Pettigrew?" Pauline asked, trying not to let her reluctance show. She had promised Peter she would observe all proprieties, and visiting an unmarried man, even with her companion and all the servants, both his and hers, was stretching the boundaries. Still, much though she liked the governess, she would prefer to talk to John without a chaperone.

Miss Pettigrew did not disappoint. "I will sit on that seat just outside of the garden doors and contemplate the stars," she said. "I shall be able to see you from there, so no one could take the least exception."

"If you walk a few steps with us, Miss Pettigrew," suggested John, "there is a pleasant seat just inside the walls of the formal rose garden. You will be able to see everything within the walls, and we will be in your view the whole time. You can supervise us and contemplate stars to your heart's content."

SOME OF THE tumult in John's heart eased as he strolled the paths of the garden, Pauline's arm tucked through his. He knew what was being said about Pauline's last visit to Rosewood Towers. They would probably say worse about this visit, even though she had brought a chaperone, even though he slept in a completely different building.

To be honest, if only to himself, he had already thought of a number of ways to get from his tower to her room unseen. Not that he would. He would treat her with every respect, at least until this situation with Augusta was resolved.

Or until the gossips forced his hand, for if they shredded her reputation, he knew the remedy. He had used it before. *I married Augusta to redeem her reputation when I didn't even know her.*

He must have said that out loud, for Pauline commented on it.

"I realize that," Pauline said. "I was at the house party. Peter and Arial thought she had created the whole scenario in order to trap you. They were furious about it. You had shown the lady no particular attention, and you did not strike me as the sort to dally with an innocent."

John shrugged. "She admitted trapping me. She said her parents were attempting to broker a marriage with an old man. She seemed amiable enough, and I thought her honest. I thought we could make it work."

"She would not try." Pauline stated that as a fact.

John nodded. "Not even as much as necessary for there to be a possibility that I fathered her child." She had vomited when he first approached her to consummate the marriage. Not realizing she was with child, he had believed she needed time to get to know him. They had been married three months when he surmised the significance of her rounding belly.

Augusta claimed that the child was mine, conceived on the night I couldn't remember, the night she climbed into my bed at the house party.

He found it hard to believe her; didn't want to believe that, if he'd been conscious enough to perform, he'd have been insensible enough to bed an unmarried lady and forget all about it afterwards.

Then she'd accused him of drugging her, abducting her, and taking her against her will. John had bitter memories from his time in the army of the evils men could perpetrate upon women. All the anger at those past injustices had rendered him blind and speechless for a moment.

Had he truly been such a monster? He'd left, afraid of what he'd say or do if he remained. Hours later, he had ridden his way to some peace, but one accusation stayed with him. She'd claimed to have been drugged, but in the morning, she was clear-eyed and composed. He was the one with the heavy head, the dry, foul-tasting throat and mouth.

He'd confronted her again when he'd returned home, walking into her bed chamber unannounced for the first time since their wedding.

"Who drugged me?" he asked. "Was it you or your lover?"

She'd shaken her head, but her blush had given her away, as did the way her eyes had searched the room for a lie.

He'd had another thought. "Is that why your parents were planning to marry you off to a friend of your father's? Because they knew you were with child?"

He had learned to read her face in the three months of armed truce that had passed as a marriage. "That was a lie, too. I was the target all along. Were your parents in on it?"

She'd shrunk away from him, the color ebbing from her face as he'd loomed over her, near shouting. He'd lowered his voice to a growled whisper. *No need to alarm the servants*.

"Just you and your lover, was it? A married man, I take it, for your birth and dowry were good enough for anyone short of a peer."

Tears jumped to her eyes and the rest of the clues fell into place.

"Spindler."

Spindler had challenged him to a game of billiards that night, after his brother Deerhaven and his friend Peter Stancroft had gone up to bed with their wives. Spindler, as he recalled now, had attended the party without his bride—some story about her being sickly and hints regarding the condition that made her so. Truth, possibly, since the woman had presented him with a son a few months later.

Spindler had clapped him on the shoulder, and left him with a scratch that was still visible the next day. *A loose claw on the stone of a ring*, Spindler apologized. *Very sorry*. John vaguely remembered feeling dazed shortly after, and Spindler seeing him to his room. *I thanked the swine*.

Augusta had stared up at him, eyes wide, lip trembling. He had frightened the usual defiant confidence out of her. He'd decided he would feel guilty about it tomorrow, but he had been determined he was going to have the truth.

"The child's father is Spindler," he'd barked. She'd nodded.

"Spindler drugged me so you could trap me into marriage."

She'd nodded again.

He'd straightened and wondered, *Now what?*

Augusta had wondered the same thing. "What are you going to do?"

John had sighed. What could he have done? It wasn't as if he could turn Augusta out into the cold, baby and all. Not after the way his mother had been treated.

"Spindler would have married me if his grandfather had let him," Augusta had whispered. "He loves me. He doesn't love her."

He'd felt a surge of pity. What a fool he had been.

"He cannot marry you, Augusta. He has a wife. You have me and I have you. It is over to us what we make of it."

He had tried. He had really tried. Especially after he held Jane for the first time.

"Nothing I did suited her," he told Pauline. "Even the time I spent with Jane. She was jealous of her own daughter, even though she did not want my attention herself. How is a person supposed to make sense of that?"

"She wanted to be first with everyone," Pauline said. "Some people are like that."

"Then Kingston died and the rat became heir to the duchy. He abandoned his wife and children and came for Augusta, and that was the end of our marriage," John said. "She left Jane without a backward glance. Even when she wrote to me after Lady Tenby died, she didn't ask about Jane. All she wanted was a divorce."

Pauline lifted one eyebrow. "She asked for the divorce?" A thoughtful nod. "I see. She wanted to marry Tenby."

"We already had an ecclesiastical separation. That was enough for me. I had Jane, and I had no intention of ever wedding again." He met Pauline's eyes and added. "Not at that time."

Pauline didn't respond to his hint that he had changed his mind. "You could have refused her."

"If I had, it would have been less expensive and lot less embarrassing. After it was over, she fled to Paris, and I came up here, to Cumberland, away from all the people who thought they knew everything there was to know about our lives. I did it to protect Jane, but I might have known that Augusta would not keep her word."

"She had already lost custody," Pauline mused, "so… Oh! I see! You made her promise she wouldn't challenge your claim to be Jane's father."

John nodded. "I would give her the divorce and leave her free to marry Tenby, and in return she and Tenby promised to keep quiet about Tenby's role as Jane's progenitor. I won't say *father*."

"No more you should. He is a father only in the most physical of senses. He calls her 'the brat', John, but he is quite under Lady Tenby's thumb, and for some reason, she has made this ridiculous claim. She must know that she has absolutely no legal right."

They continued their stroll as they talked, making three circuits of the outer path of the garden before John turned them down one of the paths that cut diagonally across its center.

Pauline had put her other hand on the first, so she was clutching his arm, and he put his own free hand over hers. It was a comfort to have her so close while he talked about the worst disaster of his life.

"She does know," Pauline decided. "That is why she decided to go public. She hopes to embarrass you into giving up your daughter. She has not the least idea what love is. Why, I could almost feel sorry for her if what she was doing was not so evil."

"I *am* sorry for her," John said, though it surprised him to discover it was true. "I think Tenby is the only person she loves outside of herself. You say he is under her thumb. Others have told me the same thing. That does not change the fact that she is besotted with him. He feeds her ego. He will make her a duchess one day. But it is more than that. She needs him, in some way. Needs his adoration, I suppose."

Pauline gave his arm a squeeze. "They will not succeed, John. Captain Forsythe, I mean."

On the other side of the fountain in the center of the rose garden, they were briefly out of view of their chaperone. John took advantage of the moment to drop a kiss on Pauline's hair. "I have been thinking of you as 'Pauline' these three months," he confessed. "I would be honored to have you call me 'John' when we are private."

"I should like that," she murmured, the husky tone that entered her voice reminding him of bedroom matters, with the inevitable effect on his anatomy. Not that it hadn't already been responding to her nearness.

He led her back onto the path to avoid, as his old regiment's chaplain put it, the *occasion of sin*. "Pauline, then," he said.

"John."

PAULINE HAD NO opportunity the next day to call John by his

personal name. No private moments. Miss Pettigrew and Jane both accompanied them on the daytime tour, as did John and his part-time gardener, who turned out to be the churchwarden whose wife had been so helpful when they first arrived in the village.

Pauline told the gardener she wanted to see everything: not just the rose garden but all the other roses that were growing over arbors, up walls, and semi-wild along the edges and in clearings in the woods.

"A powerful lot of roses," the gardener said.

"Yes, and I have limited pots and space for cuttings, so must choose carefully. I would like to view everything first, and then make my decisions."

The man was useful, though he did not have Pauline's love of roses. "Powerful lot of work, and for not much of a flowering season. And ugly things in the winter."

"The Chinese roses flower continuously from spring until autumn," Pauline told him. "But I think the old-fashioned roses also have their charm."

He shrugged, unconvinced. Pauline didn't need his agreement, just his knowledge. This plant was subject to the blight. That one struggled in the wet. She questioned their growing habits, their hardiness, their susceptibility to pests and disease, when they flowered and for how long, and everything else she could think of.

She also shared what each different variety might do for her breeding program, and which different parts might be used in a household: to flavor food and drink, for perfume, soaps, oils, hand creams, and medicine.

By the time they had finished, she had a notebook full of plant characteristics, and had already decided on the plants she would most like to reproduce. Jane and Miss Pettigrew had long since grown bored. Miss Pettigrew had produced sketchpads for an impromptu art lesson, which moved from place to place as Pauline and the gardener left one group of roses for another.

John was still with them, asking intelligent questions about what she hoped to achieve, and showing every evidence of interest in the answers.

"That's the lot, then, Miss," the churchwarden said at long last. "And right interesting it has been. I never thought that much of roses, but I'll think about them different now."

"Thank you," Pauline said, sincerely. "I should let you get about your work, but I am very grateful you have taken the time to share what you know."

He touched his cap and made his farewells, and Pauline shared her intention of beginning immediately to collect the cuttings from the plants she had selected.

"Something to eat first," John declared, as Miss Pettigrew and Jane folded away their sketchpads and joined them. "It is noon, Miss Turner. Let us all be fed, and then you can return to your task with renewed vigor."

It was a long afternoon, but by the end of it, the Cumberland cuttings had joined those she had taken in Lancashire. The carriage that was to carry Pauline's finds back to Leicester was full of safely-secured pots of damp river sand, each with its set of carefully selected cuttings buried two thirds deep, tagged with the date, the place, and a code of letters and numbers that designated the rose of origin.

The carriage would leave in the morning, and Pauline's own gardener would know exactly what to do with its contents.

She had just enough time before dinner to write a second copy of her list of rose descriptions and codes to send with the roses, so her gardener had one in case anything happened to her. A foolish precaution. If she fell off a cliff or was run over by a racing carriage, no one was interested enough in her rose-breeding program to carry it on. She had better avoid cliffs and racing carriages, then.

There were no private moments with John after dinner, either. They agreed on going straight up to bed to be ready for an early start in the morning.

Despite the busy day, Pauline lay awake for some time, having nothing left to do but to ponder the words that had been echoing in the back of her mind all day.

I had no intention of ever wedding again. Not at that time. Did he mean that he had changed his mind? Was that the significance of his look? Of his hand on hers? Of the brief kiss? They were friends. Could Pauline dare to believe that John wanted something more?

Chapter Fifteen

THEY MADE AN early start the next morning, and reached Carlisle in the mid-afternoon, stopping only to change horses and eat from a basket that Mrs. Thorne had packed. The weather was fine, and the road was tolerable. Pauline found it hard to believe it was the same road she had traveled in reverse all those months ago in that dreadful storm.

She saw little of John all day, for he and Thorne rode on their horses. Mrs. Thorne sat up with the coachman while Pauline, Miss Pettigrew, Jane, Jane's nursemaid Cassie, and Pauline's maid Betsy occupied the carriage.

John spent little time at the inn, once they arrived. He confirmed that the rooms he had reserved were available, and then apologized to Pauline. "I hope you will forgive me if I rush off. I wish to check that the installation was completed as planned. All going well, I will be back in plenty of time for dinner."

He was not. In fact, he did not come in time to read Jane her bedtime story. Instead, he sent a messenger saying there was a problem, and he did not know when he would be free. Pauline offered herself as a substitute, and Jane accepted, though she was inclined to be sulky about her father's defection.

"Papa always reads to me when we are at home," she complained.

"He loves to read to you," Pauline pointed out. "He must be very upset he has been forced to miss it. You will need to let him read you two stories tomorrow night to make up."

Jane was content with that solution. Pauline hoped John would also approve.

He had still not arrived when Pauline and Miss Pettigrew went up to bed. The next morning, when they came down to the private parlor where breakfast was set out, she found that he had been and gone.

"Something about a bent shaft," Mrs. Thorne explained. "Thorne says it took them a long time to find out just what the problem was. Someone must have been a bit rough, apparently. The captain had to wake up a watch smith to heat the piece and straighten it. Told Thorne to stay and watch, and come and get him when the job was done. He came back here for a couple of hours sleep, and then sent Thorne to bed when the man woke him with the mended piece. The captain is over there now, putting his device back together again."

Poor John. With the opening at one in the afternoon, Pauline hoped nothing else went wrong.

She, Miss Pettigrew, and the nursemaid took Jane out for a stroll. They found the marketplace, with the town hall along one side. "Your Papa is in the clock tower," Pauline told Jane. "We can't go up there, but this is where we shall come to look at the display this afternoon."

They stopped to admire the market cross, then walked on to see the cathedral before returning to the inn so they could eat and then dress for the event.

John was there before them, looking weary but triumphant. "Fixed it," he said, "and just in time."

"Shall we see it, Papa?" Jane asked. "Can we come with you to see it?"

He swept her up into his arms and kissed her nose. "You can, my princess. I am going to have a bath and dress in my best clothes, but I would be proud to escort such a lovely lady to the opening."

"Then we shall go and dress in our best, too," Pauline told Jane and him both. "Your Papa is going to love your new dress, Miss Jane."

QUITE A CROWD was gathered when John's party arrived at the market square. As the minute hand moved towards the top of the dial, the mayor gave a speech, speaking of John's brilliance and praising himself and the town council for their own cleverness in choosing John to create something that would rain down credit on the whole town.

He had not quite finished his speech when the minute hand reached the twelve. A single bong for one o'clock attracted everyone's attention. It preceded a peal of bells that accompanied the opening of doors below the clock face.

The mayor fell silent. The crowd gazed expectantly.

Apart from a brief glance to check that the little soldiers were performing as expected, John studied the crowd, who were as rapt as he'd hoped, as the Romans marched back and forth across the scene. Another peal of bells and the scene changed, to a group sigh of awe.

Jane was dancing with delight, and beside her, Pauline was grinning. She cast John a glance and mouthed, "Wonderful." His heart swelled, and he felt the sudden urge to kiss her again. *Not a good idea, John. Don't spoil the friendship.*

Two more peals of bells, two more scenes, and then the doors closed again to another peal, a deep collective sigh from the crowd, and then applause.

"Make it go again, Papa," Jane begged.

"I cannot, Jane," John told her. "It will go again in one hour." Then the mayor called him to come and be introduced to the crowd, so he had to leave Pauline and Mrs. Thorne to explain to Jane why he couldn't change the sequence or timing to please his little princess.

From the platform the mayor was using as a stage, John looked back to see how she was reacting. She was smiling up at Pauline and nodding, so she must have accepted his edict. He would have to bring her back later. After he had caught up on his sleep. He suppressed a yawn, and acknowledged the applause of the crowd.

As he said the few words he had prepared—just an explanation for his choice of the four scenes—he scanned the crowd, his eyes again and again returning to his own people. To Jane, the Thornes and Pauline. Betsy and Miss Pettigrew were Pauline's, he supposed, and through her, part of his party. The nursemaid was one of his, though he couldn't say he knew her. Where was she? Ah. A few steps behind them on the edge of the crowd, and just beyond her… *That man looks like Lord Tenby.*

Someone passed in front, blocking John's view for a moment, and when he looked again, the man was gone. He didn't think his tired eyes had conjured a man out of thin air, but he might have put Tenby's face on a stranger of approximately the right size. Must have. Tenby was a creature of the ton, a lover of parties and gambling dens. He and Augusta were made for one another in that way. Tenby would not be in Carlisle.

John shook off his discomfort as people came forward to meet him, to ask him questions, to praise his work. It wasn't Tenby.

Chapter Sixteen

ONCE THE CROWD broke up, Pauline and Miss Pettigrew remained in the square while the rest of the party returned to the inn. John had declared his intention of going back to the inn to catch up on his sleep, and Mrs. Thorne insisted that Jane, too, would benefit from a rest.

Pauline was not tired, and this was her opportunity to take a closer look at the rose garden she'd glimpsed when they had gone walking that morning. Miss Pettigrew wanted to browse the market stalls, but was happy to accompany Pauline first.

The roses were pretty, but none of them had characteristics that Pauline needed. "Which is as well," Miss Pettigrew teased, "for we would spend the rest of the day searching town for someone who could give us permission to take cuttings, and I wish to see if I can find a little something for the children." The children were the current occupants of the Stancroft nursery.

"That's a good idea," Pauline said. "You miss them."

Miss Pettigrew sighed. "I do. I have enjoyed my holiday with you, Miss Turner, but this is the longest I have been away from my schoolroom since your stepfather employed me to be governess to Lady Vivienne and Miss Rose. Lady Douglas, now. I will be pleased to be home."

"That must be twelve years ago, now," Pauline realized. Miss

Pettigrew was still a relatively young woman, though older than Pauline's thirty years, but she had been governess to Peter's family for most of her adult life.

Pauline's stepbrother and his wife were not uninterested and distant parents. They gave the children a lot of attention, even having the older ones at meals when they did not have guests. Pauline, too, enjoyed time with the children. But she had never really spent much time with Miss Pettigrew until this trip.

"Will you not call me Pauline?" she asked, impulsively. "I like to think we have become friends during our travels."

Miss Pettigrew's eyes lit up, but she said, "You are the sister of an earl, Miss Turner. One, furthermore, who is my employer. It is kind of you to suggest it, though."

Pauline dismissed that argument with an impatient gesture. "If not for Peter's generosity, I would have been yet another of that army of indigent gentlewomen seeking genteel employment, and I cannot think I would have been as successful as you. I would be proud to be called your friend, if you could bear to consider it."

Miss Pettigrew blushed. "You are very kind. Millicent, if you please. Just while we are on holiday and when we are in private."

"Millicent. Here we are in the market again, Millicent. Oh, look. It is almost the hour again."

A crowd was gathering at the best spot for viewing the clock automatons, but with another five minutes to go, Millicent was determined to look at as many market stalls, barrows, and carts as she could. "I will just check who is selling what, Pauline, and then we can make any purchases after the show."

"I will hold a good spot for us," Pauline suggested.

Millicent looked a little uncertain.

"You will be able to see me and I will be able to see you," Pauline pointed out, and Millicent nodded and wasted no more time before setting off around the square to do her survey.

Four more minutes to go. Pauline chose a spot up a slight rise, looking over the crowd towards the clock tower. She had a good view of the crowd, and amused herself by picking a group and imagining a story for them.

This couple, arm in arm and their heads close together, were newlyweds. That one, not touching but sneaking glances at one another, must still be courting. There was a group of apprentices. Were they on an errand for their master? Their hunted expressions hinted that they hoped not to be noticed until the display was over.

Perhaps that maid creeping through the far side of the crowd, her face turning from side to side as if she was searching for someone, was also playing truant. Pauline toyed with the idea that she was meeting a lover, but lost all interest in her frivolous imaginings when she caught a clear sight of the girl's face.

Jane's nursemaid Cassie! What was she doing here? Pauline's heart leapt. *Perhaps John has brought Jane to see the display again*?

As she set off to make her way to the front of the crowd, where the maid was headed, a peal of bells announced the hour and the watchers all took a step closer. Pauline lost sight of the nursemaid, but never mind. Jane would surely be near the front where she could get a clear view.

The town was delighted with its new toy. The crowd was larger than it had been for the official opening, and the watchers did not want to make room for Pauline to get through. The third scene had started when she heard Jane's voice raised in loud complaint. "Leave me alone. Go away. Help!"

Another voice, soothing those who might leap to a child's defense. "Nothing to worry about. I am her father. I am taking her home." It did not sound like John.

The nursemaid's voice saying, "He is her father," made her question her own frightened assumptions, but still the fear drove her. As precocious as she was, Jane would never tell John to leave her alone and especially would never tell him to go away, or cry for help.

She pushed her way between people, forgetting manners for the sake of speed, and broke free of the crowd in time to see a wailing, struggling Jane being carried down the street beyond the town hall, the nursemaid trailing behind the man who had seized the child.

She couldn't see the man's face, but it was definitely not John. Pauline was already running before she made the conscious decision to follow. Should she stop and tell Millicent what had happened?

I don't have time. The man was turning a corner. If she didn't go after them, she might lose them, and sure enough, when she reached the corner, they were gone. *No!* There was the nursemaid, peeking back from yet another lane.

Pauline put on extra speed, but as fast as she ran, they were still ahead of her, until she burst out of an alley into an innyard, where the man was forcing Jane into a carriage. The child yelled at the top of her voice and scrambled to cling to the doorframe. In the struggle, the man's hat had fallen off and she recognized him by his white-blond hair. It was Lord Tenby.

Pauline shouted. "Stop that man. He is abducting my child!"

Tenby gave Jane a hard shove so that she fell in through the door and leapt in after her. The maid began to follow, but Pauline grabbed her by the shoulder and shoved her out of the way, throwing herself into the vehicle, falling forward onto the floor at the feet of the occupants just as the coach driver whipped the horses into a fast start.

Tenby pulled the door closed, but Pauline only had eyes for Jane. She was being restrained by Lady Tenby, who held the poor little girl with both arms behind her back.

"Miss Turner," the child wailed. "I want Miss Turner."

"It looks like you have Miss Turner," said Tenby, dryly. "So stop that infernal noise."

The conveyance was rocking and lurching as it raced over the road. Even if Pauline could get the door open without Tenby stopping her, she and Jane would never survive a leap onto the roadside.

The point became moot when Tenby announced, "I am

pointing a pistol at your Miss Turner, Augustina. If you do not stop that noise immediately, and sit quietly next to your Mama like a good little girl, I shall shoot a bullet into her."

Jane's loud complaints stopped abruptly. "My name is Jane," she said. Pauline, who had shifted enough to see that Tenby was, indeed, pointing a coach pistol at her, was pleased to hear Jane's tone: defiance and anger. Better anger than fear.

But Jane's voice shook when she added, "Don't hurt my Miss Turner."

Tenby's nostrils flared as he made a harrumphing noise. "I won't have to if you are good. Get up, Miss Turner. You can sit next to Lady Tenby and take Augustina on your knee. I will still be able to shoot you in the leg if you or she should cause any trouble."

"You will not get away with this," Pauline said as she obeyed, adding—more to comfort Jane than to defy the Tenbys—"The Captain will come after us." Jane climbed willingly onto Pauline's knee, and Pauline put her arms around the child.

"He won't," Tenby insisted, but he did not sound certain. He turned to Lady Tenby for reassurance. "Will he? Why should he? She's just a girl brat, and not even his."

"She is *our* daughter," Lady Tenby soothed Tenby, then glared at Pauline. "He will not find us."

Jane opened her mouth, her eyes defiant, then looked at Tenby holding the pistol and back to Pauline and subsided. Just as well. Pauline would not be able to run with a bullet in her leg, and she was determined that she and Jane would escape as soon as possible.

Chapter Seventeen

JOHN SURFACED FROM fathoms deep to the call, "Captain! Report to battle stations!"

He was out of bed and pulling on his trousers before he was awake enough to remember that Thorne had last woken him for a battle call eleven years ago and that his army days were eight years behind him, something he forgot in his sleep, which would be why Thorne called from the door, and waited there till John was fully awake.

The manservant moved forward as John did up his fall, and held out a waistcoat.

"What's afoot, Thorne?" John asked. From the grim set of Thorne's jaw, it was bad.

"Our Miss Jane, Captain. She's been taken."

John froze, warring instincts rendering him immobile as his brain sent competing signals to fight someone, to run in search of her, to question Thorne and find out more. His rational brain won, barely. He forced himself to continue dressing as he barked, "Explain."

Thorne came to attention. "Miss Jane is not in her bedchamber. Wasn't there when Mrs. Thorne checked on her a few minutes ago. Maid wasn't there neither, and we was just about to wake you, Captain, when the maid came back. Said she'd chased after Miss Turner and Jane, and seen them get into a coach down by the town hall. Said she thought she'd better come back and tell you, Captain.

His first thought was that Jane would be safe if Pauline was with her. Pauline was their friend. Pauline was perhaps becoming more than a friend, if he let his wayward anatomy have its way. Those thoughts were swamped by blinding rage, all the worse for the pain that was ripping his heart to shreds. Pauline had betrayed him. It was all a façade.

He shoved away his hurt at being taken in by another deceitful bitch, and steeled himself to ignore the grief. She wasn't what mattered.

"She must be working with Lord Tenby. I thought I saw the villain at the opening of the clock automaton," he told Thorne. "Ignored my own eyes, dammit, but Jane should have been safe there. Why was she alone, dammit? Where was Mrs. Thorne?"

Thorne, his eyes as bleak as John had ever seen them, said, "Doing the laundry, and left the maid to look after Miss Jane. Feels terrible about it, she does, Captain."

John led the way through to the next room, saying, "Where was the maid?"

Cassie was collapsed on her knees, her head in Mrs. Thorne's lap. The room resounded with her noisy weeping. Tears ran down Mrs. Thorne's face, too. She was pale, but composed as she said, "The girl stepped out for a moment, she says. Came back to see Miss Turner, leaving with Miss Jane." Some of her outrage and anxiety colored her next words. "She should have called me or Thorne, stupid girl."

The maid sobbed harder.

"Miss Turner has been abducted," said a voice from the door. "Is Jane safe? The witnesses said there was a child, too."

Miss Pettigrew stepped into the room, Miss Turner's maid behind her.

"Miss Turner has kidnapped Jane," John told her, coldly. "The maid saw her take the child from her room."

Miss Pettigrew's tone was equally chilly. "That is a lie, Captain Forsythe. Miss Turner and I were together from the time you left the market square until we returned to it just before three, when the display was about to begin again. We separated briefly while she watched the display and I checked the stalls. Witnesses saw a man put a struggling child into a carriage several streets away from the square as the last bell sounded, and Miss Turner threw herself into the carriage as it moved away. It is not possible for her to have returned to the inn, collected Miss Jane, and taken her to the other side of the market square between two minutes to three, when she was no longer in my view, and five minutes past, when she leapt into the carriage, presumably to *protect* your daughter, Captain Forsythe."

"But the maid said..." John trailed off. It was Cassie's word against Miss Pettigrew's. His fear of being hurt again was screaming that Pauline was working with the Tenbys, but that wasn't fair. Even if he could believe that Miss Pettigrew was also part of the conspiracy, Pauline had not given him any cause to doubt her since they met again in February.

Miss Pettigrew was not waiting for him to make up his mind. She walked up to the weeping maid, and pulled her head back by the hair. "Yes, you might well cry. You are in serious trouble, young woman. Helping someone to kidnap a child is a hanging offense. And blaming Miss Turner for your crime will not help you, for I have the names and addresses of people who can prove you are lying, and I have given them to the constable."

Cassie tried to pull away, but her wailing did not cease.

Miss Pettigrew commanded her, "Stop that noise this instant and tell the truth. Perhaps the Captain may be inclined to mercy if you help him get his daughter back."

"She's not his daughter!" the maid screamed. "I did nothing wrong. The lady told me. The lady said he wouldn't let her have her own daughter, and I wasn't doing wrong to help her get her little girl back."

"The lady lied," Miss Pettigrew told her. "What were you

told to do?"

The maid gave a gasping sob, and then answered the question. "Take Miss Jane to the street that goes past the cathedral."

"Was that where they were going to pay you?" Miss Pettigrew asked.

The maid nodded. It was all John could do to keep his hands off the little liar, and Thorne did jerk forward, to be stopped by his wife's touch on his arm.

"But they didn't pay me," the maid complained, "because Miss Jane wouldn't go past the market square because the bells were playing. I knew she'd make an awful fuss if I dragged her or picked her up and carried her, and people would notice. I went to get the lord, but he wouldn't pay me till he had Miss Jane, and then Miss Turner chased them, and they all drove away with my money." She raised her voice in another wail. "I was going to buy a new dress." And she buried her face in her apron to grieve the loss of that dream.

"They took the road west, towards the coast," Miss Pettigrew said. "Now that we've established that my charge needs rescuing as much as yours, Captain, you had better be after them. Leave Mrs. Thorne and me to hand this little fool over to the constable."

The little fool raised her head for a louder wail, but was ignored.

"Pack two sets of saddle bags," John told Thorne. "My pistols, a change of shirt. You know the sort of thing. I'll go and order horses. Buy some, if our own are too tired." He took a stride towards the door, then turned back to Miss Pettigrew. "Thank you," he said. "I'll get them back."

Chapter Eighteen

THE APPEARANCE THE Tenbys presented to Society was of a devoted couple who lived in blissful domestic harmony. That appearance dissolved in private when they disagreed, at which point they bickered like children, as they did as soon as Lord Tenby opened a hatch between the carriage and the driver and instructed the man to slow down.

"Tell him to spring them, Tenby," Lady Tenby demanded. "John will be after us."

"Stop fussing, Augusta," Tenby growled. "He is not a magician. Who is to tell him we have the girl, or which way we went?"

"The maid will," Lady Tenby retorted.

Tenby scoffed. "Not her. If she has an ounce of sense, she'll disappear so she doesn't have to answer questions."

Pauline's own assessment was that Cassie had no sense at all, but she said nothing.

Tenby thought for a moment. "In any case, we won't get there at all if we keep the horses at a gallop. They'll founder on the road, and if we don't make the tide, Lady Tenby, then your ex-husband may well catch up with us."

"You love your horses more than you love me," Lady Tenby complained.

Tenby cast his eyes up to the ceiling and muttered something

Pauline thought might be, "The horses are better tempered."

Lady Tenby chose to ignore the remark, but five minutes later, she complained again. "You should have waited for the maid, Tenby. Do you expect *me* to look after the child?"

"Miss Turner was screaming blue murder," Tenby pointed out. "Did you want to be caught?"

That distracted Lady Tenby, and she returned to worrying that John was on their heels, but in only a few more minutes, she fretted that she would not be able to find a nursemaid until they reached France. Possibly not until they arrived in Paris.

"Miss Turner will look after the child," Tenby pronounced.

Lady Tenby's eyes widened, and she looked Pauline up and down. "We are not taking Miss Turner with us, Tenby."

Tenby raised his eyes ceilingward again. "We are taking her now, Augusta. You just told her we are going to Paris. We cannot leave her to send Forsythe in the right direction, and I am not going to kill a female, even for you. She might as well be useful."

Pauline made no comment, but she was relieved. She had not intended to leave Jane, unless they dragged her from the child's side. If they willingly took her with them, she would be right there when the chance came to take the little girl and escape.

Perhaps at the port they must be heading for, if the tide was a consideration.

Meanwhile, she held Jane on her lap, and Jane sat with her arms around Pauline and her head on Pauline's chest. They stayed quiet, and the Tenbys, after the conversation about taking Pauline to care for Jane, ignored them. Their lack of interest begged the question of why they had stolen Jane away.

It seemed a long time until the horses slowed. Tenby took a watch from his pocket and said, "Quarter past four. We have made good time. The tide turns not long after four thirty."

We have been travelling just over an hour. If this is the port, it is not far from Carlisle.

The coach drew to a stop. Tenby, who had all this time kept his hand near the pistol, picked it up again. "Remember, Miss

Turner and Augustina, if either one of you misbehaves in any way, I shall shoot Miss Turner in the foot."

He waited while a footman assisted Lady Tenby out of the carriage, and then descended himself, keeping the pistol on Pauline the whole time.

Jane whispered, close to Pauline's ear, "I am not Augustina. I am Jane."

Pauline gave her a loving squeeze and set her down on the floor of the carriage. "I shall climb down, darling, and then I shall lift you out. I shall not let go of your hands. Not once."

Jane nodded, though a tear trembled and spilled from each eye as Pauline set her to her feet. She clung tightly to Pauline's hands while Pauline backed awkwardly down the carriage steps. In moments, Jane was in Pauline's arms again, and Pauline was able to take the time to look around.

They had stopped at a bustling wooden jetty on a broad river. Stevedores were moving barrels and crates from canal barges to larger ocean-going vessels, and from other vessels to the barges.

Tenby didn't give her time to look around further. He waved the pistol in the direction of a path along the shore. "That way," he instructed.

Pauline obeyed the order, hurrying as fast as she could with an eight-year-old girl with legs wrapped around her waist and head buried in her shoulder.

Tenby offered his arm to his lady and set off behind her, while servants offloaded a trunk and a couple of bags from the luggage rack at the back of the carriage, and followed along.

They didn't go far. Just to where a rowboat was pulled up on the river bank a little beyond the busiest part of the village.

A large man lifted himself from where he had been leaning against a stack of rocks. "Lord and Lady Tenby. You are just in time. My instructions were to give you until the half hour then leave." He spoke like a gentleman, but was dressed like a common sailor—like the four other ruffians who were picking themselves up from the ground around the boat.

"We are here," Tenby said, shortly.

"And you have your daughter, I see," the man observed. "Do you normally hold your nursemaid at gun point?" His tone was inquisitive rather than censorious.

"You are not being paid to ask questions," Tenby grumbled, and Lady Tenby said, "Do let us get on, Tenby." She cast a glance up river towards the road, obviously still concerned that John would appear at any moment.

Pauline wished he would, but she did not believe he would know which direction to chase them, if he even knew yet that they were missing. If the maid had not gone back to the inn, Jane might not even have been missed, though Miss Pettigrew—Millicent—would be looking for Pauline.

The inquisitive gentleman gave his fellows a nod, and in moments, the rowboat was in the water, with one of the sailors aboard wielding oars, one thigh deep in the water holding the boat steady, and the other approaching Pauline and Jane.

Pauline clutched Jane more tightly, her heart pounding. She could not let them be separated.

"If you will hand the child over, nursemaid," said the inquisitive gentleman, "my friend here will carry her to the boat."

"I can carry her," Pauline insisted.

The man waved towards the boat. "I will carry you," he said," and keep you from the waves." He narrowed his eyes at her, as if trying to see into her mind. "I give you my word that you will be within reach of her at all times, and together again in half a dozen paces."

Another sailor was carrying Lady Tenby, and Tenby was following, grumbling about the impact of sea water on his boots.

Farther down the shore, Tenby's servants were helping two other sailors to load the Tenby's baggage into a second boat.

With all of them but these two occupied, could Pauline escape with Jane?

"You cannot run," said the inquisitive man.

"Let me," she begged. "They kidnapped Jane from her real

father, and when I tried to stop them, they kidnapped me, too. Let us go, please."

His face changed, hardening into a grim mask. "I am truly sorry. I cannot do as you ask. I have my orders. Come. Give the child to Murphy, here. We must not miss the tide."

"Her father will follow," Pauline warned. She kissed the little girl's hair. "He will find us, Jane darling. He won't give up."

She handed Jane over to the sailor called Murphy.

"Put your arms around my shoulders," instructed the gentleman. He scooped her up with one hand under her knees and the other around her back. "Does this father have a name?"

"Captain Forsythe. Captain Lord John Forsythe. Brother to the Marquess of Deerhaven," she said. "Why? Do you want to know who will be hunting you for aiding in abducting his daughter?"

He grinned. "Smart mouth for a nursemaid. Who are you really?"

She lifted her chin. "Pauline Turner." He had not blinked at Deerhaven's title. She would throw another title at him. "Sister to the Earl of Stancroft."

"My, we are moving in exalted company! Helping to abduct two aristocrats! The Earl of Tenby claims the child as his own, and she has the look of him."

Pauline had nothing to say to that, and besides, they were at the boat. He put her over the side. True to his word, he had not let her touch the waves, all but a scrap of her hem, which would have got wet anyway. Lady Tenby was currently complaining bitterly about the inch or so of water that sloshed at their feet.

Pauline squeezed onto a bench next to Jane and put her arm around the child.

The inquisitive man was still in the water, whispering to Murphy.

One of the rowers called out, "Lieutenant?"

"Ready," the man said. "All aboard." He clambered into the boat himself, as Murphy waded back to the shore. "Murphy will come with the luggage. Pull away, boys."

Looking down over the side, Pauline could see the wide strand that would be exposed as the sea retreated with the tide. The rowers were pulling strongly and the boat was gliding above the mud towards a ship out in the channel, presumably their destination.

It was a three-master, stern towards them, with what seemed like dozens of men swinging through the bewildering web of lines from the deck to the top of the tallest mast—*the rigging*, she had heard it called.

All too soon, Pauline was in a cloth sling, Jane on her lap, as they were swung aboard the ship. The Tenbys had gone ahead of them, and were being ushered below as she clambered from the sling. The lieutenant, whom she had left in the row boat, was waiting for her. He must have scurried up the rope ladder the men were using fast as a monkey! The thought brought a smile to her lips, and he smiled in return.

"A nice ship, isn't she? Come this way, Lady Pauline. You and Miss Spindler have a cabin together."

She followed behind him, "Miss Turner," she corrected. "And Miss Forsythe."

Another man stepped in front of the lieutenant. He was slender to the point of gauntness, with a large beak of a nose and fiery eyes under black bushy eyebrows. "So, this is the brat," he said, glaring at Pauline. "You, girl! Keep the little chit below deck and quiet, or I'll toss you both overboard."

"Lady Pauline," said the lieutenant, flashing his charming smile, "allow me to present Captain Diablo of the Retribution. Captain, Lord and Lady Tenby apparently thought the sister of the Earl of Stancroft would make a good nursemaid for the girl—who, according to Lady Pauline, has also been abducted."

Diablo was a good name. The captain looked like a devil, Pauline thought, though—like the lieutenant—he spoke the English of a cultured gentleman.

She clutched Jane to her side, and acknowledged the introduction with a stiff nod. This was no time to argue about the courtesy title she didn't have.

"I don't care if they've abducted the queen and one of the royal princesses," Diablo told the lieutenant. "We've been paid well to take them to France, but not enough to have them walking around my ship. Stow them in their cabin, Mr. Benedict. And make sure they stay there. The Tenbys, too. I want this ship underway in ten minutes."

"Aye, aye, Captain."

The lieutenant hurried them down a steep, narrow ladder and along a passage not much wider than the lieutenant's broad shoulders to a tiny cabin—two slender bunks against one wall, and an even more confined space alongside them that comprised the remainder of the floor space.

A lantern hung from a hook on the far wall. Mr. Benedict lit it using a spill from the one by the ladder. Light didn't improve the space.

"Stay here," he warned. "You heard the captain. His name is no mistake, Miss Turner. He is the very devil, and he means every word he says."

"Then why do you work for him?" Pauline couldn't help but ask.

His grin this time was rueful, but he did not give her an answer. He just shut the door.

JOHN LED THE way as they rode through Drumburgh village. As the road emerged from the houses and turned towards the water, they could see Port Carlisle in the distance. Out in the Solway Firth, several tall ships lay at anchor, and closer to shore, lighters were unloading from barges and on to other ships. John's heart clenched. If Jane and Pauline were on one of them, he'd have them back before night fall if he had to search every nook and cranny on every vessel.

Pray heaven they were not on the ship almost out of sight at the mouth of the Firth, hauling sail as it swept out to sea on the tide.

"Captain, the carriage." Thorne's shout drew his attention from the water to the carriage on the road below. Miss Pettigrew's description of the carriage and the team that drew it had been meticulous. Three chestnuts and a bay, all with white socks, the bay with a blaze on the nose and two of the chestnuts with stars. The carriage was a coach in style, painted green with red wheels, with a perch in front for the driver and another above a luggage rack at the back.

John could see all the details as the equipage turned with the road and began to climb the hill.

He rode partway to meet it, Thorne a pace or two behind. Without a word spoken, they set their horses to block the road, and waited. It was to be hoped those with the coach kept calm, for John didn't want to have to shoot. Nor, for that matter, to be shot.

"Here now," said the driver, as he pulled up his team. "What are you about?"

"Do you have passengers?" John asked. "I'm looking for a couple, a girl of eight, and another lady."

The driver nodded thoughtfully. "You would be Captain Lord John Forsythe, then," he said. "A sailor from that ship said you might be along." He pointed back toward the firth. No. To the sea beyond. *Curse it!*

His heart sinking, he asked, "They're on that ship?"

The driver nodded again. "That's right, my lord. Lord and Lady Tenby, and the girl and the lady. Paid to bring them to Port Carlisle, I was, and that's what I did." He shook his head. "They said the girl was their daughter, and that she was having a tantrum over being made to leave the clock."

He whistled. "Something wonderful that clock is, sir. Little people marching and dancing. Never seen anything like it. But then the lady came running and shouting, and threw herself into the carriage. Didn't smell right to me."

"It wasn't right," John told him, coldly. "You assisted in the abduction of my daughter, and of the sister of the Earl of Stancroft."

The driver was inclined to argue. "Well, how was I to know, my lord? I was told what to do by an earl, even if he is a queer fish, and paid well to do it, too. And rightly speaking, my lord, we didn't abduct the lady, since she jumped aboard herself."

John took a deep breath to calm himself. Strangling the driver, or even punching his smug face, would not bring Jane back. "Do you know where the ship is going?" he asked.

The driver brightened. "That I do, my lord. The sailor told me." He looked up into the sky, pressing his lips together. "Ah yes. That's it. *On the road back to Carlisle, watch for Captain Lord John Forsythe. He will be looking for the party you delivered here*. That would be to Port Carlisle, he meant, my lord," the driver added, pointing back to the port.

"He is the true father of the girl. Tell him that she and the lady are on The Retribution. *Lord and Lady Tenby have paid for passage to Brest*. That was the message I was to deliver, sir."

"Brest, France?" John asked, though he didn't know of any other. *France*! When he got his hands on Augusta and her lying cheating worm of a husband, he'd—he didn't know what he would do. He fought back the violence that wanted free rein against an enemy who was out of his reach. The sails on the distant sea slid beyond his sight.

His poor little girl must be so frightened. *At least Pauline is with her*. It would be a consolation if he could be certain that Miss Pettigrew spoke the truth. What the driver said, too, implied that Pauline was an unexpected addition to the party. Surely, he could trust her to look after Jane, at least to the best of her ability?

"What can you tell the Captain about *The Retribution*?" Thorne asked.

The driver denied any knowledge, as did the guard, when

applied to. They had been hired from Preston, and knew nothing more than that Lord and Lady Tenby had stayed in Penrith last night, and demanded to be at Port Carlisle by four this afternoon.

John and Thorne let them go. "We'll ride on to Port Carlisle, and see if anyone there can tell us about *The Retribution,*" John decided. "Then back to Carlisle to tell Miss Pettigrew and Mrs. Thorne what we've discovered. After that, Thorne, it's you and I for France. We'll just have to work out the quickest way."

Chapter Nineteen

JOHN AND THORNE arrived in Brest seven days later. They couldn't be much behind *The Retribution*, though it was not in Brest's harbor. They'd taken the fastest horses they could find across Cumberland and Northumberland to Newmarket-Upon-Tyne and caught the afternoon mail coach to London, arriving the following evening, two days after the abduction.

Deerhaven was out of London, so they went to Peter Stancroft. When he heard their news, he'd wanted to join the rescue mission, but his countess was with child and nearing her time. John assured him that he and Thorne would bring Pauline home.

Peter reluctantly agreed, but did his best to help, with maps, money, weapons, and other supplies. By the time John and Thorne left London the next morning, Peter had contacted several friends with yachts, and begged the use of one that was standing ready at Portsmouth. The messenger sent from London had reached Deerhaven, and he was waiting to farewell them at the wharf, with letters of introduction that might be helpful and a heavy purse.

Thorne took the time aboard to catch up with his sleep. John studied maps and fretted. Why Brest? And where would the Tenbys go from there?

What the yacht's captain knew of *The Retribution* and its captain was not reassuring. "Diablo is a pirate, and his crew are thugs. I'm not surprised they're assisting a kidnapping. They will do anything that someone is prepared to pay them for."

John had visions of the captain deciding to sail off after another prize, taking Jane and Pauline with him. He hoped Tenby had paid well enough for his entire party to be delivered to their destination.

Their first stop was the Harbor Master's office, where they were able to confirm that *The Retribution* had arrived the previous night, and left this morning.

"Can you tell me whether his passengers disembarked?" John asked, but the Harbor Master shrugged and said something fast and dismissive. At least, that's what John picked up from the man's tone. John's French wasn't up to a direct translation, but he was sure he'd been told that passengers were not the Harbor Master's responsibility.

Still, he was hopeful as he and Thorne began canvassing the best inns. "If they arrived last night, they might still be here," he said to Thorne.

At the third place they tried, the innkeeper recognized the name Tenby, and suddenly developed a fluency in English he had denied to that point. "The English milord and his lady? Gone, Monsieur, this morning, and good riddance. I spit on them, and on their ancestors." He lifted a pugnacious chin, challenging John to disagree with him.

"Lord and Lady Tenby kidnapped my daughter and a friend of my family," John told him. "I am here to take them back. I would very much appreciate any information you can give me."

The innkeeper's hostility evaporated. "So, Mademoiselle Turner spoke true! You are Monsieur Forsythe, yes?"

John couldn't help but smile. "Miss Turner spoke of me?"

The innkeeper nodded, even as he seized John's hand. "I will tell you all I can, Monsieur. *Moi?* I am a father myself. Mademoiselle Turner told my wife that the English milord and his lady had stolen the little girl from her father, and her father—that would be you, Monsieur—would pursue." He leaned backward and shoved open a door in the wall behind the desk. "Gwennin!" he shouted. At a more moderate volume he told John, "You must meet my wife, Monsieur, for it was to her that the mademoiselle spoke."

A little woman almost as round as the portly innkeeper came through the door and began to berate the innkeeper for shouting, then stopped when she realized that John was standing before them.

John had enough French to follow what the innkeeper told her. "Gwennin, this is Monsieur Forsythe, the little mademoiselle's Papa." To John, in English, he said, "Monsieur, this is my wife, Madame Peress. She speaks not the English, so I will translate."

John bowed. "Madame." Madame Peress pattered off something very quickly. John looked to Monsieur Peress, who obliged with a translation. "My wife says that you have come very quickly. Mademoiselle Turner was worried that much time might pass."

"Mademoiselle Turner's companion saw her being kidnapped. I followed, but I arrived too late at the port where they caught their ship. It had already sailed. Mademoiselle Turner managed to leave a message with the carriage, so I knew the Tenbys were bound for Brest."

Monsieur Peress spoke to his wife in French, and John heard the names Turner, Tenby, and Brest. Madame Peress spoke briefly, and so the conversation went, with the innkeeper conveying remarks back and forth.

The inn had already been predisposed to dislike the English milord and milady before they disembarked from *The Retribution*, for their servants had arrived before them, and thrown the place into turmoil with demands on behalf of their employers.

On arrival, Lord and Lady Tenby had done nothing to endear themselves to the household, instead expecting instant attention to their every need. They were not the ones who needed attention, since their own servants were at their beck and call. John ached to hear that Jane had been carried ashore wan from a week of seasickness, but was not surprised that Augusta and Tenby had shown no concern for the little girl.

"They sent her off to a room with Mademoiselle Turner, and did not enquire about her again," Peress translated, while his wife's eyes flashed her indignation.

Mademoiselle Turner had won hearts by her devotion to the little mademoiselle, especially the heart of Madame Peress, who had helped Mademoiselle Turner to coax some soup into the child. "Some of my wife's special chicken soup, Monsieur, which she makes only when people are sick. Very tasty. Very gentle on abused digestion."

"When Mademoiselle Jane was asleep, Mademoiselle Turner told her story," Peress continued. "My wife believed her. She went to the *commissaire de police*, but he declined to take any action. He said that my wife had only the word of a nursemaid, that the party was, in any case, English, and therefore out of his jurisdiction, and that they had left town. Which they had, Monsieur, by the time he sent a *gendarme* to enquire."

John had expected no better of the authorities. Whether in England or in France, they would hesitate to challenge the party of a wealthy peer. His indignation was at the Tenbys, as he protested, "They traveled even though my daughter was sick?"

Madame beamed her approval at him when her husband translated this, and leaned forward to pat his arm, soothingly. "Mademoiselle Jane was much better after her sleep, and ate a good breakfast," Peress told him. "Mademoiselle Turner says that she travels well in a carriage; it was only the sea that sent her poor insides into rebellion."

Poor Jane. John, who had given up expecting anything from God on a battlefield in Spain more than a decade ago, but who had been praying for the past week that he would recover his daughter, sent up his first prayer of thanksgiving in more years than he could remember. "Thank you for Pauline." Only the

Divinity knew what would have become of his darling girl if Pauline had not hurled herself into the abduction.

PAULINE FELT IT best not to attempt to escape until they reached Paris. Without money or friends, she and Jane would not get far, but in Paris, she could appeal to her mother or her sister. And, if they would not help, to the British Embassy.

She also wanted to leave a trail for John. She was certain he would leave no stone unturned until he found them. Sooner or later, he or someone he employed would track them to Brest, and when he did, Monsieur and Mademoiselle Peress would remember her and Jane, and would let him know what she had told them.

Whenever she could, she would share the story of their kidnapping and their destination to those they met along the way, leaving a trail the searchers could follow. During a long day on dismal roads, Pauline pinned her hopes on each stop to change horses, only to be disappointed. On the occasions that Tenby allowed her and Jane down from the carriage, Lady Tenby's sour French dresser followed them everywhere, expressing with every snort and sneer how annoyed she was at being dragged from Paris to attend her mistress and then assigned the task of jailer to a nursemaid.

On the first night, they were guests in a private home. Not merely a home, but a castle. They had come through an arched gatehouse to a magnificent L-shaped stone building. The main wing towered three stories high, with a higher circular tower anchoring the corner with the lower and more modern two-story wing. At the end of each wing, a smaller tower echoed the large one.

Their carriage—they had been relegated to the servants' carriage with the dresser and Tenby's valet—pulled up beyond the main door where the Tenbys were being enthusiastically greeted by a couple of about the same age.

"Come along," the dresser grouched. "I have to see you upstairs to the nursery before I can attend to my mistress."

Pauline was not to be introduced to the host and hostess, then. No chance to tell her story. She refused to be disappointed.

They are Tenby's friends. They would probably not have believed me, or cared if they did. There will be other opportunities.

They followed the dresser along a passage and then up long, winding stairs. They must be in one of the smaller towers. The center of each stone step curved into a shallow hollow, worn by centuries of feet.

At the top of the stairs, the dresser opened the door and led them along another passage. The next door she opened led into a spacious, airy nursery, where a maid waited. The dresser spoke to her in French, saying, "This is my lady's daughter, and her attendant."

Pauline pretended not to understand. The Tenbys and the dresser had assumed she could not speak French, which gave her an advantage she did not intend to waste, but the dresser lowered her voice for whatever she said next.

While the maid and the dresser spoke, footmen appeared with the bags the Tenbys had given them, which contained the clothes the Tenbys had purchased for them in Brest. In Pauline's case, two nursemaid gowns and four aprons and caps. Pauline's own afternoon gown, refurbished overnight by Madame Peress, was hidden at the bottom of the bag, ready for their escape in Paris.

A larger bag contained gowns for Jane; half a dozen fussy confections, all in pale pastels and covered with lace, ribbons, and flounces. "How is one meant to play in these?" Jane had asked.

The dresser finished whatever she had been saying to the maid. She addressed Pauline.

"You and the little miss will stay here until it is time to leave in the morning. Yanna will make sure you have anything you need."

Pauline smiled at the maid. "Yanna," she repeated, and the maid smiled back. Another ally, perhaps? Though what good it would do, she wasn't sure. It would be hard enough for their pursuers to question the servants at every inn on the road from here to Paris, let alone the private houses.

Jane was kneeling on a window seat to look outside. "Miss Turner," she said, "I can see the sea. Or is it a river?"

Pauline leaned over her shoulder to look. "An inlet, I think, Jane, like the Solway, where we boarded *The Retribution*."

Jane shuddered. "I did not like *The Retribution*, Miss Turner. I hope I never have to go on the ocean again."

Pauline hugged her. "We won't need to cross the ocean again until it is time to go home to England, darling, when your Papa finds us. It won't be a long trip, either. There is a short way from France to England. And you won't have to stay in a stuffy horrid cabin. You will have too much to see to be sick, and scarcely time to know you are out at sea before we reach the other side."

Jane thought about that, then nodded, judiciously.

Pauline hoped she could make good on the promise.

Chapter Twenty

THE POST RIDER who had gone with the horses told John that the Tenbys had finished their first post at Landeneau. Apparently, Tenby's servants had brought three carriages to await their master's arrival.

The post rider was able to give John a good description of them, the first and most luxurious carrying Lord and Lady Tenby, the second with, so the post rider said, the little mademoiselle, her attendant, and two other servants. The dresser and the valet, he gathered.

The baggage carriage followed behind with lesser servants.

John set out the next morning, confident he'd have little trouble following their trail. All he had to do was ask after an English milord and his lady traveling with a little girl and an entourage in a procession of three carriages. Even a blind man would probably be able to tell him and Thorne which way their quarry had gone.

He started at Landivisau, where he and Thorne changed horses at the same inn as Tenby had used the previous morning. These horses carried them east to the next posting inn at Landeneau, where John received his first check. Tenby's party had not changed horses at that inn or any other before or after the town.

He wasted nearly an hour making sure they had gone no farther before retracing his steps to the road that ran south from Landivisau. He had a piece of luck after an hour on this new road, when he stopped in front of a tavern in a little village, where several old men sat on benches in the sun smoking their pipes.

In his halting French, he asked after the carriages he was following. "They have kidnapped my daughter," he explained.

One of them spat on the ground at his feet and muttered something that John could easily interpret, having heard more than his fair share of French expletives. It translated, roughly, as an instruction to go away and commit the solitary sin, and was followed by the epithet *rostbif*.

One of the others, however, admitted to seeing the *cortège*, the previous morning. They had over a day on him, but surely, he could catch that time up? He and Thorne pressed on.

A barrow holder in the marketplace at Quimper had seen the three carriages stop at the largest inn in the town, and the innkeeper confirmed that the Tenby party had eaten lunch before proceeding. John paid them both for their information, and bought pastries from the innkeeper for him and Thorne. They had cut an hour off the Tenbys' lead, and would cut another by not stopping to eat.

A boy sweeping the inn at Rosperden said they had not stopped there, but he had seen them pass. They had changed horses again at Quimperle, in the middle of the afternoon. John and Thorne rode on through the Breton countryside, confident that those they pursued had stopped at Hennebon, perhaps for the night.

But there was no word of the three carriages at Hennebon, where John and Thorne faced another choice of roads. They tried Baud, on the direct route to Rennes, and then Landevan towards Vannes. No one had seen the Tenby cavalcade. Not at the inns. Not on the road.

"We could carry on to Paris," Thorne suggested. "Wait for them there, if they haven't arrived ahead of us."

"We cannot be sure they are going to Paris," John objected. "They have a house there, true. But if that was their plan, why land in Brest? Why not Le Havre? It's not much farther by sea, but the road trip is a third of the length."

By now, it was getting dark. John and Thorne retraced their steps a little way towards Hennebon, but saw no one they could ask about the carriages. In the end, they had to give up and take a bed for the night. In the morning, they would start again with fresh horses, and cast along all possible routes until they found word of the Tenby carriages again.

THE NEXT DAY, they went all the way to Vannes without finding a trace of even one of the carriages. "We'll have to go back to Quimperle," John said. "That's the last time anyone reported seeing them. They must have turned off the post road after that."

But when they stopped in Hennebon to return the horses that had carried them to Vannes and to hire new ones, the stable master remembered them from the day before, and asked them to wait a moment. "Briac!" he shouted, then turned back to John. "The boy had a half day yesterday, to go to his sister's wedding, or I could have asked him then."

The *boy* turned out to be a hulking fellow in his thirties, with a hank of light brown hair and dark eyes. He apparently spoke only Breton but, between the stable master's halting English and John's imperfect French, they managed to establish that Briac lived along the road that headed north-west from Hennebon. He had been walking to work the morning of the day before when he was passed by three coaches that fit the description of the three for which John was searching.

"They must have stayed at a private chateau," the stable master suggested, which made sense. More importantly, they were heading in the direction of Paris. John was happy to pay both stable master and groom for the information. Their quarry had gained another half day's lead, but he and Thorne were back on the trail.

The carriages had been noticed in each town along the road from Hennebon to Ploermel, where they stopped to change horses the next day at the same inn the Tenbys had used the night before last. The innkeeper remembered the party, including the little girl and her nursemaid, but he had no message for John. However, when John and Thorne were about to leave, a maid came hurrying out and asked John if he might be Monsieur Capitaine Forsite?

"I am Captain Forsythe, yes," he said, his chest hollow with expectation and hope. Had Pauline found another ally?

Yes, she had, or so he understood from the volley of French the maid fired at him before handing him a note. He beamed at her. "Est-ce bien mademoiselle?" he asked, desperate for information.

"Oui," she agreed, patting his arm, and gave him to understand that both mademoiselles were well. Both. That was a relief.

"Give her some coins, Thorne," he said, as he broke open the seal on the letter and left the pair to a teasing conversation conducted more in gestures than in words while he read what Pauline had written.

"John, if you are reading this, I must suppose you somehow discovered we were landed in Brest. We are bound for Paris, to Lord Tenby's house there, and afterwards to Calais, and on by sea to Italy. I do not want to say too much, in case the maid betrays me and gives this letter to Tenby, but Jane is well, and I will not leave her until I can restore her to you. Pauline."

John closed the letter and tucked it into his breast pocket inside his jacket, comforted to have the paper Pauline had touched and the words she had written as close to his heart as he could manage. "Thorne, you were right. They are bound for Paris, but after that, they are going to Calais and then by sea to Italy."

"So, it's straight to Paris for us, my lord?" Thorne asked.

"Yes," John agreed. "Paris, and a reckoning with Tenby and his wife."

Soon, he would have his little girl in his arms again. As for the woman who had protected her so valiantly, he had a place for her in his arms, too, if he could just persuade her to take a chance on a sour old hermit who lived so far from the temperate south.

TENBY'S PARTY MADE a leisurely journey to Paris, stopping twice in private homes and once at an inn in Pre-en-Pail. At the inn, Pauline passed a note for John to the maid who waited on her and Jane. The girl took Pauline's coin, and passed the note to Tenby, who confronted Pauline the following morning as she and Jane came through the inn common room on their way to the carriage.

"You have betrayed us," he complained, waving the note at her. "I should put you out in the street."

Jane immediately hurled herself at him, kicking at his shins and screeching at the top of her voice. "No! You mustn't!"

Tenby's valet pounced on Jane to try to detach her from his master, and Tenby gave the child a slap that shocked her into silence.

"Let me," Pauline said to the valet, and gently took Jane's hands from Tenby's coat. She led her several steps away, kissed her red cheek, and enfolded her in an embrace. "A man who will strike a child is a bully and a coward," she told Tenby. If he was going to throw her out anyway, she had no need to mince her words.

From Pauline's arms, Jane turned on Tenby, and said, in a cold, clear voice, *and* in French, "I hate you! I hope my Papa kills you!"

Tenby's eyes widened, and he took an angry step towards the

child, but someone in the crowd of onlookers gasped. Realizing the scene had gathered an audience, he stopped.

"You are a very naughty little girl, Augustina Spindler," he told Jane.

"My name is Jane Forsythe," she replied, lifting her chin.

Lady Tenby intervened. "Tenby, darling, get them into the carriage. We can deal with this when we are in our own home." The look she shot at Pauline and Jane was venomous. Pauline resolved not to wait around in Paris to find out what punishment the foul woman had in mind.

"I don't want to take the Turner bitch," Tenby whined.

Lady Tenby tugged on his arm so that he bent for her whisper, which was just loud enough for Pauline to hear it. "Do you want to leave her here to tell her story to the authorities?"

The argument convinced Tenby, and Jane and Pauline were hustled into the carriage, while Tenby's valet moved amongst the crowd, saying, "What are you all gawking at? Nothing to see here."

They were escorted everywhere for the remainder of that day, and locked in their room at the chateau where they stayed the night. The next day was another long and boring carriage ride, with the dresser and the valet hovering over them at every stop. The servants liked it as little as Pauline and Jane. Less, probably, for the dresser, in particular, glared across the carriage whenever the games and stories with which Pauline was keeping Jane amused became a little loud.

The rain started shortly after midday, which slowed the trip as the road became bogged, and made the trip more boring for Jane by removing any possibility of seeing things out the window.

Towards the end of the day, Jane fell asleep, her head in Pauline's lap. Pauline was pleased for the opportunity to wedge her own head in the corner between the back of the seat and the wall of the carriage, and to close her eyes.

The dresser must have thought she slept. "Thank goodness we will be in Paris in an hour or less," she said to the valet, speaking French. "No more *Who can be the first to see three sparrows*. No more nursery songs."

"After Paris, we go to Calais," the valet pointed out.

"I have told my lady, I will not again travel in the same carriage as the little miss and her nursemaid. If they do not have another carriage, I leave. Someone else will have to care for my lady's hair and her skin, and look after her gowns. Without my special recipes." She made the noise that always accompanied the decisive nod she used when she had made a statement that, in her view, finished a discussion.

"I do not suppose her ladyship liked that," the valet commented.

"That is nothing to me. I can walk out of their townhouse tomorrow and find another position. And my lady knows it. Indeed, she has begged me to stay, and I will, for the pay is very good and my lady offers me much scope for my work. *If* they get a proper nursemaid for Miss Augustina and *if* I am never again expected to be a jailor for such as Miss Turner or a travel companion for a child I will stay."

The valet said, gravely, "Himself wants a new nursemaid. Says that Miss Turner is nothing but trouble, for all that she's good for the girl. Would have left her along the way if he didn't think Miss Augustina would throw a tantrum the rest of the journey to Paris."

He snickered. "Even if she didn't look just like Himself, I'd pick her for their daughter, our lord and lady. Behaves just like them in a temper, she does."

"She is a badly-behaved child, and I hope her new nursemaid beats her," the dresser declared.

The valet disagreed. "She's not too bad. She's always good for Miss Turner, and I guess any child would be upset to be stolen away from everyone else she knows. I can't see that his lordship—or her ladyship, for that matter—have much interest in her."

Pauline thought the same. *Why did the Tenbys go to such trouble to steal Jane away?*

The dresser had a theory. "It is my lady's pride," she said. "She has been telling all her friends how broken-hearted she is to have been forced to leave her daughter. His lordship's mother believed her, and told him off for agreeing not to dispute guardianship."

So that was it. Pauline wondered if there was money involved. As far as she knew, the Tenbys lived on income from the estate Tenby had inherited from his grandfather, but perhaps his father had some authority over it, or perhaps—in fact, probably—they had overspent.

"Anyway, Miss Turner will be out on her ear as early as tomorrow, if my lord has his way," the valet said. "And the poor little girl will be left for some other servant to raise."

"As long as I do not have to look after the child, I care not," said the dresser.

Chapter Twenty-One

THE NURSERY AT the Paris townhouse was ruthlessly clean and sparsely furnished with a random collection of unmatched items. Against one wall two beds, made with fresh sheets, sported a continental style of comforter each. Between the windows stood a table with two chairs. The wall opposite the beds had fitted shelves, which stood empty. A circular rug, the colors faded except where someone had darned a couple of worn places, covered the center of the wooden floor. And that was all, apart from Pauline's and Jane's bags, which a footman had deposited just inside the door.

No pictures or ornaments softened the room, which held no toys to play with or books to read.

"It is not very nice, is it?" Jane murmured to Pauline.

The footman shut the door as he left, and she heard the tumblers of the lock fall as he locked it. Pauline felt the strain go out of her shoulders. She had been afraid they might be separated straightaway, or that one of the maids might be assigned to stay with them. She was determined to escape tonight, and to take Jane with her.

"It is very bare," she replied to Jane, "but we will not be here very long. I wonder what we can see out of the windows?"

Other buildings, it transpired. But Pauline drew Jane's attention to a flock of pigeons.

"Look. I think they might be nesting on that building. Watch, and you might see which ones belong to which nests."

While Jane occupied herself watching the birds, Pauline examined the bars that, as in most nurseries, prevented children from taking a head-long fall from a high window ledge. They were mostly firm, but she found two that shifted slightly when she tugged at them. She might possibly be able to work them loose if her first plan didn't work.

She had more plans after that, from sneaking back into the house after she was evicted, to appealing to the authorities (unlikely to be helpful against a pair of English nobles), to following after the carriages and seizing an opportunity to free Jane. But all of them would leave Jane alone in the hands of the Tenbys until she could manage a rescue. Tonight was her last chance for them to leave together.

Nothing else in the room lent itself to escape. There was nothing to do but wait for nursery tea to arrive, and after that to try, if she could, to get Jane to sleep.

"Shall we make a story about the pigeons?" she said to Jane.

AT SAINT-CYR-L'ECOLE, THEY'D told John it was twenty-two miles to Paris. He and Thorne could have reached there that night, if the weather had not been foul. Without the light of even the stars, it would be foolish to continue, so instead they took a room for the night and ordered dinner, which was served in the public room.

"They can't be that far ahead of us," Thorne said. "We'll get to Paris before they can leave again, Captain."

"First stop, the British Ambassador," John said. "If we leave at dawn, we can be at the Hôtel de Charost by nine."

"Get him out of bed, do you think?" Thorne asked.

John shrugged. "There'll be an attaché on duty, I imagine, to whom I can give Deerhaven's letter with my credentials." John's brother had been at Oxford with Viscount Granville, the current ambassador, which John hoped would count more with the local authorities than any social cachet the Tenbys might have with the court of Charles X and the Paris expatriate community.

"We'll not succeed in retrieving Jane and Miss Turner without the support of the authorities," he said, though if it came to that, he'd find a way.

Thorne must have been thinking along the same lines. "It'll be easier to do it legal-like, Captain. Beyond a doubt."

"Capitaine? Un capitaine anglaise?" The speaker was a beefy man in his late middle years, who marched up to their table, gave it a shove, and spat on John's boots.

John stood; his hands spread to show that he had no weapons. "Pardonez-moi, monsieur—" He got no further, for the man punched him in the belly. Thorne leapt forward; his tankard raised to clock the man on the head.

"Thorne! At ease!" John roared, but it was too late. Several other patrons of the inn leapt into the fray, and John found himself separated from Thorne and fighting to defend himself, even as he tried to protest that he wanted peace.

Things got serious when several of the assailants pulled knives, and then men in uniform burst into the room, and John and Thorne were dragged away.

WHEN PAULINE HEARD the key in the lock, she hurried to the door, whispering to Jane, "Stay sitting at the table, darling."

Jane, thank goodness, did as she was told, and Pauline made another prayer of thanks as whoever was in the passage knocked on the door. Pauline opened it, and stepped out of the way as a maid entered with a tray, followed by a footman with a jug of hot water.

As the footman passed Pauline, the maid sneezed, and nearly dropped the tray. The footman put out a hand to steady her, and Pauline took advantage of their distraction to find the hole the lock latch would go into. *There!* Quickly, before the servants could turn, she pressed into it the ball of clay and gravel that she held. She had collected it two days ago by pretending to trip on her way back from an inn's necessary when she saw the kind of clay she needed in a bank beside the path. She had managed to hide enough, as she cleaned her hands, to block several of the largest latch holes she could imagine.

The maid set the tray on the table and whipped the cover off, coughing as she did so. "I will deal with that," Pauline said. The maid shook her head and opened her eyes wide, then turned away to cough again, this time bending in two with the force of the cough.

"You should be in bed," Pauline observed, though there was no point, since the maid clearly didn't understand her. However, the footman said the same thing in French, cupping the maid's elbow as he led her from the room.

"And lose my job?" The maid responded. "No. It is just a rhume. I shall be fine in a day or two."

After the servants left and closed the door behind them, she listened as the lock tumblers fell. Had the latch been blocked? She resisted trying the door to find out. If someone happened to be in the passage when the door opened, she would have lost her opportunity. Instead, she turned her attention to helping Jane wash her face and hands, and serving their evening meal.

The evening dragged more than usual. A dozen times, she nearly told Jane of her hopes for the night and caught the words back. She didn't want Jane to suffer the wait with her, made all the more agonizing by not knowing whether they would have their chance or not.

At last, Jane showed signs of being sleepy, and Pauline soon had her changed for bed. They knelt together for Jane's prayers—

as well as her usual list of *God bless Papa and Thorne and Thorny*, she prayed every night that, "Papa is well, and not too worried, and he will soon find us and take us home."

Pauline tucked her between the sheets and kissed her goodnight, then sat back at the table with her own thoughts, fears, and plans to keep her company as the last of the light faded outside.

It was still raining, but that wouldn't stop her.

She had no idea where in Paris she was now, let alone how far or in what direction they would have to walk to find her mother's house, but that wouldn't stop her, either. Should she change her clothes or stay dressed as a maid? Which would attract the most attention? A maid with a child or a lady with a child?

Both would be odd walking the streets in the middle of the night.

What if her mother turned her away? It was not unlikely. Perhaps she could beg for help at the British embassy? But Tenby was the son of a duke, and she was only the step-sister of an earl. Would they believe her?

She eventually decided to dress in the gown and redingote she had been wearing when she'd inserted herself into the kidnapping. They were clean enough, thanks to Madam Peress, to look respectable, and Pauline had begged a needle and thread from the dresser to mend a tear in one of Jane's new dresses, which she had also used to mend her own.

She set them out on the bed, together with the clothes Jane had been wearing on the day of the kidnapping. Then she repacked her bag with changes of undergarments for each of them, and two spare gowns for Jane.

After that, she sat again to wait until it was early morning, when all in the house would be asleep.

She must have nodded off, for she jerked awake from a dream that shredded in her memory even as she woke, leaving only a few wisps of impression. Jane being torn away from her, and an overwhelming fear that still had her heart thudding in her ears. The candle she had left alight was all but spent, so she took another and lit it from the dying flame.

She walked for a while. Back and forth. Back and forth. Many of the lighted windows she'd been able to see were now dark and the house was quiet. She had no idea, however, what time it was.

Eventually, she decided to try the door. It caught. Her heart sank.

She tried again, jiggling the handle a little in the hopes that she might shift the latch enough for it to slide over the latch plate. Suddenly, the door's resistance gave way and she pulled it halfway open before she was able to stop the momentum.

Carefully, she looked through the gap, both ways up and down the passage. Darkness. No sound.

She carried the candle to the door to check the passage more carefully. No one was there, but the key to the door was on a table a few feet away. She scooped it up. If their escape was foiled tonight, perhaps she could use it.

Another idea occurred to her. With the key safely in her apron pocket, she used a knife from dinner to clean as much clay out of the latch hole as she could. Now she could lock the door on her way out and leave the key on the table. They would not know how she and Jane had got away.

She changed into her own clothes, then woke Jane, cautioning her to be quiet. She helped Jane to dress, and they tiptoed out of the door, down the servants' stairs, and out the back door into the garden. After all the dreadful scenarios Pauline had imagined, the actual escape was something of an anti-climax.

Chapter Twenty-Two

THE ALLEYWAY BEHIND the building was a dark and noxious place, but at least the rain had stopped at some point during the night. Pauline led Jane along the center of the way, glad they both had half boots to protect them somewhat from the puddles and whatever fouled the standing water.

When they came to the end of the row of houses, another lane led up to the street. Should they continue on in the alley, hidden by the darkness, or take to the street where the oil lamps would provide them with light to walk by but also make them easier to find?

The light won. *Everyone who might know us is asleep*, Pauline reassured herself. "We'll go down here, Jane," she said.

The light did allow them to travel more quickly. Pauline could only hope that they were moving in a useful direction. They saw no one she could ask, which at least had the advantage that no one saw them.

As they walked, the sky began to lighten over the houses to the left of them, so that must be the east, and the hour must be even later than Pauline thought.

The street joined a broader avenue, where carts were already rumbling along on their way to the city's markets or warehouses. Markets, Pauline hoped, for there she might find someone to direct her to the Rue du Saules, where her sister lived with her sister's husband. She could not remember the number. She hoped it was a short street, and she would not have to ask at too many doors to find them.

If they still lived in that street. Her mother and her mother's third husband, Wilbur Edwards, also lived with them, or they had, four years ago.

It had been four years since Laura wrote to Pauline to boast about catching a husband. And not just any husband, but an Italian conte! Perhaps they had returned to Italy?

Well. If they were not at the house Laura had written about, or if they turned Pauline away, she would just have to try something else.

They must have walked for forty-five minutes and spoken to a dozen people before they found a woman with a barrow full of vegetables who could direct them to the address. She pointed north. "That way until you reach Rue St Martin and turn left. Take the sixth." she narrowed her eyes, considering. "No, the seventh on the left. Maybe the eighth? No matter. Look for Rue Du Nord. Follow until you come to..." Pauline listened carefully, trying to remember all the names.

Another long walk, and Jane was hungry, but Pauline had no money to buy food and therefore no choice. They continued on their way.

As they walked farther from the center of Paris, the houses were better. Detached and set back off the road in their own gardens. Then she passed a street name she remembered. She had corresponded with a rose breeder who lived on this street. They had exchanged advice and cuttings.

For a moment, she hesitated. But after all, she did not know for certain that her mother and sister were still at the same address, or that they would help her if they were.

Then there was the thought she had been trying to suppress—that they might immediately betray her to the Tenbys. They would do it, too, if they thought it was to their advantage.

It would be much safer to throw herself on the mercies of her rose breeder colleague.

"Jane, we are going to turn around and go down the street we just passed. Monsieur Lavigne lives down there. He breeds roses, and I'm sure he will help us." Or at least give them breakfast and a place to rest for a while.

It was a charming detached house, not too large, set in a splendid garden.

Monsieur Lavigne was in his greenhouse, the maid who opened the door told her, "but Madame is at breakfast. Does Madame have a card?"

Pauline threw caution to the wind. "I am Mademoiselle Pauline Turner, and this is Jane Forsythe. Monsieur knows me through letters, for we both breed roses. Jane and I were kidnapped and brought to Paris against our will. We have escaped, and we hope Madame and Monsieur will help us."

The maid's eyes widened in alarm, and she appeared to consider shutting the door on them. Then she took another look at Jane, who was drooping beside Pauline, and her eyes softened.

"I will inform Madame," she said. "Mademoiselle Turner, is it?"

She left them in the porch but did not shut the door, so they could see her enter a room off the hall and moments later, a lady erupted from the room and hastened towards them, already talking in voluble French so rapidly that Pauline had to strain to keep up.

"Mademoiselle Pauline! The creator of the Countess of Stancroft! Such a beautiful rose. My Charles has grown it for me. And you are in such trouble! Come in, come in. This is the little one? My, you are a pretty child. Kidnapped! Whatever is the world coming to? Are you hungry, my little one? Lisette, another two place settings. Quickly, quickly."

In no time at all, Jane was satisfying her hunger while Pauline was telling the whole story of the kidnap and the flight from Carlisle to a rapt audience of two, for Madame Lavigne had sent immediately to the greenhouse. "Monsieur must hear your story," she said. "We will help, of course. Without a doubt."

It had never occurred to Pauline, when she brooded about who she might appeal to in Paris, that she had her own community of rose enthusiasts to which her credentials would matter far more than those of a pair of idle English aristocrats.

JOHN COULD USUALLY sleep anywhere. Tonight, locked in a police cell, he tossed and turned, kept awake by his aching head where someone had bashed him with a tankard, and his worry that Jane and Pauline might be taken from Paris before he could get there.

"We didn't start the fight," he grumbled to Thorne as dawn lightened the sky beyond the barred window.

Thorne shrugged. "We're English."

There seemed little else to be said. John put his arm over his eyes and lay feeling miserable.

Some time later, a clang at the door heralded a *gendarme* with a covered tray. John bestirred himself to ask to see the magistrate or whoever was in charge, but the man shook his head. "Je ne parle l'anglais," he insisted, and John's faltering French just produced more shakes of the head.

The tray proved to contain pastries and coffee, so at least they would not starve.

Two cups of coffee fortified John enough to approach the window, but that was not much help, since the view it gave was of a wall a few feet away. At least he could see that the rain had stopped. Once they had paid whatever fine was imposed for defending themselves against an unprovoked assault, they could resume their trip to Paris.

At least, he hoped it would be nothing more than a fine.

By the time the second meal of the day arrived, his headache had receded to a dull ache and he was considerably more impatient. He hoped whoever was in authority, when he finally got to see the man, would at least allow him to contact the British Ambassador. The Tenbys must not be allowed to remove Jane from Paris before he got there!

At last, partway through the afternoon, the same polite gendarme came to fetch them from the cell and conduct them up several flights of stairs and along a passage that appeared to be in a private house of some stature.

The room into which they were ushered confirmed the theory. It was a gentleman's study, and behind the desk sat a gentleman of about Deerhaven's age, fashionably dressed and smiling warmly.

The innkeeper from last night leapt up as they entered. "Monsieur Forsythe, I trust you are unharmed. I am désolé. How do you say it? Sad is it? Your stay in my inn to come to such an end. Monsieur Arechambeau," he addressed this salutation to the man behind the desk, "this is Monsieur Forsythe and his servant, Monsieur Thorne. Monsieurs, Monsieur Arechambeau is the juge de paix."

"Justice of the Peace, you English would say," Monsieur Arechambeau translated, with a shallow bow.

"Monsieur le Juge," John addressed the gentleman, "I assure you; my man and I did not start the fight. We merely tried to defend ourselves."

"I know, Monsieur," Arechambeau said. "Indeed, Monsieur Blanc, here, has told me all. Alas, it was your misfortune to be caught up in an old man's grief. I must explain, Monsieur, that the gentleman who accosted you lost all three sons in Napoleon's wars, and blames the Anglais very much." He shook his head, sadly.

"He comes once a year, with his brothers and nephews, on the anniversary of the day his sons graduated from L'Ecole."

"The brothers and nephews being the men with whom he was drinking," John said.

"Far too much," the juge de paix acknowledged, his expression a mix of contrition and amusement. "They were, as you English say, deep in their cups. He accosted you, an innocent gentleman enjoying his dinner, and his brothers and nephews, seeing your servant intervene, joined the fight on his behalf. It was wrong of them, and reprehensible to draw knives, and so I told them. Had it not been for Monsieur Blanc's quick thinking in rendering you unconscious, we might have been laying you out this afternoon, Monsieur, not releasing you."

"You are releasing us?" John asked.

The magistrate shrugged. "You have done nothing wrong, Monsieur, but I thought it best to keep you safely locked up until after the family had paid their fines and gone home. You have my profound apologies, Monsieur, and I trust we have not too greatly inconvenienced you."

"My business in Paris is urgent," John told him. He hesitated for a moment, then added. "I go to rescue my daughter and a dear friend from villains who kidnapped them from England, before the villains can take them further away. What you call an 'inconvenience' may have dearly cost me, and the little girl I love. If our business is finished, I will thank Monsieur Blanc for the horses we ordered last night, and we shall be on our way."

Arechambeau's expression had changed as John explained his errand, the amusement gone entirely. "What is this you say? A kidnapping? Monsieur, but this is a police matter." He held up a hand. "Un moment. Monsieur Blanc, the horses, if you please, and the baggage of Monsieur and his servant." Monsieur Blanc, his face a picture of concern, hurried out. Thorne muttered, "I'll check the baggage myself, captain," and hurried after him.

The magistrate said, "You shall be on your way as quickly as we can devise, Monsieur, but I must know more. If what you say is true, then the police in Paris will help you to apprehend these villains, and I can write them a letter to ensure their help."

John thought quickly. He didn't believe the police would take his word over that of the Tenbys. He had his hopes pinned, rather, on Deerhaven's letter to Viscount Granville. However, he couldn't leave until the horses had been saddled and he trusted Thorne to check that all was as it should be.

He'd be a fool not to take assistance when it was offered. "It is a sordid story, Monsieur. I divorced my wife after she ran off with her lover, who is an English earl, the son of a duke. Now, six years after she left me and our daughter—who at that time was just a year old—she has decided she wants the child back. The earl is inclined to give her any toy she wants, and then buy her another when she tires of the first. I refused to let them take my daughter, so they kidnapped her." That was it in a nutshell.

"Les femmes," said the magistrate, sympathetically.

"They took her from a town near where we lived. It was well planned. They had a ship standing ready to sail them to France. Fortunately, the friend I mentioned saw them take my little Jane, and leapt into the carriage with them. She somehow managed to persuade the driver with the carriage they had hired to tell me they were bound for Brest." It was his one comfort. Pauline was with Jane, and would look after her.

"In Brest, my friend told the landlord and his wife, at the inn where they stayed, what had happened. They promised to carry a message for me: that they were safe, though Madame the innkeeper's wife said Lady Tenby showed no interest in the child, which was no more than I expected. In an inn along the way, a maid gave me a note saying they were bound for Paris, and then to Calais and beyond that to Italy. I would have continued last night, and perhaps caught up with them, if not for the rain. And now…?"

He trailed off. Logic told him they would rest a day or two—perhaps more—in Paris. He was surely close behind them, despite the misstep on his first day out of Brest.

"It is a touching story that you tell, Monsieur," the magistrate said. "This woman, your friend. She is your chère amie? Your, ah, mistress?"

"My…" John drew himself up to his full height and frowned. "Mademoiselle Turner is a lady, and the sister of my dearest friend. I hope to ask her to marry me, Monsieur." It was the first time he had said it out loud, and it sounded so good to him that he wanted to say it again. Pauline had intelligence and a curiosity about the world equal to his own. She was kind and thoughtful and—though she called herself "plain"—was quite lovely. And—this was very important to him—Jane loved her, and Pauline put Jane's welfare above her own.

"Ah," said the magistrate. "It is a romance, then, as well as a family quarrel. Very well, Monsieur, you have convinced me. Give me the address of your faithless wife and her husband, and I will write a letter to Monsieur Devalau, the Prefect of Police for Paris, asking him to give you every assistance. My letter may not persuade him without further evidence, but I will ask him to at least keep the little mademoiselle in Paris while your claims are being investigated."

That would be a help. With that and the support of the British Ambassador, John could hope to delay the Tenbys until his legal proof of guardianship arrived from England. "I would be very grateful, Monsieur. And my brother has promised to send the divorce papers to the British Embassy. They include Lady Tenby's agreement that she has given up all rights to my daughter, and that I have sole guardianship and custody. Indeed, the papers may be there already, if they came straight across to L'Havre or Calais."

"Excellent. Give me a few minutes, Monsieur, and you shall have your letters."

Not fifteen minutes later, John and Thorne set out for Paris. The unintended and enforced stay might have proved to be a blessing in disguise.

Chapter Twenty-Three

By the time John had presented his credentials at the embassy and the magistrate's letters at the Préfecture de Police, it was evening, so it was in the light of Paris's famed oil lamps that he, Thorne, an attaché from the embassy, and four police officers arrived at the house on the Rue du Chat, which was the address on the papers Augusta's solicitor had sent.

"My lord and my lady are not at home," said the English butler, who did his best to shut the door in their faces, but could not prevail against the two police officers that held it open.

"You cannot come in," the butler objected, loudly, and Tenby emerged from a room to the left of the entry hall.

"What is going on?" He paled when he saw John and then flushed bright red. "Forsythe! Have you taken the child?" he demanded. He spoke over his shoulder. "Augusta, Forsythe is here."

John looked at Thorne and saw his own distress reflected in his man's eyes. Taken? No, it must be a trick.

"You have my daughter, and I want to see her."

Tenby shook his head as Augusta come out of the room behind him. She slid her hand onto Tenby's arm and pouted at John. "Lord John. You are too late. That terrible woman has run off with my Augustina. Lord Michael, what are you doing here?

Who are all these other people?"

The attaché bowed. "Lady Tenby, I am here at the request of His Excellency the British Ambassador to ensure the safety of Miss Augustina Jane Forsythe."

The senior police officer stepped forward. "I am Laurent, Brigadier of Police, here on orders of Monsieur Le Prefect to make certain that Mademoiselle Forsythe is not removed from Paris until the law has decided whether she should be returned to Capitaine Forsythe."

"You are too late," Augusta repeated. "You should have come last night."

"I don't believe you," John said.

Augusta shrugged, but Tenby said, "It's true, Forsythe. When the maid went up this morning with nursery breakfast, the door was locked, but no one was inside. We have no idea how Miss Turner got a key. We've questioned all the servants, but they insist that the door was locked and the key was outside."

Good for Miss Turner. John had no doubt Miss Turner had done something brilliant. Her agile mind was one of the things that he loved about her.

"We should have left Miss Turner in Brest," Augusta complained, "or at least along the way when we caught her leaving a note for you. And now she has spoiled everything."

Tenby turned on her. "I wanted to throw her out several times, Augusta. But you insisted on waiting until we could employ a nursemaid."

"What did you expect me to do?" Augusta snapped. "Look after her myself? My dresser wouldn't do it. And when we arrived here, the housekeeper insisted she could not spare a maid, which I thought very insolent."

John broke into the bickering. "But where have they gone?" he asked.

Augusta shrugged. "Tenby, you said you'd take me to the opera," she whined. She must have seen the attaché's expression, for she produced a handkerchief to touch to her dry eye. "I need distraction from my worry," she explained, then spoiled any positive impression by adding, "If anything has happened to the little br—little darling, it will be Miss Turner's fault. Augustina was perfectly safe with her mama and her dear father." She wiped at her eyes again.

John ignored her. "Tenby, I want your authority to talk to the servants and to search the nursery to see if they've left any clues. Do you have any idea where they might have gone?"

"Lincoln," Tenby said to the butler, "make sure Lord John has anything he wants. Ask and look away, Forsythe. If you see something I've missed, I'd be glad of it. The wee mite might be a hell-born brat, but I can't help but worry about her." The brigadier spoke to his officers, and they went off with the butler.

"Tenby," Augusta complained, "the carriage is here."

"With you in a moment, my dove," Tenby told her. "Forsythe, we thought Miss Turner might have gone to her mother and sister, but they haven't seen her."

"They're here in Paris? Can you give me an address?"

Tenby rattled it off. It was a lead, and John was willing to follow any lead there was. A big city was no place for a gently-born woman and little girl on their own, and if Pauline had not gone to her family or to the embassy, where was she?

THE QUESTION REMAINED unanswered.

He felt some hope the following afternoon when Miss Turner's sister refused to see him, but the Conte Di Positano, her husband, did receive him. The conte was a short plump man of about Deerhaven's age and dressed immaculately in the latest fashion. He was friendly enough, and appeared anxious to help.

"You must be concerned," he said, sympathetically. "If my little Maria Genevra was missing, I would be out of myself. No. It is 'beside myself' that I should say. No?" He explained that Maria

Genevra was his daughter by his first wife, safe at her convent school in Italy. "The contessa and I are anxious to return to her, but Lord and Lady Tenby are coming with us, and we are told that they may not leave Paris until your little girl has been found."

He assured John that Pauline had been in touch with neither Mrs. Edwards nor his wife the contessa. "I know," he said, "for they have talked much about where she might be since Lord and Lady Tenby called in the hopes that Signorina Turner might have brought the little signorina here."

Nonetheless, the police insisted on questioning the servants, who of course clammed up and denied all knowledge of everything, including the conversation between Lady Tenby and the Contessa Di Positano that the conte said had taken place in the entry hall in front of the butler, a maid and two footmen.

The staff at the embassy were far more willing but no more helpful. No one answering to Pauline's description had visited. Several people had sent notes asking for help with repatriation, but all had since visited the embassy, or had met elsewhere with embassy staff. None of them could be Pauline.

Two days after the disappearance, John met with the brigadier of police to hear the latest results. All he had, though, was a list of avenues that had been tried and failed.

In his excellent English, the brigadier explained, "We examined the nursery and found nothing. We questioned the servants. The maid and the footman who delivered tea to the nursery insist they locked the door as they left. That was at about six in the evening. No one checked the nursery again until the maid came with washing water and petit dejeuner in the morning. That was at eight. The door was locked. The key was on the table where they had left it. No one was inside. The window was shut, and the bars were intact. At some time during those fourteen hours, they disappeared from a locked room."

The police had searched for a secret passage. It seemed unlikely, since the row of townhouses had been built in the past decade, but what other explanation was there?

However, the most strenuous of tapping, the most careful of measuring, disclosed no hidden door and no space for a hidden passage.

"What about once they left the house?" John asked. "Did anyone see a woman and child walking about at night, unescorted? Is there no nightlife in Paris?"

The police officer took that as a joke, and laughed politely. "No nightlife in Paris; that is a good one, Monsieur. We asked questions, of course. No one we spoke to reported such an odd couple. We will keep asking, but you must prepare yourself. We may be looking at something far more sinister. We are keeping a close watch on Lord and Lady Tenby. Someone must have let the lady and little girl from that room, and since they have disappeared, it can be for no good purpose."

John had been desperately fighting that conclusion himself, but hearing it from the brigadier crushed the confidence he had been trying to maintain. He fought the constriction in his chest to say, "I cannot believe it. They can have had no reason to hurt Jane. If they no longer wanted her, they had only to drop her at the British Embassy with my address. As for Miss Turner, she is a competent and capable woman. I am positive she has thought of something we have not yet imagined and taken Jane into hiding because she does not know who she can trust."

The police officer did not argue, but his look of pity conveyed his opinion. John feared that the man was right, but he refused to give up. He took rooms a few minutes' walk from the British Embassy, and in the following days he and Thorne continued to follow every possible sighting of an unidentified woman with a girl.

His dwindling confidence took blow after blow with repeated visits to view unidentified bodies that had been found in the street or recovered from the Seine. The servants at the morgue grew used to him arriving with one policeman or another to see whether the latest arrival was his daughter or the woman he loved. Time and again, he braced himself as they pulled back the covering sheet, and time and again he turned away filled with a horrible mixture of relief and pity.

The brigadier's suspicions of the Tenbys had borne no fruit. Augusta was continuing to enjoy all her usual entertainments, but had ordered a new wardrobe in half mourning.

The attaché saw her at an embassy soiree, and said to John, his voice heavy with irony, "She was there in full regalia, lapping up the sympathy. She says that she retains a small fragment of hope, and will not go into full mourning until that is dashed. She hopes it will be soon, for she and Lord Tenby have been invited to stay in the chateau of the Conte Di Positano." He shuddered. "Dreadful woman. If we find—*when* we find Miss Jane, I will gladly stand witness as to her rank unsuitability to be responsible for a child."

John couldn't spare the energy to be disgusted by his ex-wife. Every particle of his being was focused on hunting for clues as to the whereabouts of his missing daughter and the lady with whom he hoped to build a future.

Chapter Twenty-Four

HOPING HER MOTHER and sister would offer her a place to stay, but fearing they would betray her to the Tenbys, Pauline asked the Lavignes if Jane could stay with them for the afternoon. Jane, who had seen in Madame Lavigne a kindred spirit to her beloved Thorny, was willing enough, and Madame pronounced herself ecstatic. "Monsieur and I were never blessed with children, and my sister's babies are long since grown. I miss having a little one around."

Monsieur Lavigne insisted on bringing out his smart little gig and driving her to the address—or at least the road—she remembered from Laura's letter. "I do not know if they still live here, or even what house it is," she told him, as they approached the row of smart townhouses, thankfully quite short.

"Ça n'a pas d'importance, Mademoiselle," Monsieur assured her. "It does not matter. We will knock on doors and ask. If they do not live here, we will go home."

A town coach was parked in front of one of the townhouses, and as they drew nearer, Pauline recognized the driver. "Monsieur, drive on past," she begged. Monsieur Lavigne did as she asked.

"That driver works for Lord and Lady Tenby," she explained, once they were beyond the carriage.

"They are visiting your family, do you think?"

"Looking for me," Pauline stated, certain she was right.

They turned a corner out of sight, and then continued around in a large square until they were back at the corner that led to the townhouse. Looking towards it, they could see several people on the steps.

"Lord and Lady Tenby, with my mother and my sister," Pauline explained to Monsieur, as the little group hugged one another in farewell. "I cannot go there."

"Then we will go home, Mademoiselle," Monsieur Lavigne said, giving a light shake to the reins to set the horses walking past the street where Pauline's family lived. "I regret it did not work for you, but to me, you are a very welcome guest."

Madame Lavigne agreed, saying she was delighted to have Pauline and Jane to stay for as long as they liked.

"I hope I will not have to impose on you for long," Pauline told them. "I have written to Jane's father, Captain Forsythe, and to my own brother giving your address and asking them to send money so I can buy us passage home."

Madame shrugged. "Family is what matters n'est ce pas? Meanwhile, Théo will greatly enjoy long conversations about roses, and—" she smiled at Jane—"Jeanne my little, you shall keep me company and we shall have such a good time, no?"

Jane and Madame Lavigne had already conspired over a cake for afternoon tea. Jane was currently sitting next to Madame with a little square of linen on her lap, onto which she was attempting to embroider a daisy, in imitation of Madame, whose own far more ambitious table runner bloomed with thread-painted flowers of all kinds.

"I would like to stay here until Papa comes," she said, firmly.

Madame patted her hand. "There, Mademoiselle Turner. It is settled."

Pauline debated sending a note to the embassy, but she did not know what influence the Tenbys had with the ambassador. She could not risk it, and it would gain nothing, since she was certain John would come for them soon, or Peter, if John was out of touch searching for them. One thing she knew beyond all shadow of a doubt, John would never give up until his daughter was restored to him.

Meanwhile, all they could do was wait. If not for her concern about how John was feeling, to remain in one place after all the travel would have been a delight, even without a hospitality precisely calculated to delight them both.

The house was modest—five bedrooms for family and guests, and two reception rooms, as well as a long sunroom built onto the back of the house. Madame Lavigne was her own housekeeper, and managed the maids and the cook with a firm hand, not ashamed to turn her own hands to any work that was needed.

"I am not one to sit around doing nothing," she declared, when Pauline came in from the garden to discover her at the kitchen table with Jane. Jane was stringing beans while Tante Marie, as she had asked to be called, was deftly fitting pastry into pie tins.

Nor was Oncle Théo above turning his hand to anything his small squad of gardeners did. He was usually found in his garden or his succession houses, and Pauline was more than happy to assist him.

Pauline had never had an aunt or an uncle. She could barely remember her father; perhaps one thing he had had in common with her mother's second husband was the disinclination to spend any time with her mother.

Indeed, all of her family relationships had been tainted in one way or another. Her mother took delight in setting her and Laura at one another's throats, while still expecting them to combine forces against Peter, and his little sister Rose.

As for Peter, Arial, Vivienne and Rose, Pauline could never forget her sins against them. Desperate for their love, she was certain she did not deserve it. They gave it, anyway, though she could not quite believe it and was always slightly on edge for fear that today would be the day they changed their minds.

Her gratitude had her performing any service she could think of. Her guilt made her wince when they thanked her.

Spending time with two people who knew nothing of her history and who sincerely liked her for herself was a wonderful holiday. The only thing to taint the pleasure of her visit was knowing how worried John must be.

One morning, Oncle Théo announced that he had arranged a treat for them. "We are to go to the École des Rosiers, Pauline, to meet with the Director! What do you think of that?"

"Julien-Alexandre Hardy? At the Garden of Luxembourg?" The chief gardener of that wonderful garden had, so rose lovers in England said, amassed an amazing collection of roses and was having great success in breeding new ones.

"You are pleased?" Oncle Théo's smile said that he knew she was.

"Shall I come?" Jane asked.

Tante Marie patted her shoulder. "You and I shall both go, and we shall walk in the gardens, sail a little boat in the fountain, and admire the statues while these two talk roses, shall we?"

"Should Jane go out?" Pauline asked Tante Marie. Jane had woken that morning with a runny nose and a tendency to cough.

"If she wraps up warm, and is not running a fever, it shall do no harm," Tante Marie decreed, which seemed reasonable.

The next question was what to wear. Jane had several suitable dresses, since Pauline had not scrupled to take two of those Augusta had ordered for her, and Tante Marie had removed many of the frills and furbelows that made them impossible to play in. And, she had provided more frocks that had belonged to her niece.

Pauline had scorned the maid's uniforms that Tenby had supplied, but Tante Marie had managed to find her some simple dresses to wear in the garden, and she had been dressing for dinner in the gown she'd been wearing on the day they were abducted.

It had been mended and cleaned, but was it fit for an introduction to Monsieur Hardy? It would have to be, for she had nothing else.

However, she felt more confident when they set out in the

Lavignes' comfortable little gig. Tante Marie had used a ribbon that matched Pauline's gown to refurbish a bonnet of her own, and had also provided clean gloves and a shawl. Pauline might not be in the first stare of fashion, but she was tidy and respectable.

As it turned out, it was of no importance. Monsieur Hardy was delighted to meet her, and she and Oncle Théo spent a very happy hour in his succession houses and nurseries.

They left the head gardener's domain and turned into the path that led to the gate where the gig had been left in the care of a groom. "If my wife and little Jane are not there, we will wait for them," Oncle Théo said.

"Look, Monsieur." Pauline pointed. Tante Marie was running towards them, her bonnet hanging from her neck and flapping at her back.

They hurried to meet her, and she fell into Oncle Théo's arms, terribly upset, and incoherent in her distress. Oncle Théo persuaded her to sit on a nearby bench and to take deep breaths, but Pauline had already guessed what she had to say. Jane was nowhere to be seen.

Even so, she waited for Tante Marie to explain that an elegantly dressed woman had approached her and asked the way to the Notre-Dame.

"She was English, the lady. I explained, but she asked me to come and speak to the driver. He was just outside of the gate, she said. She would only keep us a moment."

But as Tante Marie spoke to the driver, she heard a shriek from Jane and the driver sprang the horses.

"I chased it, Pauline," Tante Marie insisted, "but it was too fast."

Pauline fought for calm. The carriage would be long gone. She had to figure out where to. Was it Lady Tenby? It seemed obvious, but she couldn't make assumptions for fear of being wrong. Jane would be frantic. *Think, Pauline. Think.*

"Tell me what you can remember of the carriage," she said. If it was the Tenby's town carriage, Pauline would march to the embassy and demand people storm the Tenby's house. Perhaps she should do that, anyway.

The carriage Tante Marie described sounded like a traveling carriage, but not any of the ones Pauline remembered so well. "What did the English lady look like?" she asked. Tante Marie described the woman as slender, fair-haired, and magnificently dressed.

That sounded like Lady Tenby, certainly. "Very beautiful?" Pauline asked.

Tante Marie shook her head. "Fashionable, and not ugly. But I would not say beautiful." She frowned, obviously trying hard to remember. "The carriage. There was a crest on the door," Tante Marie added. "A gold shield, almost square, with blue stripes on the diagonal, and a black eagle. A crown above, also in gold, and blue dolphins on either side."

Laura, in her letter announcing her marriage, had boasted of her husband's crest—gold and blue with a royal eagle and a royal crown, she had said, though she had not mentioned dolphins. It was something to check.

Tante Marie confirmed Pauline's suspicions, saying, "She looked a little like you, Pauline, although you are prettier, I think. This one looked as if she had sucked on lemons."

It had to be her sister. Or her mother. If that was the case the Tenbys were definitely involved, though how any of them had known where to find Jane was a mystery and not one she had time to solve. The traveling coach made it urgent. They were on the move, and not planning to stay in Paris.

"I must go to the British Embassy," she said. "Perhaps it will serve no purpose, but it is at least a chance. Oh, how I wish that Peter or Deerhaven had answered my letter!"

"I sent a boy for the gig while you were talking to Marie," Oncle Théo told her. "We shall go to the British Embassy immediately, and then to the police, where my wife will tell them of the child's abduction."

"Again," Pauline commented mournfully. Twice she had

been nearby when Jane was abducted, and twice she had failed to stop it. She feared that John would never forgive her.

THE SUMMONS FROM the British Embassy was delivered by the attaché who had been assigned to help John, Lord Michael Finch-Western. "We have two VIPs who want to see you, Forsythe," Finch-Western told him. "Your brother the Marquess of Deerhaven and your friend, the Earl of Stancroft. I am to tell you that Miss Turner wrote to them five days ago. She took refuge with friends, and sent letters to England for help. You're to come to the embassy, and we shall all go to collect the child and the lady."

The news was so unexpected and so welcome that John's knees buckled, and he had to sit down for a moment. "Safe? They're safe?" He leapt up, suddenly full of energy. "Let's go."

He ran the distance from his rooms to the embassy, dodging other pedestrians and traffic, Thorne beside him. Finch-Western kept pace and still found enough breath to complain about being made to run in the heat.

John passed under the arch between the two pavilions that guarded the courtyard to the building, and saw Peter and Deerhaven standing with Lord Granville on the steps outside the front doors. "They are safe? Is it far?" He called out as he approached.

His friend and his brother came to meet him, each hugging him in turn. "She is staying with a rose breeder friend," Peter told him. "A Monsieur Lavigne. She did not want to go to the authorities for fear her voice would not be believed against that of an English lord and an Italian conte. My former stepmother, Mrs. Edwards, and her daughter and son-in-law, the Conte and Contessa Di Positano, are also in Paris, and she saw them with the Tenbys."

John nodded, grinning. She had a good head on her shoulders, did Pauline. And a rose breeder! *Of course.* He should have thought of it.

"How far is it?" he repeated.

At that moment, a commotion at the arched entry caught his attention, as a woman raised her voice. A very English voice. A voice he knew. "You must let us in. My daughter has been kidnapped."

Pauline! John outstripped his friend in reaching her, and pulled her into his arms. "Pauline. Thank God you are all right. What is this about Jane?"

Peter tugged her away and into his own hug, then held her at arms-length. "You are well?"

"That is not important," Pauline protested. "My sister Laura has taken Jane." Quickly, she explained what had happened, introducing the couple she had been staying with, who were as distraught as she.

"It was their traveling carriage, John," she added, when she'd disclosed the whole. Somehow, the skills of an officer had come back, shoving his roiling emotions into a locked compartment in his mind so he could deal with the immediate situation. Pauline must have done the same, for her report was remarkably concise and comprehensive, despite the tears that continued to roll down her cheeks.

Deerhaven and the ambassador had joined them in time to hear the account. "They might not have left," Deerhaven said, "and if they have, we will find them if we have to send riders down every road from Paris. We will have her back by nightfall, John."

"An English marquess and an Italian count," said the ambassador. "Hmm." He called the attaché. "Michael, hop over to the Austrian Embassy, will you? Let them know that the English wife of the Conte Di Positano has absconded with the niece of an English marquess, and we're about to visit the conte with the Paris police, if His Excellency would like to send a representative."

The attaché bowed and took off at a run.

"Well then," Deerhaven said. "John, I suggest you, the ambassador, and I go to the conte's house, since that is probably where my niece is. Miss Turner, perhaps you would be good enough to accompany Peter to check the house of the Tenbys, in case they have gone there?" He raised his brows in question at the ambassador. "Can we borrow horses, dear boy? And can someone advise the Prefect we will need policemen at both addresses?"

"Of course," the ambassador agreed, and gave the orders.

John did not want to be separated from Pauline, but Deerhaven's suggestion was far more proper than John's preference: to keep at least one of his womenfolk within arm's reach while he searched for the other.

Not that she was his yet. To think he looked forward to spending the rest of his life alone. Instead of the disgust he used to feel at the thought of any woman in his life, he was filled with hope that he could face the future with Pauline at his side.

It felt good and right. Pauline was his, or at least, he was hers. As soon as they found Jane, his next mission would be to persuade Pauline to agree to give him her heart as he had given her his.

"Look after her," he told Peter, fiercely.

Peter looked surprised, but he nodded. "Of course."

Pauline came back from a hasty discussion with her friends. "They will go home and wait for news," she said. She reached to touch John's hand. "I am glad you are here. I am so sorry I could not keep her safe." She lowered her gaze to the floor, but John couldn't allow it. She'd done the best she could, perhaps more than he could have done for his daughter in such circumstances.

"You've done well," John assured her, catching her hand in his and hoping his eyes showed all the feelings he could not express in front of their interested audience. "I blame Augusta for this, and Tenby. Not you. Never you."

Grooms hurried up with horses, and John, Deerhaven and the ambassador mounted and cantered out of the courtyard, followed by several English soldiers.

Chapter Twenty-Five

PAULINE WASN'T DRESSED for riding, but Peter took her up before him. She sat across the pommel with one hand on Peter's waist and the other holding her bonnet. They also had some of the embassy guard as outriders. It was a short ride—less than fifteen minutes, despite the traffic, and if people stared at the mad woman in a shabby day gown and perched sideways on a horse, never mind. All that mattered was making sure they retrieved Jane before her kidnappers could take her out of Paris.

"Are you well, Pauline?" Peter insisted as they rode. "Have you been hurt?"

"Frightened, uncomfortable, indignant, but not hurt," she assured him. "But Peter, I am so sorry that my sister took Jane. I should have realized that the Tenbys would not give up and that Laura would help them. I cannot imagine how they found us! How she must feel!"

"From what I remember of Jane," Peter told her, "she will be exceedingly cross, and is undoubtedly making the contessa sorry she ever involved herself."

That made Pauline smile. He was probably right. Indeed, even the threat of losing Pauline had not kept Jane from showing Lord and Lady Tenby her temper from time to time.

"I should never have agreed to the outing, or to letting Jane out of my sight," she sighed.

"You thought you were safe. You should have been, too," Peter said. "We'll find out how they discovered your presence when we find Jane."

Somewhat comforted, Pauline suddenly remembered the reason she had not expected to see Peter. "Peter, I should have asked you before, how is Arial?"

Peter's face lightened. "Arial is well, and so is our new son. He arrived a week ago, and his brother and sisters are delighted with him."

"That is wonderful news." It went some way to warming the chill of her fear for Jane.

"Do you think there is a chance we will find Jane at the Tenbys?" Pauline wondered. "I suppose it was only fair that John went to the most likely place."

"I think Deerhaven wanted each party to deal with the other party's unpleasant relatives," Peter retorted. "Is this it?"

A few houses farther down the street, a row of coaches stood outside the Tenby's townhouse, the steps for one at the head of the queue down and awaiting those who had just exited the doors: Lord and Lady Tenby, dressed for travel.

"There they are," Pauline said, then had her attention distracted as a troop of mounted police came around a corner just a few hundred yards down the street, slowing to allow a pair of approaching carriages to precede them. Two men were riding beside the first, one of them a man she had seen at the British Embassy.

"The approaching carriage!" Pauline told Peter. "I think it is the conte's"

It slowed and pulled in behind those outside Tenby's, and the one that followed did the same. The police troop split into two, three coming ahead to meet Peter and Pauline, and three remaining behind the new arrivals.

"Monsieur Milord Stancroft?" asked the lead rider. "Are the miscreants attempting to flee?"

"Apparently so, Monsieur," Peter replied. "And my sister, Mademoiselle Turner, believes that the kidnapped child is in one of the carriages that has just arrived."

"Take me to the coach at the back," said Pauline, urgently. A man she assumed was the conte had assisted a woman from the carriage, the two outriders had joined them, and they were walking towards the Tenbys. Meanwhile, at the door to the vehicle behind, a little girl struggled to escape a servant.

"And there she is," Peter told the policemen, even as he touched his heels to his horse.

They passed the carriages in a few swift strides, and Pauline slid to the ground and strode towards the foot path, calling out as she did so, "Jane! To me!"

The servant holding Jane spun around, but did not let go of the coat the little girl wore. That didn't stop Jane. She suddenly dropped, wriggling to free her arms from the coat, and dove out from under it to speed to Pauline. "Miss Turner! You came for me!"

Pauline wrapped her arms around the dear child as a footman leaped from the carriage and approached, only to be felled by a blow from a policeman's baton. Another footman jumped down to assist, and was joined by the servant who had been holding Jane.

"Arresto!" The man Pauline assumed to be her sister's husband was hurrying towards them, gesturing to his servants as he issued a stream of Italian that had them withdrawing with their hands up in a signal of surrender.

"Sir?" the conte asked, offering his hand to shake. "Do you represent Signor Forsythe? I return to you his *figlia*, his daughter. My contessa did not have my authority to take the little girl from her *bambinaia*, her nursemaid."

"It is true," said the man from the embassy. He and the other outrider had followed the conte. "The Conte Di Positano and his wife were at the Austrian embassy when I got there, trying to find out where Miss Turner was staying. So, I told him Captain

Forsythe and Miss Turner were looking for the little girl, and brought them here." He looked around. "Is Captain Forsythe here?"

The conte glowered at his servants. "My servants meant no harm. I had instructed them to protect the little *signorina*, and they did not think."

He did not pause for breath. "*Signorina*," he bowed to Pauline. "I believe that I am addressing my sister, *Signorina* Turner. Is it not so? I apologize for my contessa. I have reminded her that her duty is to please me, and not her friend."

Peter ignored the hand. "Captain Forsythe will be with us shortly. I am Stancroft and, if I am addressing the Conte Di Positano, we are in somewise related."

Positano bowed again, with a grand sweep of his arm, "Lord Stancroft," he said.

Pauline was looking beyond them. "Laura," she said.

Her sister shot her a fulminating glance from under her lashes. "Pauline. I hear you have set your sights on Augusta's discarded husband. One must do the best one can, I suppose." She sniffed, and her husband muttered to her in irritated Italian.

"Do we arrest the gentleman?" asked one of the police officers, sounding revoltingly eager. Pauline suppressed the urge to tell them to arrest her sister, and instead focused on Jane, who was trembling, and snuffling, as she said, over and over again, "I thought I would never see you again. I thought I would never see you again."

Pauline crouched over her, holding her tight. "I'm here, darling. I am here."

Peter put a comforting hand on Pauline's shoulder. "You are safe now, Jane. Your Papa will be here soon, and so will Uncle Deerhaven."

Jane did not loosen her limpet grip, but she lifted her head from where it had been buried in Pauline's shoulder. "Uncle Peter! Did you come to rescue me? *He* said I did not need to be rescued. *He* said I am like his own *figlioletta* and he would make the lady give me back to Miss Turner."

"That is true, what the little one says," the conte insisted. "See? Now you are back with *Signorina* Turner."

Jane regarded him seriously, then turned her gaze back to Pauline. "Is he really your brother? Like Uncle Peter?" She sneezed, and Peter gave her a handkerchief.

"He is married to my sister," Pauline explained, "so he is my brother by marriage, though I have never met him. Like my sister Rose's husband Ruadh Douglas is my brother by marriage, though I do not know him very well."

Jane must have accepted that, for she shifted her gaze to Laura. "I do not like your sister," she confided to Pauline.

Pauline ignored Laura's indignant snort. "I do not like her either. We cannot choose our relatives, however."

The conte made another sharp remark to Laura in Italian.

Jane's eyes moved beyond Laura to Lady Tenby, who was approaching, stiff with indignation as the three mounted police herded her and her husband along the footpath towards her. "I do not like my mother, either. I do not want her for a mother."

Lady Tenby was close enough to hear the remark. "I do not like you, either, you brat."

Jane started to stick out her tongue then changed her mind and closed her mouth. "I will not be rude to her," she told Pauline, "because I am going to be a lady, like you, Miss Turner. But I will not stay with her, either. If anyone tries to make me, I shall scream, and fight, and run away." Poor lamb. Her speech was a little muffled by a blocked nose. Also, if Pauline was not mistaken, she had a slight fever.

"You will not stay with her," said a new voice. "You are coming home with me." John had come up from the other side of the carriages, undetected until he spoke. Jane gave a glad cry, released Pauline, and in two bounds was in her father's arms.

Pauline felt oddly bereft as she accepted Peter's assistance to stand. The Marquess of Deerhaven and Thorne had arrived with John, as well as the ambassador and more of the Paris police.

"Perhaps," said Deerhaven, "we might impose on Lord and Lady Tenby to undertake the rest of this conversation inside their house."

It was not a question. Deerhaven led the way along the footpath past all the parked carriages, and the entourage followed, John carrying Jane and holding her as if he would never let her go.

Peter, with Pauline on his arm, stopped at the carriage with the conte's coat of arms. "Come along, stepmother," he said to Mrs. Edwards. "You will want to be part of this conversation."

Ahead of them, John had stopped on the steps to the house. Jane was sobbing loudly, and wailing whenever he tried to take an additional step upwards. The wailing made her cough.

"If she were mine," Mrs. Edwards told him, "I would beat her."

"No one who knows any of your daughters would take your advice on child raising, Mother," Pauline told her.

Mrs. Edwards sent her a lethal glare and swept past John into the house.

Pauline reached to stroke Jane's hair. "What is the problem, my darling? Here is your Papa, come for you, just as I told you he would."

Jane was sobbing too hard to answer.

JOHN LOOKED AT Pauline, helplessly. "She does not want to go into the house," he said.

"I do not blame her," Pauline told him. "Last time we were here, we were prisoners, and Lord Tenby threatened to shoot me in the leg if Jane did not do what she was told."

"I'll kill him," Peter insisted, his voice low and furious.

"You'll have to wait your turn," John said.

"John, shall I take her with me to the Lavignes?" Pauline

offered. "We need to go back, anyway, to let them know she is safe and to collect our bags. She is comfortable there. You can deal with these people and come to fetch her."

John hesitated.

"It's a good plan, Captain," said Thorne. "I will take your ladies to Miss Turner's friends' place, and stay with them. You give those Tenbys what for."

"Jane?" John stretched his head backwards so he could see his daughter's face. She had calmed since Pauline had joined them, and he had to admit he felt calmer himself, with one of them in his arms and the other within reach. He was tempted to leave the coming interviews to Deerhaven, Peter, and the police, but he supposed it was his duty to see it through. "I have to go inside, darling, to make sure that Lord and Lady Tenby can never take you away from me, ever again. You can come with me, and I promise I will keep you safe, and Miss Turner will stay with you the whole time."

He met Pauline's gaze, hoping she would not gainsay him. She nodded. Reassured, he continued. "Or you can go back with Miss Turner and Thorne to Monsieur and Madame Lavigne's house, and I will come for you when I am finished."

Jane let go of the death grip she had on his neck and reached out her arms for Pauline. "Miss Turner and Tante Marie," she said.

John sent a boy who was loitering in the street to find a *cabriolet de place*, one of the light two-wheeled conveyances on which the carriage maker Davies had based the London cabs. Peter sent a scoffing Mrs. Edwards ahead of him into the house, kissed Pauline on the check and entered the house himself. "I will tell them you are on your way, John," he said.

John waited in the street to hand his ladies into the cabriolet, though Thorne assured him he could go on inside, and that he would make sure they were safely delivered to the Lavignes.

John shook his head. He couldn't walk away from them. In truth, he wished he was going with them. He didn't want to let them out of his sight. Either of them, though he had no right to keep Pauline close in his embrace as he longed to do. *No right yet.*

Her attention was all for Jane. Did she burn for him as he did for her? She showed no sign of it. She had returned that long-ago kiss, but she had been excited about the automaton. She'd thrown herself into a moving vehicle to save his daughter, and protected her through a kidnapping, a sea voyage, and then during a long journey. But that was for Jane's sake, surely?

He watched the cabriolet out of sight, then entered the house, where the butler showed him into a crowded parlor.

"Ah," said Deerhaven. "John. The ladies safe, are they?"

John nodded as he looked around the room. They had arrayed themselves according to their allegiances. Lord and Lady Tenby sat hand in hand on the sofa even as they argued about whose idea it was to kidnap Jane in the first place.

The Conte and Contessa Di Positano occupied two matching chairs, him talking rapidly to her in an undertone, and her listening with a frown, her chin set and her lips in a pout. Mrs. Edwards was on her own, ignoring everyone else.

Three men stood by the fireplace, surveying the room: Finch-Western, from the embassy, the other man who had ridden beside the conte's carriage, and the police brigadier. Two policemen who had been brought inside stood one each side of the door, presumably to ensure no one left before the meeting was over.

John joined Deerhaven and Peter, who had taken up a stand before the window.

"Well, John," Deerhaven said. "This is your show. You have the Tenbys and the contessa, both of whom have kidnapped your daughter. What do you want to have done?"

"Don't forget that the Tenbys also kidnapped my sister," Peter growled.

"Not on purpose," Tenby protested. "She threw herself into the carriage. What were we supposed to do? Shove her out? She would have been hurt, Stancroft."

"That is correct," Augusta agreed. "We did not abandon her along the way, even when she deserved it. We fed her and housed her. We even bought clothing for her."

The sound that came from Peter before he spoke was definitely a growl. "You threatened to shoot her if Jane did not behave."

Lady Augusta shrank in her chair. "Tenby," she pleaded.

Tenby rose to the occasion, John was intrigued to note, standing and putting himself between Augusta and Peter. "Wouldn't have done it, of course. Not right. Would never shoot a lady. It was just the child. Very annoying, all that complaining and screeching and calling names. It was upsetting for Lady Tenby. Couldn't think of anything else to do. It worked, though."

The frown he directed at John was bewildered. "Wouldn't have taken her if I'd known what she was like. Not even for Lady Tenby. You *do* want her back, don't you, Forsythe?"

"Not even for me?" Augusta demanded, sitting up in her indignation.

Tenby instantly turned to soothe her, kneeling at her feet with his arms around her, ignoring the rest of the room. "I want only your happiness, my dove. You know that. But you have to admit, Augusta, the child does not make you happy. Forsythe wants her. You don't. Heaven knows, I don't. So, we'll just apologize, and promise never to do it again, and toddle off to Italy, and everyone will be happy. You want to go to Italy, do you not, my dove?"

"As simple as that?" Deerhaven demanded, but was so surprised when Tenby waved him to silence that he actually complied.

Augusta didn't notice. "People will think I am a bad mother, Tenby," she complained.

"You *are* a bad mother," Deerhaven snapped.

Tenby half-turned. "You are not helping, Lord Deerhaven. Lady Tenby is upset."

Deerhaven turned red and Peter, who was normally of an

easy and equable temper, clenched his fists and widened his eyes. "Lady *Tenby* is upset!" Deerhaven stuttered. "*I* am upset! Lord Stancroft is furious at being dragged away from his wife and his newborn child. My brother is desperate to be reunited with his daughter and is instead here watching you fuss over that dreadful female as if she is not the cause of all this upset. Lady Tenby is upset, indeed!"

"Sir," said Tenby, "if you continue to insult my wife, I am going to have to call you out."

The brigadier of police, who had been watching the scene with the air of a man at the opera, came to life at that. "Dueling is illegal in France," he reminded the room. "You must not arrange a duel in the presence of a police officer."

Technically, dueling was illegal in France, but from what John had heard, the law was largely ignored. Perhaps the brigadier was merely hinting they should make arrangements for any duel where the brigadier could not hear them. The whole scene was descending into farce.

The conte clearly agreed. "Signors, let us leave Contessa Tenby to her husband for the moment. Signor Forsythe, what is required for your honor to be satisfied regarding the trespass by my wife against your little daughter? Whatever it is, if it is in my power and does not touch on my honor, it is yours."

"I was only trying to help my friend," the contessa whined. "She was really upset. My sister had no right to take Augusta's daughter away from her."

The conte turned on his wife. "Upset? Upset! Yes, and consoling herself at the modiste and the opera and the afternoon promenade. *Santi ci preservano*!"

"But Cosimo—"

"*Silenzio*! I am very disappointed in you. Not another word."

Pauline's sister opened her mouth, but closed it when her husband intensified his glare.

"It is true, Forsythe," said Finch-Western. "His lordship was at the Austrian Embassy when I got there, seeking their help." He gestured to his companion. "This is *Signor* Martinengo, an attaché with the Austrian Embassy, responsible for Italian citizens of Austria. *Signor*, meet Lord Deerhaven, Lord Stancroft, and Lord John Forsythe. Lord John is the little lady's father."

Signor Martinengo bowed.

John returned the courtesy. "In that case, I have no quarrel with you, sir," he told the conte. "Indeed, you have my thanks."

It was the conte's turn to bow. "You are very kind, *Signor*. I trust your daughter has suffered no harm through her adventures."

"So do I, *Signor*," John replied. If she had not, it was every credit to Pauline for protecting her, and none at all to Augusta and Tenby. "I would like to know how your wife found my daughter. I have been searching Paris for her these last five days."

The conte shrugged. "An accident, *Signor*. A lady we know grows roses. She asked if my contessa was related to the Pauline Turner who was visiting the head gardener at the *Jardins de Luxembourg*." He spread his hands to indicate his surprise. "She wanted an introduction, *Signor*. Something about a rose called Rosalind something."

"The Rosalind Douglas," Peter supplied. "One of Pauline's."

Mrs. Edwards stirred. "If anyone wishes to know what I think—"

Peter cut her off. "I do not."

At the same time, the conte ordered, "*Silenzio*. I blame you, too, *Madre* Edwards. You should have stopped your foolish daughter. *Signor* Forsythe, you may be certain that my wife and her mother will do penance for their sins. Nor will they trespass against you again, for tomorrow we leave for Italy."

He bowed to Peter. "*Signor* Stancroft, I am pleased to have met you and regret that we do not have time to become acquainted."

Another bow, this time comprehensively including everyone in the room. "Good afternoon. Come, Contessa, Madre Edwards."

As the two women leapt immediately to their feet, John reflected that, short and stout as he was, the man had presence. He would not look out of place in a toga and laurel leaves.

"But Cosimo, we were not planning to travel to Italy until the end of the week," Augusta protested.

Di Positano stopped his progress across the room. "Tenby, your wife is not good for mine, nor do you do anything to check her mischief. I am reconsidering your welcome to visit my family in Italy." With that declaration made, he sailed out of the room. The Italian attaché, with a commiserating look at his British colleague, bowed his farewells and followed.

John restrained the urge to clap.

"No Italy?" Augusta gasped. She appealed to her friend. "Laura!"

"Contessa!" shouted the conte from outside of the room.

"Sorry, Augusta," said the contessa, and followed her husband, arm in arm with her mother.

"Tenby!" shrieked Augusta, and collapsed into her husband's arms, weeping hysterically.

"Was she like this when you were married to her?" Deerhaven muttered to John.

John nodded. "I used to leave her until she got over it," he admitted.

"Perhaps we should do that," Peter suggested. Apart from Tenby, all of the men in the room, including the police officers, were obviously wishing themselves somewhere else. In fact, all the men in the room appeared to share those sentiments. Tenby himself kept glancing for the door, as if planning to escape.

"She cannot get away with kidnapping," Deerhaven insisted.

Tenby glared at him as Augusta wailed louder.

"Gentlemen," he said, "with your permission, I shall send for Lady Tenby's dresser. She will be able to put my lady to bed and give her something to calm her. I will then make myself available for your questions and your judgement."

Despite his dislike for the man, John had to acknowledge his request was fair. "Yes," he said, without consulting the others.

Tenby looked around the room. "If you would pull the bell chain, Lord Michael?" he asked the attaché. The attaché obliged.

Tenby sent the footman who responded for the countess's dresser, and the woman must have been waiting for the summons, for she was there in moments, murmuring soothingly to her mistress in French, as she helped her from the room. John made out, "A bath, Madame." What *allons, allons* meant, he had no idea.

Chapter Twenty-Six

"RIGHT," SAID DEERHAVEN, as the door closed behind Augusta. "Let us get down to it. Tenby, you and your wife kidnapped John's daughter, even though you had both agreed to never challenge his rights as part of the divorce settlement. What do you have to say for yourself?"

"You have the child back, Forsythe," Tenby pointed out. "Is that not enough?"

"No," John replied, waving his brother to silence. "I want to know why you did it. You didn't want her then, and neither did Augusta. What changed?"

Tenby nodded. "Fair enough. I know I owe you an explanation. Do you mind if I pour myself a brandy?" He didn't wait for permission but crossed the room to where a row of decanters stood on an ornate sideboard. "Does anyone else want one?"

One by one the other men agreed. The brigadier denied the privilege to his men, saying they were on duty. However, he sent them from the room so they were not forced to see others drinking. Everyone else accepted a glass, and the whole gathering took on a surreal aspect, as everyone sat, their brandy glass in hand, their eyes on Tenby, who stood near the fireplace, as if about to recite a poem for their entertainment.

He swallowed his brandy in two or three gulps. "You need to

understand one thing about my wife," he began. "She lives for admiration. I saw no harm in her seeking sympathy for losing any rights to her daughter—"

"Not losing," John corrected. "*Giving up*."

Tenby ignored him. "The problem was, she began to believe she wanted the little chit. I mean, the little darling. I blame myself. I know her. I should have known she would talk herself into believing what she was saying."

Deerhaven made the grumpy sound that tended to presage a roar. John put a hand on his brother's arm to stop him exploding.

"I blame you for encouraging and assisting her," he said.

Tenby poured himself another brandy, and took a sip before he responded. "Quite fair," he acknowledged. "But what else can I do? It has always been the two of us, you see, Augusta and I. Since we were small children, I could always go to her when my parents ignored me, or my tutor beat me. I was there for her when her governess or her mother made her cry. We promised we would always support one another against everyone else. It doesn't matter whether I am right or wrong, or whether she is. We support one another." He grimaced. "I do not expect you to understand."

John understood. He disagreed with the man, but he understood. Tenby and Augusta were trapped loving one another as they had when they were children, each making excuses for the other, each preventing the other from taking responsibility and growing up.

Maybe he would not have realized that before Pauline, who always tried to see the best in people and understand what was behind their actions. If he were fortunate enough to win her as his wife, he knew she would always support him with her love, but support actions that were wrong? Not likely! She would challenge him to be a better man.

In a mild tone, John said, "So she made up her mind to lay claim to Jane, and when I refused, she wanted to take her anyway."

"Yes," Tenby replied with a nod. "That was partly my parents' fault. My mother's, anyway. We were staying with them, and Augusta told them how awful you were. You made her unhappy, Forsythe, and she—I guess she overdid it. She thought you must make Augustina unhappy, too. But you don't, do you? I see that now."

He sighed. "Anyway, my mother was up in arms that Augusta could leave her baby with such a brute, and they both nagged at me, and it seemed easier…" he spread his arms in a helpless gesture. John noted that the glass he still held was empty again.

"If it helps," Tenby added. "I was sorry even before we reached Port Carlisle, and I did my best to keep Augustina and Miss Turner together."

"Jane," said John. "Her name is Jane." He had an overwhelming need to be with her. Yes, and with Pauline, who had become as necessary to his daughter as she was to him. He didn't want to waste time taking revenge on this overgrown boy and the pathetic child who was his wife.

"Finch-Western, does the embassy have a lawyer?" he asked.

The attaché was startled to be addressed but replied, "Yes, several."

"Tenby," John said, making it up as he went along. "You and your wife will stay out of Great Britain for the next five years or until you become Duke of Kingston, whichever comes first." *Yes*. That was a good start.

Tenby was watching him without reaction beyond wary eyes and several gulps of his third glass of brandy.

Now for the lawyers. "The lawyers will draw up a confession that will outline your kidnapping. Everything you did. Every law you broke. Every threat you made. And you and Augusta will both sign it."

Deerhaven nodded. "Good," he said.

Tenby downed the rest of his glass and poured a fourth.

John hadn't finished. "I shall give you a copy of the document and my solicitor will get another. I shall keep the original. Never attack me or my family again. Don't let Augusta do so, either. I don't care what title you hold, Tenby, or how much wealth or influence you have. Leave me alone, and I shall leave you alone. But touch Jane again, or any other member of my family, and I shall marshal all of my allies. I *will* destroy you."

Tenby gulped. "What if I don't sign," he mumbled into his glass.

"Then I shall prefer charges against you in a French court for kidnapping," John replied. He caught the brigadier's eye. "Please make sure that he and his wife don't leave Paris until the matter is resolved," he said.

The brigadier bowed. *"D'accord, monsieur."*

"Then, gentlemen, we are done here. I am going to my daughter." *And Pauline.* His steps quickened as he left the room, Peter and Deerhaven following behind.

JANE REFUSED TO eat, complaining that she wasn't hungry and that her throat was sore. Tante Marie declared that chicken soup would be just the thing, and bustled off to the kitchen to make it herself.

Pauline took Jane upstairs and tucked her into bed, worried when the child did not complain, as she normally would that it was still afternoon, and she was not a baby. Tante Marie sent a maid up with a posset made of lemon and barley, and sweetened with honey, and Pauline managed to coax Jane into swallowing about half of it.

After that, Jane drifted into a restless sleep, and Pauline sat and watched her. She wondered what was happening at the Tenby's townhouse. In the cabriolet, on their way to the Lavignes, Thorne had told her of their journey, and of how he and John had searched Paris for her and Jane. Thorne was now back at wherever John was lodging, packing their bags ready for their journey home.

Poor John. No wonder he looked tired! If only she had not escaped her first night in Paris, he and Jane would have been reunited the next day! Pauline could not have known that, but she could not blame John if he was angry about it.

His eyes had been all for Jane, of course, while hers took their full of him. She smoothed a fallen lock of hair on Jane's face, touching the child's forehead and confirming that it was warm but not, thank the dear Lord, hot. How she loved the little girl!

Be careful, Pauline. It was too late. In the nearly three weeks they had been together, Jane had seized a firm hold of a heart that had been half-given to her already. As for the little girl's father, she had been attracted to him from the first and then infatuated since their kiss. That sense of attachment had grown with each letter they'd exchanged.

Hopeless and helpless. He had shown her nothing but gentlemanly courtesy. Even returning the kiss she initiated was, she supposed, a matter of kindness, for Pauline had no illusions about her appeal to men. She was not even the type of woman men propositioned, let alone the type they married.

Even if he felt for her a particle of what she felt for him, he would not act on it. The women in his past had turned him off of marriage, and he was too honorable a man to bed a lady without wedding her.

Now she would lose them both. The child she loved and the man she yearned for. John would arrive soon and take Jane with him to wherever he was staying, and Pauline would need to smile, and be happy for them.

You must never let anyone know how you feel, she told herself, fiercely. People would laugh. Not Peter or Arial, of course, but they would pity her. Or worse, they would assure her that she was worthy of marriage, and that John was a fool for not seeing it, which would only serve to make her bitter. She had resolved years ago that she would not allow herself to be bitter, and she had no cause to believe that the man owed her anything.

As if thinking about him had conjured him up, a knock on the door proved to be the man himself, arrived to collect his daughter.

Pauline managed to curve her lips in welcome. "It is good to see you, John."

For a moment, she thought he was going to hug her, but if he'd had the impulse, he checked it. "It is good to see you." His eyes drifted past her to his daughter, and he beamed to see her asleep before turning the smile to Pauline.

"Pauline, I can never thank you enough for all you have done."

"If only I had stayed at the Tenbys instead of escaping," she mourned. "You would have had her back the day you arrived in Paris, and saved a week of worry."

"You did the right thing." John sounded convinced of it. "Who knew, with that pair, whether they might have thrown you out and left Jane to the maids? Or taken off for Italy immediately, so I was behind them again? Besides, you could not have known that I would get your messages and be on your track so quickly. Indeed, if they hadn't told me in Port Carlisle that you were heading for Brest, it might have taken me months to find you. How did you persuade the carriage driver to watch for me on the road and give me your message?"

Pauline stared at him. "I left no message in Port Carlisle. I did not have the opportunity. Tenby had a gun on me the whole time."

"Someone left a message," John insisted.

Pauline frowned. "I left one in Brest and another at an inn along the way. The third time I tried, I was caught, and they did not give me another opportunity."

"I got them all, then," John said. "You cannot know what a relief it was to know how you both were and where you were going."

Pauline shrugged and changed the subject, uncomfortable with the praise. "Jane is a little unwell, so I persuaded her to have a sleep. Shall I wake her up? She will be glad to see her Papa. She has longed for you."

"Not well?" John said. "I thought she was a little warm when I was carrying her, but I put it down to her upset." He laid gentle lips on his daughter's forehead. "Just a little fever," he said, with some relief.

"She also has a runny nose and a sore throat," Pauline said. As if the words brought on the symptoms, Jane started to cough, and woke herself up.

She smiled when she saw her father leaning over her. "Papa!" Her dear voice was hoarse.

"Sweetheart." John gathered her into his arms. "Miss Turner tells me you are not very well, my chick."

"I feel bad, Papa," she croaked. "I have a tummy ache in my throat."

"Poor sweetheart." He kissed the top of her head and held a handkerchief for her to sneeze into. "I have someone who wants to see you," he told her, pulling the little girl's rag doll from the pocket in his coat tail.

"Clementine!" she exclaimed, and hugged the doll to her. She kissed the doll on the forehead. "She has a bit of a fever," she reported. "Perhaps she can have some of Tante Marie's soup." The talking set off her cough, and she clung to her father until the coughing fit ended.

John's total focus was on his daughter, as hers was on him. Pauline began edging towards the door, but John noticed and turned towards her as Jane called, "Miss Turner, I want you."

He held out a hand to draw Pauline back to them both. "Yes, Miss Turner, please stay, if you are able."

"I thought to pack my bag," Pauline explained. "I suppose you will be taking Jane with you and Lord Deerhaven. I should be ready when Peter comes for me."

"No!" Jane cast herself from her father's arms onto Pauline's chest. "No. Miss Turner." She attached her arms around Pauline's neck so tightly that Pauline had to beg her to be careful.

"Darling girl, a little looser so I can breathe!"

Jane's choke hold eased, but she still clung. "Don't leave me, Miss Turner," she begged.

"You don't need me now, Jane darling," Pauline pointed out. "You have your Papa."

"I want Papa," Jane acknowledged, tearfully. John put the handkerchief into play again. "But I need you, Miss Turner."

"Could you stay?" John asked. "I don't want to move her while she is ill, and when she is feeling better, she will take the separation more easily. Do you think Madame Lavigne would mind if we stayed one more night? That is, if she can make room for me, as well."

MADAME AGREED IMMEDIATELY, when John went downstairs to ask her—Jane being unwilling to let Pauline out of her sight. "Of course, the precious little one must not go anywhere while she is sick. I will make up a bed for you, *Capitaine* Forsythe."

Peter, who had accompanied John to the Lavignes, frowned, and Madame hastened to add, "Mademoiselle Pauline shares the room of the little Jane, for Jane has *des cauchemars*." She looked to Monsieur Lavigne, who translated.

"Nightmares, Monsieur."

"It is not that," Peter said. "I am wondering if… John, has Jane had the Boulogne sour throat? The malignant croup?"

John shook his head. "She has just got a sore throat and a bit of a sniffle," he reassured Peter.

"Yes, I hope so, but it's best that you know—as I was leaving, Tenby was asking the police brigadier if Lady Tenby could stay with friends while the man decides if there are to be charges. Apparently there has been malignant croup downstairs. It started with one maid, and now several others are sick. His wife hasn't had it, apparently."

"Pauline and Jane were only there for one night." John spoke mostly for his own comfort.

"Yes. That's good," Peter agreed. "Is Pauline coming down? I've barely seen her, and I have messages from her sisters and the children."

John shook his head. "Jane cries when she tries to leave," he explained.

Peter's smile was fond. "All our children want Pauline when they are sick. Madame Lavigne, may I go up and speak with my sister?"

John showed Peter up to the bedroom, and persuaded Jane to accept his arms instead of Pauline's by promising that Miss Turner would not leave the room. That, and his sharp ears meant he was an inadvertent eavesdropper on the low-voiced conversation between Pauline and her brother.

Peter asked after her wellbeing, and gave her messages from Arial, Vivienne, Miss Pettigrew and the children, and some family news in which the new baby dominated.

"I want to get back to Arial as soon as I can, Pauline, but I cannot leave you to travel on your own."

Pauline was firm. "I know, Peter, but I have been the only familiar being in Jane's world for the past three weeks. I cannot abandon her tonight. By tomorrow, when she feels better, she will find it easier to let me go."

"Poor little mite. She really is snuffly, isn't she?" said the fond father. "Madame is happy for you to stay another night, and so am I. It's too late to leave today, in any case."

Pauline kissed her brother's cheek and came back to the bed.

"Will you go to Miss Turner now, princess, while I walk Uncle Peter down?" John asked. The child happily held out her arms for Pauline.

"Goodnight, poppet," Peter said. "Sweet dreams. I hope you feel better in the morning."

Jane's hoarse little reply barely crossed the small room. "Goodnight, Uncle Peter."

"Do you think I should get a physician?" John asked Peter, as they walked down the stairs.

"I would, but only if she is not better tomorrow," said the more-experienced father. "Best to be careful. John, I'll let Deerhaven know what's happening. Do you want me to send Thorne to you?"

"That would be best. He might as well check us out of our *hôtel* and bring our bags. I'll ask Madame if he can have some blankets to make up a bed in my room, if space is short. We've shared a room many times over the years."

John spoke to the Lavignes, saw Peter to the door, and returned upstairs, trying not to let his mind dwell on the Boulogne sore throat. *Malignant croup* was another name for the wretched disease, and so was *the strangling angel of children*. Surely, it was just a cold?

Chapter Twenty-Seven

After a restless night, Jane was no better in the morning, so John asked a physician to call. Peter arrived to collect Pauline just after the man left. Since the physician had insisted that Jane and those caring for her must not come in contact with the rest of the household, she spoke to Peter from the stairs.

"I cannot leave, Peter," she told him. She hurried on to explain before he could object. "The physician thinks Jane may have the Boulogne sore throat. There's an outbreak in Paris at the moment, and John tells me that some of the servants at the Tenbys have it. The maid who brought us our tea the night we arrived in Paris? She was sneezing and coughing. John has sent to ask Tenby if that maid is one of the sick servants."

Peter frowned. "I cannot stay, Pauline, and I promised Arial I would bring you home."

Pauline shook her head. She felt guilty for bringing Peter all this way, especially when Arial had just had her baby, but she couldn't leave Jane while she was sick. "Peter, I haven't told you how grateful I am that you came. I didn't expect that. I'm sorry you had to come all this way."

Peter sighed. "You are family, Pauline. Of course, I came. You are not going to come with me, are you?"

She shook her head again. "I am sorry, Peter. I really am. I cannot. When she is well again, I shall hire a companion for the trip back. Given how old I am, that would be perfectly acceptable, I am sure."

Peter was silent for a moment, regarding her with narrowed eyes. Then he looked around the hall to confirm that none of the rest of the household were within earshot. "You love him, don't you?" he said.

"Jane," Pauline insisted. "I love Jane." She could feel her face flaming at the half-lie. She loved John, too. "I know that I am old, plain, and boring, Peter. I would not be such a fool as to court heartache."

Peter mimed a hug. "You are in your prime, prettier than you think, and one of the sweetest, kindest people I know. Clever, too. But I won't tease you any more, my dear one. Just remember that your family loves you, just the way you are, and if you need me, you have only to send for me. Even if you find yourself in India! Deerhaven wants to stay on for one more day, so I shall wait and travel home with him. Expect us both to call this afternoon."

"You don't mind that I am not going to come?" she asked.

"I should have added 'stubborn' to the list of your qualities, Pauline," he joked. "Here. Put this somewhere safe." He opened a leather pouch to show her some coins. "I hope Jane will be well by tomorrow and we can all travel together, but I respect your decision." He closed it again and tossed it up to her.

A fretful wail from the upper floor interrupted them. "I have to go, Peter. Jane is afraid I am leaving with you."

Peter touched his forehead in a half salute. "That is my cue to say *adieu*, I think. I will see you later today, Pauline. Tell Jane that Uncle Peter sends his love, and is going to let her keep her Miss Turner until she feels better."

Pauline chuckled at that, and blew him a kiss, then returned upstairs to the sick room, to stay with Jane while John wrote a letter for Thorne to take to the solicitor at the British Embassy about drawing up the agreement and confession for the Tenbys to sign.

His absence sent a tired and cranky Jane into a panic, and it was all Pauline could do to console her. When he returned, she was reluctant to let either John or Pauline leave the room. John insisted that they spell one another. "If things get worse, we will need all our strength. Now that Jane knows you are definitely staying, she can let you take a walk in the garden, or visit with your brother, or take a nap. And I will do the same in my turn. Thorne has offered to sit with her, but I told him that I prefer him to stay out of isolation. He can run messages for us and help out with the household."

Pauline had to agree such an arrangement was sensible.

By the time Deerhaven and Peter called in the afternoon, she and John had each had two breaks from the schoolroom. Pauline took first turn with the callers, who were sitting in the garden having coffee and pastries with Madame and Monsieur Lavigne.

Pauline greeted the two men, and took a seat several paces away under the tree that Monsieur had designated for her and John to use while they were staying apart from the rest of the household. "Peter, Thorne will give you a packet of letters from me, for the family." She explained that she had written one each for Arial and Vivienne, and one for Rose that she asked Peter to post when he reached England, along with one for the children, and one for her gardener.

Peter laughed at the last. "Proof that she loves your niece," he told Deerhaven. "She is putting Jane ahead of her roses."

Monsieur Lavigne sent Pauline a conspiratorial grin. She had already talked to him about making cuttings to take back to England with her.

Pauline accepted a coffee and asked after Deerhaven's wife Cordelia, who was a friend of hers. They chatted about Cordelia and then about Deerhaven's children. "All going well, we could be home in two days. Three at most," Deerhaven said.

They talked of the journey, next. Jane was not improving. Even if it turned out to be a mere cold and not the dreaded

Boulogne sore throat or the equally dangerous scarlet fever, the physician advised against travel until she had been well for several days. In the next day or two he hoped to have good news for them, but if Jane's condition worsened, they could be here for weeks. Deerhaven and Peter planned to leave Paris at first light and ride straight for Calais. Deerhaven's yacht was there, and would take them all the way to London.

"I shall send it back when we arrive home," Deerhaven told Pauline. "It will wait to transport you, John, and Pauline to England."

Once Pauline had finished her coffee, she stood. "I shall go up to Jane and let John take his turn," she said. "Travel well. Give everyone my love."

Peter followed her down the path to the house. "Pauline, I called at the bank that works with mine and set up a line of credit for you." He pulled some papers out of the satchel he carried with him.

Pauline regarded him with wonder. "You didn't need to do that," she said.

Peter shrugged. "You need to be able to pay the companion you promised to hire for the journey, if you need her. Some gowns that fit. Anything you want. Having access to money gives you some protection, Pauline. The satchel also carries the account details and a letter you need to carry to prove who you are." He passed her the satchel.

"You are the best of brothers," Pauline told him.

"I am your only brother," he pointed out.

PETER ASKED TO speak to John alone, so the Lavignes took Deerhaven off to show him the succession houses.

"John, I called on Tenby. The maid who attended the nursery the night Jane and Pauline were there was the first to come down with Boulogne sore throat."

John's fear for his child kicked up another step. "That isn't what I wanted to hear, but I appreciate you telling me. The doctor says we'll know tomorrow or the next day if that is what Jane has."

"Arial and I will be praying for you. You will write and let me know how she does?" Peter asked.

"I shall," John promised. His friend didn't bother with false reassurances. They both knew that most well-fed, well-nursed children survived the illness, though it was a deadly killer in the stews. But most was not all, and Jane had been through a difficult two weeks before arriving in Paris. He didn't know how that might affect her.

"It may be just a cold," Peter said.

"I hope so." So far, Peter hadn't said anything that needed privacy. "There was something else?" John asked.

Peter nodded. "There was. Tenby also told me that Mrs. Edwards had a quarrel with her son-in-law and has been left behind in Paris. Apparently, Di Positano refused to be confined in a carriage with her for the journey. She is still heading for Italy, because apparently her husband is there. He left France posthaste as soon as he heard I was in Paris. The Tenbys have been reinvited, and will take Mrs. Edwards with them, when they go. Tenby warned me, however, because he thinks she might try to cause trouble for Pauline."

John's instant surge of protective wrath had him rising to his feet. To cover the reaction, he bent over a particularly lovely rose and inhaled its odor. "She's a sour old besom, but what can she do?"

"My stepmother's weapons of choice have always been innuendo, malicious gossip, and character assassination," Peter told him. "What is discussed by the English who live in Paris will soon be known in London. If Mrs. Edwards discovers that you and Pauline are alone together, even though it is under a respectable roof and at a child's sickbed, she is likely to cause trouble, simply because she can. If she attempts to damage Pauline's reputation, I want to know you will look out for her."

"You know I will." He hesitated, then rushed in. "Peter, I haven't said anything to Pauline. The timing is poor, when she is living under the same roof as me and cannot get away, but you should know—I want to court her."

Peter nodded, as if John was confirming something he already realized. "So, you would offer her the protection of your name, if she needs it?"

John should have expected the question. "In a heartbeat, but I would hate for her to be forced into marriage for such a reason. It is the worst kind of hell being married to a woman who doesn't want you for a husband, and I have been assured by my ex-wife that it is no treat for the woman, either."

Peter raised his eyebrows. "I would remind you that we are talking about Pauline, here. Not Augusta."

"You are right, of course. Pauline would make the best of such a situation. I suppose the truth is, I would like her to marry me because she wants to, rather than because she has no other choice." Which made him sound like a whining prat. If it came to the point, he would have her under any circumstances, and do his best to woo her into being happy.

At least she already loved Jane. He had *that* in his favor.

"Pauline will always have a choice. Social approval is not important to her, and her family—my family, not hers—will love her whatever happens. You can be very confident she would not marry someone she disliked. And, I don't for a moment think she dislikes you, John."

John was sure of that. In fact, he thought it was fair to say that she enjoyed his company. And she *had* returned his kiss. That had to count for something. "We are friends," he said.

"A good place to start," Peter told him. "Arial and I were and are friends. John, Pauline has not confided in me, but I don't think she would refuse you. You could prevent any problems, and neutralize her mother's venom if you and she were betrothed.

And if you asked her now, you wouldn't have any doubts about whether she had married you for her own sake."

He stood. "Anyway, it is up to the pair of you, and only my business because she is my sister and I am fond of you both. I should find Deerhaven and let you get back to your daughter. Is there anything else I can do for you before I leave Paris?"

"Can you..." John couldn't believe he was about to ask this. "Can you make some enquiries at the embassy about what it would take for us to wed? Here in Paris? I would want it to be legal in England." He rushed to add, "I am not saying that I'll need it, but it would be good to know."

Peter nodded. "I can do that. I cannot think of a man I would rather welcome as a brother."

John grimaced. "That's jumping the fence before the horse is out of the stable, Peter." He bowed, since the doctor had warned that those in isolation should not touch others. "But thank you. The sentiment is mutual. Which reminds me that I had better speak with the brother I already have."

Peter went to find Deerhaven and the Lavignes, and a few minutes later, Deerhaven joined John. "Madame has gone back into the house," Deerhaven told John. "I left Peter to learn all about the parentage of the blooms in Monsieur Lavigne's succession houses." He cast his eyes skyward. "I daresay Peter is more knowledgeable than I, however. How is my niece?"

"Uncomfortable and unhappy. Time will tell," John said. He asked after Deerhaven's wife and family, and did his best to pay attention to the answers, but his mind was still on his conversation with Peter. Was his friend hinting that Pauline returned his regard? Should he take the risk and ask her be his wife?

Deerhaven picked up on his distraction. "You are anxious to get back to your daughter."

He grasped at the excuse. "I am, but I know she is safe with Pauline for a few more minutes. Deerhaven, thank you for coming all this way. It means a great deal to me."

"You're my brother," Deerhaven said, simply. "And don't

give me any nonsense about half-brother, as if that makes any difference. Look at Peter and Pauline. They don't even share the same blood, and they love one another like brother and sister."

"His lordship didn't see it that way," John pointed out.

"His lordship was an ass," said the man's son. "He drove our mother into someone else's arms and then blamed you. Father never loved anyone but himself in his entire life, but if he'd given you half the attention he gave any one of his horses, he could not have helped but see what a blessing you were. You were the dearest child; you've grown up to be a fine man. I am proud to call you brother."

Deerhaven had clearly embarrassed himself with the declaration for he pasted his most impenetrable expression across his face, lifted his chin, and said, "Tell my niece that I love her, John, and look forward to giving her a hug when she is back in England."

John swallowed the lump in his throat and said, "I am proud of you, too, brother. If I have grown to be in any way a decent man, it is at least in part because I had your example before me."

And how the old Marquess of Deerhaven had produced a paragon like John's brother, he did not know.

"If I am, John, you started it. You were just a sprout when I was a young fool, feeling my oats and all ready to follow my father's example. But you admired me. How could I look you in the eye if I knew I'd done things I wouldn't want you to copy?" He shrugged. "Then Cordelia came along and I wanted to be a better man for her."

The mutual exchange of compliments had left them both uncomfortable, and Deerhaven was undoubtedly as pleased as John to bring the conversation to an end. Still, John tucked his brother's remarks away to think about later. It was not just the warmth of knowing he had his brother's regard, but also the dismissal of the old marquess's hatred that warmed him.

He had only to look at Jane, the daughter of his heart, to know that yes, the old man was an ass.

Chapter Twenty-Eight

BY THE FOLLOWING afternoon, Jane was breathing in a hoarse rattle. With Clementine tucked against her chest, Pauline on one side of the bed holding her hand, and John on the other, she submitted to the physician's examination, whimpering her objection but without the energy to resist.

The physician peered into her mouth, tapped her chest, then listened to it through a listening cone, and held her lids up one after the other to peer at her eyes.

After he had finished, he beckoned Pauline to the other corner, since John could not follow the man's rapid French.

"I regret, Mademoiselle Turner, that the little one has the *dipthérite*. The patch on her left tonsil is a strong sign, and all of the other symptoms fit."

Pauline asked, "The Dip... what did you call it, *monsieur le doctore*? Is it the malignant croup?"

"Yes, yes," he said, impatiently. "*Dipthérite*, for the leather-like membrane. It is the medical name."

"What can we do, *monsieur*?" Pauline asked.

"What you are doing. Soothing drinks for the throat, if she will take them. Ice, if you can get it. Keep her as comfortable as you can. You must watch closely and pray that the patch does not grow into a full membrane. In her favor, the illness is most dangerous for the very young and the very old. Your Jane has eight years. Also, she is in a comfortable bed and a warm house and has you and her *père* to nurse her. We have reason to hope, *Mademoiselle*."

Pauline repeated all of that in an undertone to John, while the physician chatted benignly to Jane, using his voice to cover the conversation between Pauline and John.

"Surely there is something else we can do?" John begged. But when Pauline translated the question, the physician spread his hands and shrugged, a gesture that needed no translation.

He promised to return again the next day, and took his leave, and John settled beside the bed to comfort Jane while Pauline went to the door to tell Thorne what the physician had said and to ask him to find out if Tante Marie knew where they could get ice.

The days and nights that followed blurred into one another, as Jane absorbed nearly all of Pauline's attention. What little was left was devoted to John, whom she loved more and more each day, as they worked together to keep Jane as comfortable as they could.

Jane could not eat, rejecting even Tante Marie's chicken soup, which had been so soothing for the first two days. Ices were welcome, and Thorne was kept busy traveling to and from the glacier bringing home *creme glacés* and sorbets to be stored in ice and dribbled down Jane's throat a few swallows at a time.

John refused to leave her side, making up a pallet on the floor where he slept while Pauline attended to Jane's care. Pauline went to bed in the bedchamber next door at scattered intervals through the day and night when Jane slept for an hour or two, propped up on pillows to help with her breathing, and hugging her doll.

On the third day, Lord Tenby called. Oncle Théo and Tante Marie entertained him to tea and promised to pass on his expressions of concern. When Thorne reported on the visit, he said Tenby was going to come again, and he did, too, calling every day, bringing fruit to be squeezed for juice, and books and toys that might, he said, amuse Jane in her recovery.

John grumbled about the man's audacity, but Pauline was pleasantly surprised at his persistence. Especially when he kept coming even after John received notice from the embassy that both Lord and Lady Tenby had signed the papers John had demanded, making it impossible for him to pursue custody of Jane without serious legal consequences. His concern could not be in pursuit of some nefarious plot.

The gray patch on Jane's left tonsil spread and grew, until it reached her uvula. That still left one side of her throat open, but each breath was a struggle. The air she took in whistled through the gap left between the membrane and her swollen tissues. Her lungs released the spent breath in a barking cough that hurt the muscles of her chest and diaphragm, so she curled against the pain.

She dozed fitfully, waking herself up when the cough grew worse, and drifting off after a mouthful of ice eased her throat for the few minutes that the numbness from the cold lasted.

Pauline was also worried about John. His insistence on not leaving the room meant he barely slept, though sometimes sheer exhaustion pulled him too far under to hear the sounds of his beloved girl fighting for each breath.

As for herself, Pauline was only slightly better. Deep down, she feared Jane would die if she left the room. It was silly to think her presence would somehow prevent Death from claiming the child, and so she told herself each time she retired to catch a few minutes sleep in the room next door.

But no sleep lasted for long, for Jane's cough pursued her into dreams, and she was soon back at her post.

Side by side, she and John cared for the little girl they both loved. They were so in tune with one another they barely needed to speak as they bathed Jane, coaxed her to drink another spoonful of juice or iced confection, changed her bedding and her nightrail, plumped up her pillows, and murmured comfort.

Side by side, they watched as each day the physician checked Jane's condition and shook his head.

Side by side, they waited for death and prayed for deliverance.

⋙⋘

PAULINE WAS AN anchor. Her calm reassuring presence helped John, as well as Jane. Jane relaxed more and could breathe more easily when Pauline's arm was around her, her voice murmuring encouragement.

When Pauline went next door to sleep, John felt her absence keenly, not just because Jane was more restless, but because having Pauline in the room with him gave him more confidence in Jane's recovery, as if Death could not steal his child from him if Pauline was present.

He loved her. He could admit it to himself, though he was reluctant to tell her.

Now was not the time to think of such things. Not with Jane needing them both, for if Pauline didn't want what he had to offer—and who could blame her—continuing to work at her side would be pure torture. Also, if he proposed and she refused, she might feel she had to leave, and Jane needed her.

The chance of her rejection also made him reluctant to bear his soul. Surely, when he asked her to marry him after this present struggle was over, she would understand his feelings without him needing to express them?

"I think she is breathing more easily," Pauline said one morning, some ten days after the first appearance of the patch of membrane. John wasn't sure, especially when Jane broke into a fit of coughing.

However, the physician, when he came, confirmed that the throat was a little less red and swollen, the gray occlusion slightly smaller. "The doctor is cautiously hopeful," Pauline translated.

"The danger is not over, but she may have turned the corner."

Dipthérite could affect the heart and the kidneys, according to the physician. Pauline had been told what to watch for, and she passed the information on to John, but it was with more hopeful hearts that they sat with their girl after the physician's visit.

Their girl. John opened his mouth to speak.

"He said that the *dipthérite* membrane will be gone in another few days," Pauline said, "but Jane must stay in bed and in isolation. He wants her to rest for at least four more weeks. By then, she will be past the worst of the risk of the heart being affected."

Four more weeks? That made a proposal of marriage imperative. John could not imagine being separated from Pauline now, and Jane would certainly not stand for it. But four more weeks in isolation, just him, Pauline, and a child who would certainly need to spend a lot of time sleeping? It was his duty to her brother and to his daughter to make Pauline his wife. Besides, he did not want to face life without her at his side, and could not sleep without dreams of her spread naked across his bed.

Several times that day, the words were on the tip of his tongue, but each time he swallowed them back. Thorne arrived with a noon meal for them. Jane woke from the sleep of exhaustion caused by the physician's examination, and wanted the attention of them both. When she dropped off to sleep again, Pauline's huge yawn prompted him to send her to her bedchamber.

Never mind. It was probably better to leave it until Jane was farther down the road to recovery, lest a refused proposal made it impossible for Pauline to stay.

Perhaps tomorrow.

Jane had improved a little more the next day. She was still listless and miserable, but she managed a few spoons of soup, the first food she'd taken unfrozen since the patches first appeared. John felt more refreshed, too, having submitted to Pauline's demands that they share the night nursing, and that he take himself off to his own bedchamber and get some sleep during her turn to care for Jane.

Pauline looked more rested, too, and she glowed with happiness when Jane showed some interest in the books and toys piled on the bureau by the window. Most of these were Tenby's offerings, which Jane had been too sick to bother with when Thorne brought them upstairs and Pauline added them to the heap, day by day.

John had mixed feelings about the offerings. He had to admit that Tenby's juice had been much appreciated, and he supposed there was no harm in a few books and things to play with. But he was suspicious about the man's motivation and—he had to admit it—was possessive enough to resent Tenby having anything to do with Jane, even if it was just purchasing gifts.

Still, when Jane picked one of the books and settled into Pauline's arms to listen to her reading it out loud, John had to add another tick in Tenby's plus column. Whatever his reasons for bringing them, his gifts were giving pleasure to both of his ladies.

So, when he answered a knock on the door to find Thorne waiting to say that Tenby wanted to see him, John agreed.

Tenby was waiting in the garden. He greeted John by saying, "They tell me yesterday's improvement has continued? Is she truly on the mend?"

If he was feigning concern, he was doing a good job. His expression was a mix of worry and hope. A bit of wariness, too, which was wise of him. "The doctor says she is past the danger of suffocation, but we must keep her isolated and quiet for at least another four weeks. There is a danger the illness might affect her heart or her kidneys."

In a sudden burst of generosity, he added, "I must thank you for the books and toys. They will really help to keep her entertained in the next few weeks. Pauline is reading her one of the books at the moment. And thank you for the juice, too. While she has been so sick, it has been one of the few things she could swallow. That, and ices of one kind and another."

Tenby appeared surprised at John's thanks. "I'm glad. I felt so helpless. She is so little, and I... Well. I know she is yours, not mine, Forsythe, but I wanted to help. It is my fault she is here."

His fault and Augusta's that Jane was here in Paris, but also their doing that she was born at all, and even that she was born while Augusta was married to John. When John looked it like that, Tenby had done him a huge favor. Not that he was going to tell the man that.

"I've paid the vendor to continue delivering juice every day," Tenby said. "I hope that's acceptable? Augusta and I are leaving Paris, now that Jane is out of immediate danger. We are going to join the Di Positanos in Italy. If I leave the address, would you mind letting me know how she goes on? I know I have no right—"

"Yes, of course." John could hardly believe he was agreeing. "When do you leave?"

"Tomorrow. Augusta is anxious to be away," Tenby confided. "She thinks all of Paris is laughing at her for abducting Augustina—Jane, I mean—and giving her up. I tell her that we have done the right thing, and that people don't care. But she will be happier in Italy with her friend."

"I wish you a good journey, Tenby," John said, and was surprised that he meant it.

"Don't know how good it will be. We're taking Mrs. Edwards with us. Promised Di Positano. Never should have done it. His mother-in-law, not mine. Nasty old besom. And that's what I wanted to talk to you about, Forsythe. That, and to ask you to write about Jane."

"You wanted to talk to me about Mrs. Edwards?" What did Pauline's mother have to do with him? Of course, if Pauline married him, Mrs. Edwards would become his mother-in-law as well, which was a thought to make a man shudder. Still, Pauline was worth it, and besides, Mrs. Edwards would never dare step foot in England again after she and her husband tried to kill Peter and have Arial committed.

"She has been making trouble, Forsythe. I thought you

should know."

Ah. Peter had her to rights. "Gossip?" John asked.

"About you and her daughter. I haven't told anyone that you and Miss Turner are in isolation with Jane. Not even Augusta. But Mrs. Edwards is making a meal out of what she does know. Lord Stancroft has gone back to England and left Miss Turner with only a pair of bourgeois French rose growers and your own servant to play propriety, and what are you getting up to with her daughter. That sort of thing."

"A good thing you are taking her off to Italy," John said.

Tenby shuffled a little and looked off down the garden. "Least I could do." He shuffled some more. "Admire Miss Turner, don't you know? Woman with courage and principles." Another shuffle. "From afar, you understand. Augusta is my everything. Still. Wouldn't want to see any harm come to Miss Turner. Especially by the tongue of Mrs. Edwards."

John had never expected to be amused in Tenby's company, but the man was not the villain John had believed him to be all these years. Just an overgrown and spoiled boy, used to having his own way and unaccustomed to thinking of others. Still, his feelings for Augusta appeared to be genuine. John was beginning to think that so was his concern for Jane and Pauline, though shallow and belated.

"Tenby, are you asking me my intentions?" he teased.

The man blushed and shuffled some more, looking down at his boots, but he didn't deny the charge. "No right," he acknowledged.

John was amused. "I will tell you in confidence, but you're not to say a word, for I haven't asked her yet."

Tenby lifted his head, his eyes startled. "You want to marry her?"

"I have been thinking about it for months," John confided. "Her brother helped me make arrangements with the embassy chaplain, before he left Paris. But Jane has been so sick, and Pauline so tired… It hasn't seemed the right time."

"Well, good," said Tenby. "Glad you told me. Congratulations, Forsythe. She's a fine woman. Up to your weight."

"She hasn't accepted me yet," John pointed out.

Tenby dismissed that argument. "Woman is devoted to you. Jumped into a moving carriage to look after your daughter. Looks at you like you hung the stars."

Did she? Did she really?

Tenby offered his hand. "I'll be off, then. Augusta has a list of friends she wants to visit before we leave Paris. All the very best to you, Forsythe. You will let me know how Jane goes on.?"

John found himself agreeing. As he returned upstairs to Jane's bedchamber, John was shaking his head in bemusement at the pleasant end to their conversation. Who would have predicted that the day would see him shaking Tenby's hand and wishing him a pleasant journey?

A random thought had him chuckling. In fact, if he'd wanted to see Tenby suffer for his sins, and he really no longer cared, a trip to Italy escorting Augusta and Mrs. Edwards seemed punishment enough.

Chapter Twenty-Nine

JOHN DECIDED NOT to tell Pauline about the gossip. Not until he had asked her to marry him. So, when Jane drifted off to sleep, he asked her to come and sit by the window with him where they could talk without waking the little girl.

"What is it, John," Pauline asked. "Did Tenby have bad news?"

"Not at all," John replied. "He just wanted me to know that he and Augusta are leaving for Italy tomorrow. He asked if I would let him know how Jane gets on. I said I would."

Pauline commented, "You know, John, I would never have wished any of this on you and Jane, but it may have its silver lining. I think, having seen the Tenbys together and obtaining their agreement to leave you and Jane alone, you are, perhaps, freer of the past than you have ever been. If you don't mind my saying so."

"I think you are right," John replied. "But I didn't want to talk about Tenby and Augusta, Pauline. I wanted to talk about us."

Her eyes widened. "What do you mean?" she asked.

The words John had been rehearsing all afternoon had gone completely out of his head. "Pauline." That was as good a place as any to start. "I wondered... that is to say, would you consider..." She was looking at him attentively, her brow slightly furrowed in question.

Asking this woman to marry him was harder than any battle he'd ever fought. John cleared his throat, which had suddenly grown dry, and tried again.

"I mean," he explained, "you and I get on very well together, and I would count myself the happiest of men if you would consent to be my wife." *There. It was done.* He waited anxiously for her reply.

If he had to categorize her expression, he'd call it more bewildered than delighted.

"Because we have been alone together," she said.

"No," he replied adamantly. "That's not it at all. I *know* we have been alone together, and Tenby tells me there is talk..." From the way her eyes widened, he should have kept that to himself. "I already intended to ask you, Pauline. I have been unable to stop thinking about you since our kiss."

"Marrying me?" Pauline's eyes expressed doubt, but also, if John was not mistaken, longing.

"Yes, you and I," he said. The silence stretched, until he added, "We deal very well together, you and I."

PAULINE'S HEART YEARNED to say yes, but she did not want him looking back and regretting this day. How dreadful to be tied for life to yet another woman whom he did not set out to marry.

"John," Pauline pointed out, "you were forced into marriage once, because a girl was compromised. I am not a girl, and my life will change very little if my reputation is damaged in some quarters. My family will still love me. You don't have to do this."

"This is what I want," he insisted. "Not what I *have* to do."

Pauline saw almost everything she had dreamed of within her reach. She could stay with John and Jane and have the right to call them family. She could enjoy John's kisses and more, perhaps have babies of her own. But would he come to resent her in time?

"If you are ready to marry, John, wouldn't it be better to choose someone younger, who could give you half a dozen children? I am thirty."

He rejected her suggestion with a fierce frown and a wave of his hand, as if throwing it away. "I want you. I want my friend, the lady I trust, the lady I can see as a partner for the remainder of my life." His voice turned coaxing, and he possessed himself of her hands.

"I know Cumberland has long winters but we grow good roses. I can build you as many succession houses as you want, and the garden will be yours to do with as you please. As for children, if I have Jane and you, I have enough, but you are still young enough to give me more, if we are so blessed. I will certainly try to fill you with my babies, and enjoy doing so, if you are willing."

Was the room suddenly warm? Or was it John's words, and the heat in his eyes, melting Pauline's core? She would do it, she decided. Perhaps he did not love her, but he wanted her, and she loved him. It would be enough. And perhaps they would be happy after all, for had not Arial once said that it was marrying a friend that led to love between her and Peter?

John was still trying to persuade her. "We can move from Cumberland closer to your brother, if you prefer. Or I could take a house in London so we could spend part of each year there, with Jane and any other children we have, so they can grow up knowing their cousins."

"Cumberland will do just fine, but I like the idea of visiting London from time to time," Pauline told him. "Wherever we live, I would be proud to be your wife."

John whooped, and grabbed her off her feet to swing her around in a circle, so she laughed out loud. As he bent his head to kiss her, a voice from the bed asked, "What are you doing?" They had awoken Jane.

"Miss Turner has just agreed to be my wife," John told his daughter. "She will come home with us to live with us, and we will be one family."

Jane promptly burst into tears, and both adults hurried to comfort her, but she brushed off their concern. "I am so happy," she told them.

Just then, Thorne arrived with the afternoon's mail and Jane was eager to tell him the news. From his broad grin, he was not surprised, but was delighted. He gave John his warm congratulations. "Mrs. Thorne will be very pleased," he said. "She reckoned you and Miss Turner here had something going on between you. It is a very good thing, Captain."

He told the Lavignes the news, and they hurried upstairs with glasses and a bottle of homemade elderberry wine to toast the happy couple from the doorway.

"Will you and Mademoiselle marry here?" Tante Marie wanted to know. "It would be best done without delay. There is gossip."

"The captain has a license," Thorne explained.

Pauline turned wide eyes to John. He *really* had been thinking about this!

He shrugged and gave her an adorably shy grin, very unlike the stern, stoic man she'd first met. "The Bishop of London was at the embassy, and I was able to claim us both as residents of his diocese using our brothers' addresses," he said to Pauline. "Or Peter did, on my behalf. I have a common license we can use to wed at the embassy chapel any time."

Which meant that Pauline's overprotective brother had had a hand in this. Still, John did not have to say all those lovely things to her. Or did she just want to believe it?

Jane yawned, which recalled Tante Marie to herself. "We shall leave Miss Jane to her sleep. I am very pleased for you Pauline, and you, *Monsieur Capitaine*. You will remember that this is a respectable house, if you please. You are betrothed, I know, but not yet wed." To emphasize the point, she left the door open as she, her husband, and Thorne retreated.

Pauline wondered what Tante Marie thought they might do

with Jane as their witness. However, obviously John something in mind, for he closed the door before helping Jane to have a few more sips of juice and compose herself to sleep.

"When would you like to marry?" John asked her, once Jane had drifted off again. "Tomorrow? If the chaplain can manage it?"

"We cannot leave Jane just yet," Pauline pointed out.

John grimaced. "You are right. But soon, dear Pauline." He took her into his arms and pressed a gentle sequence of kisses along her mouth. "We shall have to think of something, for I am anxious to be your husband in every way." His mouth settled over hers and Pauline was left in no doubt he was telling the truth about his desire for her.

Later, John finally opened the letters that Thorne had delivered. "Listen to this," he said to Pauline. It's from Deerhaven. *"You will be pleased to know that I am sending you the faithful Mrs. Thorne. She turned up on my doorstep to ask for my help, having braved the strictures of the mail coach. She wanted transport to Paris so she could be with her little girl. By the time you receive this, John, the good woman will be only a couple of days behind."*

"So, there we are," he said. "Would it suit you to marry three days from now?"

Pauline agreed, so John wrote a letter for Thorne to take to the embassy chaplain. Pauline went to Tante Marie for help with acquiring a suitable gown. She was still wearing made over gowns that Tante Marie had acquired for her, because she had not been able to spare time from the sick room for any shopping.

"I don't know where to start," she told the dear lady, "or even if it's possible to have something made in time."

"Leave it to me," said Tante Marie, and within an hour, Pauline was called into her bedchamber to submit to measurement by a modiste friend of Tante Marie's, who had been willing to come at short notice to assist in the romance. She brought pattern books, fabric samples, and a measuring tape, and went away with a notebook full of measurements and sketches.

"Leave it to me, Mademoiselle," she said.

By the time Pauline returned to the sick room, Thorne had brought the message that the chapel would be available the next day or the day after, and then again in a week's time. "I sent him back to book it for the day after tomorrow," John told Pauline. "If Mrs. Thorne has not arrived, perhaps Jane will accept Thorne for a time."

The next day, Jane had perked up enough to take an interest in the fabric samples that the modiste had left, and in the gown itself when the modiste pinned it on for the first fitting.

"Mama looks beautiful, Papa," she told John, when he was allowed upstairs after the gown had been unpinned and taken away. "I may call you *Mama*, Miss Turner, may I not?"

It was Pauline's turn for happy tears, as she hugged the little girl and said, "I would love you to call me *Mama*. I think I am the luckiest woman in the world to have you for my daughter."

"I think Jane and I are very fortunate," John told her. "To think none of this might have happened if your sister had not married in Galloway, and if the rain had not washed out the bridge. It doesn't bear thinking about."

A STIR THAT evening proved to be the arrival of Mrs. Thorne. Madame Lavigne brought her up to Jane's room with the courier Deerhaven had sent to be her translator and her escort.

While Jane was having a tearful reunion with her beloved Thorny, the young man introduced himself to John and Pauline as Lewis Watson. "Deerhaven instructed me to place myself and the carriage at your command, Captain," Mr. Watson told John.

He switched to French, speaking to Madame Lavigne slowly enough that John could follow along. "Can you direct me to a suitable *hostellerie*, Madame?"

Madame Lavigne protested that they had plenty of room, but Watson explained he also needed to house the driver, two guards, and the carriage. Madame Lavigne hustled him off below stairs to discuss the matter with *Monsieur*.

Meanwhile, an excited Jane had told Mrs. Thorne about the wedding, and when John turned his attention from the courier, she was hugging Pauline and expressing her delight. John came in for his share of hugs, and then Thorne arrived to enfold his wife in a hug of his own, so that she burst into happy tears.

"Maggie! You're a sight for sore eyes, and so you are!" he said. "You came all this way!"

"How could I not, Nate?" she asked, wiping her eyes. "With my Miss Jane needing me, and you and the Captain and Miss Turner."

Jane had a fit of coughing, and Pauline and Mrs. Thorne nearly bumped heads as they both rushed to the child's side. With a smile, Pauline deferred to Mrs. Thorne, but Jane, though clinging to the woman who had been her nurse since the day she was born, also held out a hand to Pauline. "Mama, you too," she demanded.

If John had allowed it, he would have had a happy tear of his own. "We're surplus to requirements here, Thorne," he said briskly. "Let us go and see what the Lavignes have recommended for Watson and his people."

The hospitable couple had organized it all. The entire party was staying here, Watson in the house, and the three other men in the carriage house. It had plenty of room for the carriage, since the Lavignes possessed only the little gig. The horses could share the stable with the Lavignes' one pony, and the carriage room had sufficient rooms above that the men could have a room each.

"It is too much trouble," John worried, but Madame Lavigne assured him it was no trouble at all. "I am having so much fun," she told him, "and less work than usual, *Monsieur Capitaine*, since you and your brother are paying for the extra servants as well as the feed for your brother's men and the horses."

She had taken on two extra two maids to help with the extra work that came from having John, his daughter, his betrothed and his manservant in the house. The maids had two sisters who also needed employment. One of the maids had been sent in Deerhaven's carriage to fetch them, and the other was already upstairs putting clean sheets on a bed for Watson.

"When they return, we shall have three rooms ready in the carriage house lightning fast, Monsieur," Madame Lavigne assured John, with great satisfaction. "For everything is clean, and it remains only to make the beds."

John had no doubt. Madame Lavigne was a prodigiously energetic housewife.

"And cook has made a large stew and fresh bread, which will allow us to feed them all tonight," Madame caroled. "I must see about something sweet to finish the meal. A clafoutis, perhaps?" She bustled off, humming cheerfully to herself.

"Madame is loving all the bustle," *Monsieur* Lavigne observed.

Chapter Thirty

THE FOLLOWING MORNING, John was cast out of his daughter's bedchamber and ordered to remain in his own or go downstairs. He was not to see Pauline before she arrived in the chapel, apparently, and Pauline was dressing in Jane's room to give their daughter a part of the wedding.

"I shall make sure Miss Jane does not overdo things, and that she rests while you are gone," Mrs. Thorne told him before he could express concern.

So, once John was dressed, he, Watson and Thorne borrowed the gig to go early to the embassy. There, John met with the chaplain to confirm everything would be ready when the bride arrived, then took a quick trip to Mellerio, on the *Rue de la Paix*. It had occurred to him, and he had checked the matter with Madame Lavigne and Mrs. Thorne, that a necklace for his bride might make a good bridal gift.

Nothing seemed quite right, until he mentioned Pauline's love of roses, and the assistant brought out the perfect item—a golden English rose descending from an intricately twisted gold chain. The petals and leaves sparkled with tiny diamonds and a larger diamond made up the center. John left the shop with the necklace, plus matching earrings and bracelet.

He gave the box to Watson, who promised to deliver it to the bride as soon as she arrived, and went to wait at the front of the chapel with Thorne. It seemed like an hour but was probably only fifteen minutes before Watson entered the chapel with Madame Lavigne on his arm, and gave John the thumbs up.

Lady Michael, the attaché's wife, who had been playing something quiet and soothing on the organ, changed to a triumphal march. Then Pauline was there, walking towards John, dressed in gold and as lovely as one of the roses she loved—a rose of rich cream kissed by sunbeams.

PAULINE HAD LONG believed she would never have a wedding day. The morning had passed in a flurry of excitement, with *Tante* Marie, the modiste, and two of the maids fussing over her, and Jane and Mrs. Thorne providing a running commentary.

Pauline kept expecting someone to stop her; to tell her it was all a mistake. But here she was, walking towards John and the altar on *Oncle* Théo's arm, in a gown of the softest silk in a warm, buttery cream, carrying a huge golden-yellow bunch of *Oncle* Théo's prize roses, and wearing John's gifts around her neck, in her ears, and on her wrist.

It was real. There he was, smiling at her, his eyes warm and welcoming. She fought against submitting to the fantasy. This was not a love match. He had been very clear. He liked her. He desired her. He wanted her as a mother for Jane. She should not expect anything more.

As she moved towards him down the aisle, she balled up those sensible thoughts and locked them away in the deepest recesses of her brain. Today was a dream. She was wedding the man she loved, and she was going to enjoy every moment. When she reached his side and *Oncle* Théo released her into his hands, she gave herself over to the fantasy.

She was determined to memorize every moment, but afterward, she mostly remembered John's voice, strong and confident, vowing to love her above all others, placing a ring on her finger and then not releasing her hand; John sneaking glances at her throughout the ceremony, glances that hinted at his own wonder and delight as they bound themselves to one another for life.

Afterward, they signed the marriage lines and then returned to the center of the church to be presented to the congregation. On the way down the aisle, they were waylaid first by the Lavignes, then by Watson, and then Lord and Lady Michael and some other of the embassy staff.

"Lady John," gushed Lady Michael, "Lord Michael and I wish you both every blessing."

"Thank you," Pauline acknowledged, conscious of John wincing beside her. Augusta, Arial had once told her, insisted on being addressed as Lady John despite John's dislike of the courtesy title. "You are very kind. Would you be good enough to call me Mrs. Forsythe? The Captain and I do not use his courtesy title, fond though we are of his brother."

Fortunately, Lady Michael took this in good part. "Of course, Mrs. Forsythe. Now that I think of it, I remember that the renowned artificer of mechanicals is always known as Captain Forsythe."

John and Pauline took the carriage back to the house, the Lavignes, Watson, and Thorne all crowding into the gig. "You shall have a few minutes to yourself," Tante Marie said.

Alone in the carriage with John, Pauline was suddenly struck mute. She couldn't help thinking about what they might be doing, alone in a carriage, if they were lovers. Already lovers. Presumably, sooner or later, they would be lovers. John had spoken of children, after all.

I will certainly try to fill you with my babies, and enjoy doing so. Yes, they would be lovers, and Pauline burned at the thought and had no idea what to say to break the silence.

They had traversed half the distance between the embassy and their destination before John cleared his throat and commented, "I appreciated what you said to Lady Michael."

With an internal sigh of relief, Pauline accepted the safe topic of conversation. "About your courtesy title? Or about your brother?"

"Both, I suppose. That you respect my reasons for not using the courtesy title, and that you and my brother are fond of one another." John put his hand on hers.

Pauline turned her hand over so she could wrap her hand around his. "He is a good man, your brother. And a good husband and father."

John nodded. "He is. He said something to me that made me think. The late marquess was an ass."

"That is evident," Pauline agreed. "Look how much joy Jane gives you and you give her. He deprived himself and you of affection because he put his pride ahead of getting to know and love an innocent baby."

"Precisely," John said. "He was an ass. I am not an ass. Rather, not quite as much as I was. If you would like to be Lady John, I shall be Lord John. For you."

Pauline was not quite sure if she followed his logic, but she appreciated his gesture. "Not necessary," she assured him. "I shall be the wife of Captain Forsythe, renowned artificer of mechanicals."

He chuckled at that. "And I shall be the husband of Mrs. Forsythe, famous breeder of roses."

They smiled at one another, in perfect accord.

Pauline remembered another gesture she appreciated. "John, thank you for my rose jewelery. It is beautiful! The wedding ring, too."

"The wedding ring is a family one. My grandmother wore it, and hers was a happy marriage, dear wife. Deerhaven sent it with Mrs. Thorne."

Pauline raised an eyebrow. "Our brothers have been matchmaking."

John shrugged. "They both knew my intentions, for I told

them when they were in Paris. Pauline, we have just turned the corner and will be home within minutes. May I kiss you before we are overwhelmed with people again?"

Pauline gladly lifted her lips. And to think she had more of this to look forward to!

AS SOON AS he escorted Pauline inside, John lost her attention to the only person who needed it more.

Jane, very excited, had been carried downstairs with the physician's approval, and ensconced on a sofa in the parlor. From that throne, she greeted her new mother with another large bunch of roses, these ones red, pink, and white for love and romance. Pauline, blushing with delight, accepted them. She bent to inhale the rich fruity smell, with touches of honey and spice. Someone had removed all the thorns.

"Look at you, out of bed and dressed in a pretty gown," she said to her new daughter, and called John to her side to admire Jane's pretty dress, made from the same fabric as hers.

"I am allowed to stay downstairs to have an ice and maybe a slice of cake," Jane assured him, looking a little anxious, as if she feared he would withdraw the permission. "Thorny says."

"As long as you stay on the sofa, and don't get too excited," John reminded her.

Madame Lavigne had arranged a magnificent spread as a wedding breakfast, and John was grateful. His wife was far from home and her own sisters, and—although she would never make a fuss—this could not have been the wedding day of which she had dreamed.

The least John could do while he waited for night to fall so that he might have his wife to himself was be a good guest. Polite, obliging, friendly. He sampled the food, laughed at the speeches, complimented the cook. But all the time, he lusted after his wife.

If this had been a wedding in England, perhaps from her brother's house in London, he would have arranged rooms in a hotel, and by now would have swept her away. But with Jane ill, there was no possibility of spending the night elsewhere.

Thank goodness for Mrs. Thorne. With Jane improving in health and Mrs. Thorne ready to take the night shift, at least they could have a wedding night.

Pauline would want a wedding night, would she not? He really had no idea how she felt about him. She liked him. She enjoyed his company. She loved his daughter. She responded to his kisses. She had promised herself to him for life. But was she ready to go to bed with him?

He should think about something else, for he was dressed as a fashionable gentleman today, and the breeches had little room to hide what he'd prefer others not to notice. Another topic. Had he told her how pretty she looked? "I love your gown," he murmured to her.

"The petticoat and stays are embroidered with roses," she whispered back.

"You will have to show them to me," he teased.

She blushed bright red and replied, "Later."

John shifted to ease the sudden constriction. Not such a safe topic after all. Jane called for his attention, then, and he went to sit on the floor with her. She had received a little puzzle box, compliments of someone called Lord Lumley, and she wanted him to show her how it worked.

Instead, he patiently coaxed her to try different steps, but all the time, he was aware of Pauline's speculative glances. When he realized it was only one in the afternoon, he barely managed to suppress a groan.

However, his new wife was braver than he was. When Jane began to yawn, and Mrs. Thorne said it was time she went up to bed, Pauline stood and announced that she and John would also have an afternoon sleep, since they had had weeks of worry and broken nights.

"John, you carry Jane up to bed, and Mrs. Thorne," she said, "if you stay with her, John and I will take it in turns again tonight."

Clever girl.

In Jane's bedroom, though, Mrs. Thorne had a whispered consultation with Jane, and then told John and Pauline, "If you please, Captain and Mrs. Forsythe, Jane will be happy tonight with her Thorny on the pallet there, and Thorne will take a turn sitting with us, too."

Pauline addressed herself to Jane. "Are you certain, darling? We shall be just through the wall if you need us."

"I am certain," Jane declared. "It is your wedding day, and you are meant to spend the night together. Thorny told me. It is the rules."

"That's settled then," said Mrs. Thorne. "Madame Lavigne says to sleep as long as you like, and to ring when you would like to have some dinner sent up."

Pauline blushed some more at the knowledge behind all the conspiring. She was still blushing as John lifted her and carried her across the threshold into what had been her room and would now be theirs.

John's things had been brought from his room, the bed was freshly made, and the room festooned with flowers. "When did they find time to do all this?" Pauline wondered as John set her on her feet.

Clearly, *Tante* Marie assumed they would share a room. John was pleased, but was Pauline? What were her expectations? Downstairs, he'd thought she was eager to begin their married life, but was that just wishful thinking on his part? Perhaps she really did intend to sleep?

He stood by the door, wondering what to say and do. Pauline surprised him, then, turning her back and saying, "It is a lovely gown, but not designed for a woman without a maid. I will need your help, John."

He took two quick strides and removed the necklace and then

the bracelet before beginning to fumble his way down what seemed like a thousand tiny buttons, his fingers suddenly losing all their skill.

"I will need your guidance," she continued, "for I know very little about what to expect. I did not like to ask *Tante* Marie, and I've never had much interest in the matter in the past."

He could not resist. He kissed the nape of her neck. "We will discover one another together," he promised.

Kissing and caressing as he went, it took a while to undo enough buttons for the gown to drop over the swell of Pauline's hips. She stepped out of it and faced him, looking shy but trusting. "Your jacket next?" she wondered.

He picked her gown up first, the pretty thing, and put it over the back of a chair out of the way, then held his arms out, inviting her to assist him.

And so it went, each of them taking turns in removing a garment. After he lingered over the corset, tracing the embroidery and scattering kisses, she followed his example, and let her hands and her lips roam as she removed his waistcoat. Her petticoat followed, and his breeches.

Stockings next, one at a time, touches and kisses moving down legs as the stockings dropped and came off. Finally, he stood in his shirt and she in her chemise. It was, as promised, embroidered with roses.

"Both at the same time?" he suggested. His face disappeared into his shirt as hers was covered by her chemise, and when he could see again, they were both bare. "Another kiss," he decided, and by the time it was over, she was spread on the bed and he was over her.

"John, I need more," she said. He gave her more, determined to see her to completion before they joined. At last, he swallowed her cries of release with his kiss, and set himself to slowly sink into her, battling his own urgent needs and taking his time. Until she urged him on, and he forgot everything but sensation, and they climaxed together.

He saw to her ablutions, tucked her into his side, and sleep took them.

They woke to complaints through the wall. Jane wanted Mama to read her a story and Papa to kiss her goodnight. From the light through the window, they had slept until evening. "It is probably just as well," John commented, as he buttoned Pauline into an afternoon gown that fitted her magnificently—Madame's *modiste* deserved a bonus. "For I want you again, and you must be sore."

Pauline smiled as she held his jacket. "Not sore so much as warm, and soft, and a little swollen, perhaps. I want you again, John. Is it always like that?"

If it hadn't been for a wail from Jane, he would have taken her back to bed immediately. "Never. But I hope it will be for us."

She must have seen the desire in his eyes, for she dropped a swift kiss on his lips. "I will look forward to having other experiences to compare," she promised. "Tonight?"

Chapter Thirty-One

IT WAS AN unusual start to the marriage: living in a foreign country in someone else's house, caring for a grumpy, convalescent child, surrounded by other people.

Nevertheless, the household conspired to give them time alone, and they made full use of it. Pauline was, though she had denied it to John, a little tender for the first few days. It was worth it, though. She had never imagined such an experience. The sensations, the emotions, being so close to the man she loved; she felt they had fused into a new person.

Outside of the bedchamber, too, John was a physically affectionate man, seldom being near Pauline without dropping a kiss on some part of her anatomy, or putting an arm around her shoulders or her waist, or touching her hand or her arm in passing. Pauline, who had lived most all her adult life without the pleasure of being held, apart from brief hugs from her sisters, reveled in the experience, and fell more deeply in love with John than before.

As Jane's health continued to improve, so did her appetite and her disposition. The physician reduced his visits to every second day, and then every third. Three weeks after the last gray patch shrunk out of sight, he gave her permission to walk, rather than to be carried everywhere, "Though you must watch like a hawk for any signs that she is tired," he told Pauline and John, "and then back to bed with mademoiselle."

He would come again in one more week, and then two weeks from now. He was confident that, by then, Jane would be ready for travel, provided that they made their way by slow stages.

"Two more weeks," *Tante* Marie lamented. "Indeed, Pauline, we shall miss you and all your family."

"Two more weeks," said John, "and then perhaps a week to Le Havre by slow stages. Let us hope that the weather holds into the autumn." He wrote to the captain of Deerhaven's yacht, arranging a date and a place. They would land on the south coast, perhaps at Brighton. From there, it was a two-hour carriage ride to Deercroft, Deerhaven's family seat and John's childhood home.

Another letter went to Deerhaven, asking for a carriage to be on standby to fetch them. "We will stay overnight in Brighton," John told Pauline. "If we send a message as soon as we arrive, they can send the carriage first thing in the morning. We can make a leisurely start and still be at Deercroft by nursery tea."

Jane was delighted to be introduced to the steady stream of callers. For John, old army friends and French automaton makers; for Pauline, Lady Michael and other diplomats' wives from the embassy as well as Paris rose enthusiasts who were keen to meet the creator of the Rosalind Douglas and the Lady Stancroft.

Letters and packages continued to arrive for the newlyweds, from family and friends in various parts of England, and from Rose in Scotland. Most included games or books or toys to keep Jane amused, until John joked he would need another carriage just to carry them.

One package came all the way from Italy. John had written, as promised, to Tenby to tell him that Jane continued to recover, and Pauline had enclosed a note to Laura, announcing her marriage.

Laura and Tenby both wrote back, Laura's note surprisingly

polite and Tenby's somewhat wistful.

"I wish you and your new wife every happiness. You both deserve it. Jane is fortunate in her parents. The painting in the crate is nothing special. A local painter was selling it in the market, and it made me think of the three of you."

Carefully packed in the crate Tenby mentioned was a set of three matching decanters in etched crystal, silver-mounted, and stoppered. The card indicated they were from the Di Positanos. At the bottom of the crate was a flat rectangular package which proved to be a painting of the Holy Family in the most saccharine of devotional styles, apparently painted by a barely competent apprentice.

"It is the thought that counts," Pauline told John.

"My thought is that the Tenbys will never visit us, so they won't know if this is relegated to the attics," John said.

The final two weeks flew by, even though rain kept them inside for much of it. The sun came out the day before they were due to depart, however, though the wind was still brisk.

"All the better to dry the roads," said Watson.

The parting from the Lavignes was tearful on both sides. *Tante* Marie, in particular, required assurances that they would write. "And you must come to visit whenever you are in Paris, my dear Pauline," she insisted.

"You and *Oncle* Théo must visit us in Cumberland," John said. "We have made ourselves family, have we not? Pauline would love to show her *Oncle* Théo her roses. You could sail directly to Newcastle and be with us that day or the next."

SIX WEEKS LATER, on a clear but crisp afternoon as October wound to a close, John's procession of carriages came over the bridge into the village, with just one last hill to climb.

"Home," Jane said to Pauline, her eyes shining. She waved

out of the window to a boy who was running down the village street, and he turned to lope beside the carriage, waving back and shouting, "The Captain is back. The Captain and Miss Jane are home!"

Pauline's mouth shaped the word *home*, and John squeezed her hand, his heart full, and his pulse beginning to beat faster as he anticipated her reaction to the surprise he had planned.

He had set it in motion even before he asked Pauline to marry him. It had been hard to keep it a secret for two months. Would she like it? He hoped she would at least appreciate his motives—he wanted her to know how welcome she was, how much this *was* her home, how needed she was.

She was leaning forward to wave out the window as more and more villagers came to their doors or their gates to greet the returning travelers. More boys had joined the first, to run alongside the carriages, shouting greetings.

"Look," she said, to John. "Some of the roses are still blooming. The late flush, it will be. If I can find a sheltered sunny spot for my cuttings, they will be able to put down some roots before the cold."

One of the carriages behind them carried a number of tender rose plants, newly rooted. Some had come all the way from France, some from Peter's London townhouse, and some from the gardens at the Stancroft estate in Leicester.

The baggage also included a couple of crates of toys—Tenby's gifts and those with which Jane's uncles and aunts had welcomed her home. There was another of wedding presents, plus the whole new wardrobes John had commissioned in Paris and added to in London for Pauline and Jane. A few things for himself, too. In Paris, and again in London, he had stepped out into Society for the first time since his disastrous first marriage. It was much more fun as a happily married man with his beloved wife on his arm.

Love. He had not expected it, but it had found him, anyway. Dozens of times the words he owed her had been on his lips, but he had held them back, waiting to gift them to her when she saw his surprise. He hoped she knew. He hoped she returned his love. But if she did not, he would love her enough for them both.

"Clementine and I have not minded traveling," Jane announced, "but we are glad to be home." She was holding the doll up to the window, using her own hand to wave Clementine's. The poor toy had barely survived the boiling the physician prescribed after isolation ended, but Pauline, Mrs. Thorne, and Tante Marie had conspired on a new face, new hair, and a new wardrobe.

"What have been your favorite parts of the traveling?" Pauline asked, as the carriage turned off the road and began to climb the carriage way to the house.

"*Tante* Marie and *Oncle* Theo," Jane answered, without hesitation. "I did not like being kidnapped or going on that horrid ship. I did not mind the ship of Uncle Deerhaven."

They had accomplished the crossing from Le Havre to Brighton on a single sunny day. Jane, permitted to sit on the upper deck with Pauline and Mrs. Thorne to watch over her, was fascinated by the sea birds, passing ships, and occasional glimpses of marine animals. At one point, a whale breeched within view, and a school of dolphins accompanied them for part of the distance.

"I liked staying with Uncle Deerhaven and Auntie Cordelia, and with Uncle Peter and Auntie Arial," Jane added. "I like the cousins." She had been immediately accepted into the large tribe of Deerhavens and Stancrofts. Most of them were older than Jane, but she was fast friends with Cordelia's youngest son and Arial's two daughters, adored Arial's baby, and was made much of by the remainder of both families.

Mindful of Jane's convalescence, they had spent a week at Deercroft, four days in London and then another week in Leicester. Though Pauline and Mrs. Thorne continued to watch the child for tiredness or any weakness, she had bounced back to blooming good health, and John gave thanks that she seemed to have escaped any permanent ill effects.

One mystery had been solved on their second night in London, when they had an unexpected visitor. John looked at the card on the butler's salver. "Do you know a Captain Lord Lumley, Pauline?"

Pauline shook her head, though she reminded John, "I do not recall meeting him, but someone of that name sent Jane a puzzle box while we were at the Lavignes."

However, when the butler showed the guest in, she recognized him immediately, though he was shaven and in a smart naval uniform. "Lieutenant Benedict!"

"About that," said the gentleman. "It is, actually, Benjamin Courtney, Viscount Lumley. I was in masquerade to bring down a smuggling operation."

"John," Pauline said to her husband, "This is the man I knew as Lieutenant Benedict, second in command to Captain Diablo." A thought occurred to her. "Was it you that left the message for John? In Port Carlisle?"

"It was," Lord Lumley confirmed. He gave Pauline a rueful look. "I'm sorry I could not compromise my investigation by doing more. I hope it helped."

John grasped the man's hand. "It did. It sent me straight to Brest, and from there to Paris."

Pauline was feeling less charitable. "I hope," she said tartly, "that it was worth it, since it cost me, Jane, and my husband weeks of worry."

He regarded her gravely. "Captain Diablo is in prison and will be hanged for his crimes, as will those of his crew who participated by choice and those at the French end of the connection, who were smuggling out of Brest. It is not an exaggeration to say hundreds of people will continue their lives oblivious to the harm he would have caused them if he had remained free, and scores, at least, have been saved from an early death."

Pauline nodded. Point taken. "It *was* worth it, then. Thank you for doing what you could to help me and my daughter, Lord

Lumley."

He flashed her a charming smile. "You are very gracious, Lady John. I am glad it worked out for you."

Pauline smiled at John. "It did," she acknowledged.

John leaned in and kissed her cheek. "Precisely," he agreed.

The drive flattened as it came out of the trees, and there it was. Rosewood Towers, the upper windows reflecting the late afternoon sun.

"Home," Jane said, on a sigh.

"Home," Pauline breathed.

"*Our* home," John confirmed.

A welcoming party waited on the steps—Mrs. Elliott with her daughters, the church warden-gardener and his wife, the youths from the village who helped with the garden, the maids and cook who came up daily from the village.

Mrs. Thorne had left the church warden and his wife in charge when she absconded to be with her beloved Miss Jane. With no-one living in the house and the increased number of servants, the workload would not have been burdensome, and they were a reliable pair.

Pauline wondered if the couple would be prepared to accept full-time work. John had spoken about her and John taking up residence in the main house, inviting neighbors to visit, perhaps having friends to stay. If the house was to come alive again, they would need a full-time housekeeper, and Mrs. Thorne's heart would always be in the nursery with Jane and any other babies Pauline might have.

That was a conversation for another day. John was handing her down from the carriage and Jane was calling, "Look who has come home with us! Miss Turner is not Miss Turner anymore; she is my Mama, and she is staying forever!"

Those waiting burst into a cheer, and John ushered Pauline down the line to receive their good wishes. "You've a good one here, Captain," the church warden insisted, and his wife wanted Pauline to know that the whole village had been praying for the little miss, and hoping the Captain would bring Pauline home with him.

"All is ready, just as you wanted," the church warden told John. Pauline wondered what that was about. Letters had been going back and forth from her party and the Towers for weeks, but John had, she thought, left the preparation of their home to her and the Thornes. The Thornes and Pauline had collaborated on letting the servants know what needed to happen in the house. Most of Pauline's correspondence, though, had been with the church warden, as gardener.

She put the small mystery to one side, as Mrs. Thorne sent the servants about the work of taking the luggage inside and preparing baths and food for the travelers. "Everything is ready just to be poured or heated as the case may be," the church warden's wife said.

"I'll just see my seedlings and cuttings to their temporary home," Pauline told John. She had ordered a number of large cloches to be made, to keep the precious plants safe until the promised succession houses could be built.

"I'll come with you," John said. He ordered the men with the plant carriage to take the wider cart track around the hill and meet them there.

"Can I come, Mama?" Jane asked. She had become Pauline's eager student, and several of the cuttings were her own.

"Of course, darling." Pauline took Jane's hand and John clasped the other. He was suppressing a grin. He must be as pleased as her to be home.

They rounded the far tower and passed through the garden and then the trees to the sunny slope that Pauline had chosen for her nursery. Pauline stepped out of the trees and stopped. Where she expected to see half a dozen temporary cloches, on a scrub and heather slope, a full-size succession house rose from the cleared ground, where the shapes of three more such structures had been marked out, as well as rectangles for the outside nursery beds.

"What? But how?" It was the plan she had drawn in Paris, and refined in letters back and forth to Rosewood Towers, already taking shape in reality. *So,* this *is what was ready*! She took a good look at John, his dancing eyes, his broad grin.

"You did this," she said. "But I cannot imagine how, in such a short time."

"I had a lot of help," he admitted. "Deerhaven has a friend with a house near Glasgow, who was willing to sell me an unused succession house, and the church warden went up there to supervise it being taken apart and transported down."

Pauline turned back to the building; a visible expression of her husband's love. She could live with him never saying the words when he went to such trouble to please her. "I love it, John. It looks perfect."

"You need to inspect it," John told her. "The carriage is nearly here."

It was just in sight, coming around the curve of the hill on a new carriage way that must have been cut to bring in the pieces of the succession house. "Come on, Mama," Jane urged, tugging on her hand, and they went together down the hill to meet the carriage.

JOHN WAS DELIGHTED at how thrilled Pauline was with her present. He'd have liked to bask for a while in her gratitude, but she and Jane were thoroughly absorbed in directing the servants, who were trotting back and forth to the carriage, bringing each item of cargo to her, so she could decide where it went.

"Is there anything I can do to help?" he asked. "We should get this done as quickly as possible and return to the house. It has already been a long day, and it will get very cold once the sun goes down."

She squinted to the southwest to assess how much time she

had. "Does the boiler work?" she asked.

John raised a brow at the church warden. They had been testing it at the time of the man's last letter.

"It do, Mrs. Captain," the man said. "It is fired up, and the water is boiling. I just have to let it through into the radiators."

John went off to the boiler house with the church warden to do that job. The boiler had been another favor called in by Deerhaven. A younger son of a fellow duke was an engineer, and knew where to source a boiler of his own design, purchased for a house in Lancaster but never fitted because the owner had died. John had a wad of notes, instructions from Lord Thomas, complete with numbered and labeled drawings.

The boiler would also serve the other succession houses to be built here. John and the church warden worked out how to direct the water to the existing one, and were delighted when they returned inside and the radiators were already warming.

"I'll come back to check on it in an hour or so, Mrs. Captain," the church warden assured Pauline, as she looked around to make sure all was in order. Her baby plants were dwarfed by their surroundings, but John saw it through Pauline's imagination, for she had told him many times what she intended. In time, they would grow fruit and vegetables for the house, as well as tender flowers. But one succession house would always be devoted to Mrs. Captain's roses.

"We'll do the check on the boiler," John told the church warden. "My wife and I will walk down after dinner. You come and see to it in the morning."

They'd done all they could here and the light was fading. They walked back up to the house as they had come down, hand in hand.

IN THE SUCCESSION house later that evening, it was pleasantly warm. "I should see to some furniture for this end," Pauline said. "Somewhere I can sit while I plant seeds or pot up cuttings."

Somewhere we can make love of an evening, John thought, *when the plants are grown enough to give us some privacy.* Perhaps she knew him well enough to follow his thoughts, because she blushed as she said, "Perhaps a comfortable sofa?"

She moved into the arms he opened for her. "Thank you, John. I love my present, but I love the fact that you thought of it, even more.

He kissed the lips she offered and murmured against them, "You said you needed at least one succession house before next winter to truly reestablish your breeding program here in the north. I did not want you to lose a year, or to spend weeks in Leicester with the stock you cannot transfer up here."

"It is wonderful," she said. "Particularly since I have been co-operating in another breeding program, which will prevent me from traveling to Leicester this summer."

John frowned, unsure what she meant. He knew the rose breeder community was both competitive and co-operative, but he was unaware of any special arrangement.

She looked up at him, her eyes shining. "You and I have been working on it assiduously since our wedding, John, but we must have succeeded almost immediately, for by midsummer, we shall be able to hold the results in our arms."

It took him a moment, but light dawned. "We are having a baby?" At her nod, he whooped, and swung her in a circle, shouting to the silent audience of cuttings and seedlings, "We are having a baby!"

"You are pleased, then." The relief in Pauline's voice indicated that she had not been certain of his reaction.

"Delighted. Thrilled. Beyond delighted and thrilled." John placed a gentle hand over the curve of her abdomen. He could not detect a change in its shape, but come to think of it, her breasts had been larger and more sensitive in recent weeks.

"Hello, little one. I am your Papa, and I love you. And I love your Mama. I haven't told her that. I didn't expect it to happen, but it has been creeping up on me for months. Your Mama is the best thing that has ever happened to me; as great a blessing as your sister, and as you will be. You are a lucky little baby, for you are coming into the world surrounded by love."

He glanced up from his hand on Pauline's body to assess her reaction. Her eyes were wide and her jaw had dropped slightly. His heart sank. "I cannot deny my feelings, dear wife. I gave you my heart weeks ago, and I trust you with its keeping, but I don't expect your heart in return. I know that wasn't part of our bargain. Still. I wanted you to know. I love you, Pauline."

She wrapped her arms around him and hid her face against his chest. "I have loved you for months, John. I never said because I am not as brave as you."

He put his fingers under her chin and lifted it so he could see into her eyes. "You love me?" The evidence shone back at him—her eyes, full of love and trust and joy. "You love me. We love each other."

He hugged her to him. "Was ever there a couple as fortunate as us? We have Jane, each other, the new baby, our work and our estate. What more could we possibly need?"

"We could do with that convenient sofa about now," his wonderful wife murmured into his throat.

John laughed. "In the meantime, my darling, we shall have to make do. Let's go back to the house." He picked up the lantern. Together, they secured the succession house doors, confirmed that the boiler had sufficient fuel for the night, and strolled arm in arm up the hill to their convenient bed.

Epilogue

Spring, 1831

OVER THE YEARS, the north end of Pauline's first succession house had become a family lounge in all seasons. The western corner was enclosed with a fence and full of baby toys, and the rest was furnished with the promised comfortable sofa, a selection of chairs, several low tables, and even a cupboard with supplies for making hot drinks on the pot belly stove they'd added two years ago for extra warmth on the coldest days.

At the moment, the people Pauline loved best in the world were either in the succession house or somewhere else about the estate. They had gathered for the baptism of the newest member of the Forsythe family, Theodore Benjamin Paul Forsythe, who was asleep in the arms of *Tante* Marie, though undoubtedly, he would soon be passed to another of his doting relatives.

The Lavignes had first visited when Thomas Peter John was born, and had since returned every year, sailing from Dieppe to Newcastle, where John's carriage collected them to bring them to Rosewood Towers. They had not been there for the winter birth of Paulette Cordelia Marie two years ago, but had arrived with presents six months later.

Lettie was in the playpen with Vivienne's toddler and Rose's youngest. Tom had insisted on joining her and *Oncle* Théo, as they inspected the aisles of plants. *Oncle* Théo had no idea of the surprise she was about to show him.

As they came back up to the north end and circled into the next aisle, Pauline noted that she'd been right; Theo the younger was now in the arms of his Auntie Arial, with Auntie Cordelia hovering, waiting for her turn. Pauline had left her son with Rose, and last time she came this way, Vivienne was passing him to *Tante* Marie.

John was over in the other corner hosting the men to a sip of the brew they had laid down last harvest—Rose's husband Ruadh, Vivienne's husband, Peter and Deerhaven all appeared to be enjoying it.

Jane looked up from the cluster of girls on the floor—cousins, other family connections, and a couple of local friends. They were chattering while supervising those children who were too old for the playpen but not old enough to wander on their own, as several of the older children had done.

Jane said a word to the others and came to join Pauline, taking Tom by the hand. This last aisle led to the surprise, and she wanted to be part of the reveal!

Here they were. *Oncle* Théo stopped in his tracks. "Pauline! Your rose!" He hurried towards it, beaming, Tom and Jane at his side. Pauline stood back and watched *Oncle* Théo examining all of the rose's features, while Tom and Jane explained its history and what made it exceptional.

The parent plant from which it had been cloned had been a seedling the year before last. Pauline had known, as soon as the first bud began to open, that she'd achieved the color she'd wanted—a deep cerise pink with streaks of golden yellow. The ensuing weeks proved it also had the fragrance, the shape, the abundance of blossom, and the growth habit she'd desired.

It still remained to test its hardiness, its disease resistance, and its vigor, and last summer that first seedling's clones thrived in the outdoor beds, confirming that she had achieved the rose she had been seeking for so long.

This year, as soon as she heard that the Lavignes planned to come in April, she brought several plants inside, hoping they would bloom early enough to show *Oncle* Théo. And they had.

"When I grow up," Jane was telling *Oncle* Théo, "I am going to have a garden full of roses."

"Me, too," insisted Tom.

"They are your children, my love," John told her, slipping her hand into his arm and pressing a kiss on her hair.

"And yours," Pauline pointed out. "Jane made an excellent job on the device she gave you for your birthday, and Tom can spend hours taking apart and putting together the model you made for him to practice on."

John's smile was proud. "He has not needed me to fix it for him for weeks."

At the other end of the succession house, the door opened, and Mrs. Thorne led in a procession of maids and footmen with refreshments, as well as some of the older cousins. Pauline was about to suggest that they join the party, when Jane asked, "Mama, will you tell *Oncle* Théo the rose's name?"

Sneaky. Pauline and John were the only ones who knew, and Jane had been agitating to be included in the secret for weeks.

"We shall go back to the others, and Mama shall announce it to everyone at once," John decided.

It had taken a long time to name the rose, Pauline reflected, as she strolled with John, Tom and *Oncle* Théo along the aisle to the sitting area. She'd wanted a name that celebrated the importance of the rose in her story and John's.

The storm may have trapped her at Rosewood Towers, but her quest for the rose had captured John's attention and begun their friendship. The cuttings he'd promised had been their excuse for a continued correspondence. Roses had given her and Jane a refuge with the Lavignes in Paris, and an honorary aunt and uncle for life. John's way of showing his love had been this building, chosen for her to grow her roses.

True love was not specific enough, and trite besides. Paris Love did not encompass all that she wanted to say. *Family Love*? Pauline wasn't satisfied with that, either. Jane suggested Starburst, which suited the color but did not hold the meaning Pauline wanted. Deerhaven thought that they would sell more plants if they called it William and Adelaide, after the new king and queen. Mrs. Thorne wondered if Cumberland Empress might suit. Everyone had an opinion.

"Marie," said *Oncle* Théo as they reached the sitting area. "You must come and see Pauline's new rose." *Tante* Marie shook her head; Theo the Younger was back in her lap, and sound asleep.

"Here is the rose, *Tante* Marie." Jane slipped past them with three roses: a bud, an opening bloom, and one full-blown. She sent a conspiratorial smile to Pauline, who had asked her to cut them.

"My wife is about to announce the rose's name," John said, and all conversations died away as everyone looked expectantly in Pauline's direction.

John pressed Pauline's hand. His support, his pride in her accomplishments, had been constant. She smiled up at him, speaking to her audience while not looking away from the love of her life.

"The rose," she said, "is *Dreams Fulfilled*."

THE END

AUTHOR'S NOTE

1820S PARIS

When I began to write the Paris section of this novel, I assumed that the local law enforcers would be called *gendarmes*. Just as well I checked. Paris has, in fact, had a police force since 1667. It was reestablished after the French Revolution, and has been headed by a Prefect of Police since 1800.

History gave me the Garden of Luxembourg, its rose collection, and its chief gardener, Julien-Alexandre Hardy, who was founder and director of the *École des Rosiers*. I hope I have been true to their reality in my depiction of them.

Viscount Granville was the British Ambassador to Paris at the time of my story. The *Hôtel de Charost* was and still is the British Embassy.

The *cabriolet de place*, which Thorne hired to take Pauline home, was a common sight in Paris in the 17th, 18th, and 19th centuries. It was a light, two-wheeled carriage, pulled by one horse and available for hire.

In the 19th century, a carriage maker named Davies introduced such vehicles to London under the name cab, and we have cabs and cabbies to this very day.

ROSE BREEDING

Wild roses grow throughout the northern hemisphere, and have been cherished and cultivated since the beginnings of human settlement. They split into two groups, both of which have helped to form modern rose breeds.

First, and most familiar to my English gardener in 1825, are the Western roses: Gallicas, Albas, Damasks, Damask Perpetuals,

Centifolias, and Mosses. These bloom once a year, in the spring.

The Netherlands, thanks to their trading ships and geography, became great producers of all sorts of flowers. They still are, with tulips being one of the most famous, of course, but also hyacinths, carnations, and roses. Where there were once dozens of cultivars, by 1810, a couple of hundred existed.

The French rose industry was fueled by the French Empress Josephine, who consoled herself with her garden at Malmaison after her divorce from Napoleon. Here, she encouraged breeding and hybridizing, and several breeders inspired by her produced several hundred new cultivars.

The second group, the Oriental roses, were newcomers to Europe between 1750 and 1824: primarily China and Tea roses. These bloom more or less continuously. Initially, they were hard to hybridize with the Western roses, and not hardy. But crosses between East and West finally happened, and by the 1830s, repeat-breeding hybrids began to appear. By the 1840s, hybrid perpetuals were the favorites of most gardeners. Experimentation continued and does to this day, as rose breeders seek to perfect color, perfume, disease resistance, length of blooming season, size, growth pattern, and other features.

THE CARLISLE CLOCK TOWER AND CLOCKWORK AUTOMATONS

The Carlisle town hall and its clock tower still exist today. The Forsythe automaton is a fictional creation. However, clockwork automata were popular from the 17th to the 19th centuries. Most were made in France. Many in Germany. While automata for clock towers were popular, complex mechanicals were made as collectors' pieces and simple ones were reproduced in quantity as toys to delight children and guests.

If readers would like to know more about this fascinating subject, I refer them to *Figures in the Fourth Dimension*, by Ellen Rixford.

DIPHTHERIA

Diphtheria, previously known as the Boulogne sore throat, malignant croup, or other names, was described by the Greeks 2500 years ago. In the year I'm writing about, 1827, it had recently acquired the French name *dipthérite*, translated into English as diphtheria, which is the name by which we know it today, but effective prevention and treatment were still a century or more away. All my characters could do was keep their patient calm and hope that the ghastly false membrane growing from one tonsil to the uvula would not close the throat entirely, and that the child's heart and kidneys did not become affected by the toxins the bacteria produces.

Sitting with my hero and heroine as they watched and worried, I once again gave thanks for the era and the country in which I raised my children. Some forty years ago, one of my daughters had scarlet fever as a complication of mumps. When I told our doctor her temperature and that she was rambling in and out of consciousness, he put snow chains on his car and drove up the hill to give her an intravenous shot of antibiotic. Within half an hour, she was sitting up complaining that she wasn't allowed to play with her brothers and sisters out in the snow.

It's an experience I have never forgotten. We live in a time and a country of miracles.

In Regency England slums, overcrowding and poor nutrition meant that diphtheria, scarlet fever, influenza, mumps, small pox, and other epidemic illnesses spread easily and killed frequently, but a wealthy home was no protection. Children died in numbers that we, who expect to raise our children to adulthood, find it hard to comprehend. One third of children born in the early 1800s did not reach their fifth birthday.

On the whole, I sanitize this world for my readers. My sick child survives, unharmed. Romance, after all, is about happy endings.

ABOUT THE AUTHOR

Have you ever wanted something so much you were afraid to even try? That was Jude ten years ago.

For as long as she can remember, she's wanted to be a novelist. She even started dozens of stories, over the years.

But life kept getting in the way. A seriously ill child who required years of therapy; a rising mortgage that led to a full-time job; six children, her own chronic illness… the writing took a back seat.

As the years passed, the fear grew. If she didn't put her stories out there in the market, she wouldn't risk making a fool of herself. She could keep the dream alive if she never put it to the test.

Then her mother died. That great lady had waited her whole life to read a novel of Jude's, and now it would never happen.

So Jude faced her fear and changed it—told everyone she knew she was writing a novel. Now she'd make a fool of herself for certain if she didn't finish.

Her first book came out to excellent reviews in December 2014, and the rest is history. Many books, lots of positive reviews, and a few awards later, she feels foolish for not starting earlier.

Jude write historical fiction with a large helping of romance, a splash of Regency, and a twist of suspense. She then tries to figure out how to slot the story into a genre category. She's mad keen on history, enjoys what happens to people in the crucible of a passionate relationship, and loves to use a good mystery and some real danger as mechanisms to torture her characters.

Dip your toe into her world with one of her lunch-time reads collections or a novella, or dive into a novel. And let her know what you think.

Website and blog:
judeknightauthor.com

Subscribe to newsletter:
judeknightauthor.com/newsletter

Bookshop:
judeknight.selz.com

Facebook:
facebook.com/JudeKnightAuthor

Twitter:
twitter.com/JudeKnightBooks

Pinterest:
nz.pinterest.com/jknight1033

Bookbub:
bookbub.com/profile/jude-knight

Books + Main Bites:
bookandmainbites.com/JudeKnightAuthor

Amazon author page:
amazon.com/Jude-Knight/e/B00RG3SG7I

Goodreads:
goodreads.com/author/show/8603586.Jude_Knight

LinkedIn:
linkedin.com/in/jude-knight-465557166

www.ingramcontent.com/pod-product-compliance
Lightning Source LLC
Chambersburg PA
CBHW071437200726
48294CB00002B/672

* 9 7 8 1 9 6 1 2 7 5 5 1 5 *